"I DIDN'T WANT TO GET MARRIED. I didn't think I was ready. It wasn't a matter of loving you or not."

"You're not ready for marriage, but you're ready to raise a baby alone?"

She snorted, her sarcasm and self-possession returning.

"Maybe I'm not. Maybe I'll do a lousy job."

"Yeah, maybe you'll wreck some baby's life as well as mine and the Sidels'. Then you can be *really* happy."

Finally I felt angry. "I *haven't* wrecked your life."

"Well, you sure haven't made my senior year a piece of cake."

"I told you I was sorry about that."

"Why don't you stop being so sorry?" Cheryl yelled. . . .

NO MORE SATURDAY NIGHTS

Norma Klein

FAWCETT JUNIPER • NEW YORK

RLI: $\dfrac{\text{VL: 5 \& up}}{\text{IL: 10 \& up}}$

A Fawcett Juniper Book
Published by Ballantine Books
Copyright © 1988 by Norma Klein

Library of Congress Catalog Card Number: 88-768

ISBN 0-449-70304-5

This edition published by arrangement with Alfred A. Knopf, Inc.

Manufactured in the United States of America

First Ballantine Books Edition: October 1989

PART ONE

PART ONE

CHAPTER 1

"I think you're crazy," my father said, turning from his desk. "I think you're out of your goddamn mind."

Though I'd been steeling myself for this conversation for weeks—my hands were ice cold—I was determined, no matter what I was feeling inside, to let none of it show. My father can make me more irritated than anyone on earth. Maybe he'd say the same for me and probably it's not that unusual, given the circumstances. Since my mother's death six years ago when I was twelve, we've been like the flip, darker side of the odd couple, two bachelors grunting and mumbling at each other, never talking about the things that matter or even about the things that don't. I doubt communication was ever my father's strong suit—he didn't marry until he was forty and somehow, though I have no hard evidence either way, I doubt he was the swinging bachelor you read about in magazines. If he hadn't been lucky enough to meet my mother, I think he would've ended up like a lot of the unmarried, nongay, male faculty at Taylor, the small college in town at which he teaches mathematics: silent, absorbed in some weird little piece of abstruse research, his social life consisting of an occasional sherry party with the students.

"Look, Dad," I said, trying to sound, if not feel, patient. "I'm not asking for your approval or money or *anything*. Okay? In a couple of months I'll be away at college. If you want, I can move out in three months, when I graduate high school. I just wanted you to know, that's all. Just a point of information."

My father's eyes narrowed. He's tall—six four, like me, and lanky with pale blue eyes, thinning gray hair, and a thin gray mustache. "Oh, just a point of information, huh? You knock up some girl, now you're taking her to court to try and get the kid to raise it yourself, and it doesn't involve me at all? I don't play any part in this?"

"You can play any part you want," I said. "I'm just saying you don't *have* to. It's my affair."

"And how about the money that's going to be needed to raise this child? The fifty thousand dollars or whatever? Where's *that* coming from? Or have you inherited money from some rich aunt I don't know about?"

"I have Mom's money," I said. "I can—"

"That's for your education!" he barked. "Don't you *dare* touch that money for another purpose!"

"Will you let me finish? I have Mom's inheritance as a foundation, I've saved money from summer jobs, I'm going to work this summer. I'm just taking it one step at a time. How many people, how many married couples who have kids, have fifty thousand dollars?"

My father began nervously shredding bits of paper, something he does when he's ill at ease. He gave up smoking years ago and tried a pipe, but you can tell that somewhere, deep in his soul, there are times, like now, when he'd kill for a cigarette. "If only your mother were here," he said. Then he gazed out the window with the haunted, tragic look I know so well; it makes me ill.

Forgive me. It *was* a tragedy. Obviously, for me, too. Believe me, I miss my mother now, and I'll probably miss her ten years from now. But I just can't stand my father's self-pity. I feel like I've been drowning in it for the past six years. The way he corners strangers at parties and tells "the story" again and again, his eyes filling with tears. "She was younger than I was," he'll say. "I was forty, she was just twenty-eight. I hesitated. Should I marry her? Was it fair? Here she'd be, stuck with an old codger like me. I might pop off at any minute. God, I worried about that till I was blue in the face. And then, thirteen years after we were married, I wake up in bed one morning and she's unconscious. A cerebral hemorrhage. Out of nowhere! She was in perfect health! No hereditary problems. Slim as a reed. A nonsmoker. And that's it. I called the hospital and by the time we got there, she was gone . . . I mean, how do you explain that? How?"

If it's a woman listening, she pats my father's hand and murmurs, "How terrible, Mr. Weber. And to leave you with a child, too. But then, that must be a comfort to you in some ways, not to be completely alone."

At that my father will stare into space. "I *am* completely alone," he will say slowly. "Before I married I didn't know the meaning of that word. Now I do."

I stared at my father, wondering if I could juggle our relationship somehow, how I would do it. Would he have been better with a daughter? Better alone, with no kids? Yes to both, probably, especially the latter. He'd lived forty years as a bachelor, then slightly more than a decade with my mother, and now, back to bachelorhood again, but with this scrawny, bright, male teenager around the house who bugs him about things or looks at him with contempt or barely concealed distaste. He didn't ask for that. Neither did I, of course.

I guess my mother was an emotional conduit between the two of us. I didn't think of it at the time, didn't think of it, period. But she was the warm, talkative one, the one who made the three of us seem like a family. She thought of herself as shy, and I guess she was in the sense that she was never the life of the party, but with a small group, or just us, she was always laughing, concerned, caring. My father never struck me as that peculiar while she was alive. Mostly I ignored him. If I thought about it then, I'd have said it was his age that set him apart. My mother was the age of many of my friends' mothers; my father was more like a grandfather. While my mother was alive, my father looked, acted, and seemed maybe five to ten years younger than he was. You can see that in photos. But after her death he just aged—boom!—overnight. Now, when I look at him, he looks like one of those wax effigies that someone's forgotten to put in a museum. He's marking time till he dies, as he'll be the first to tell you.

Now he stared back at me. "Who's the girl?"

"What?"

"The mother? The one you—"

"Her name is Cheryl Banks."

"Not Henry Banks' daughter? Our garbage collector?"

"Right." I almost had to laugh. Of all the irrelevant facts for my father to pick, that one floored me. Ask him about his politics and he'll say he's a socialist, that the Democrats are far too right wing for him to even bother voting for them. Plus, his own father was a farmer. But the revulsion he managed to put into "garbage collector" made him sound like someone in a drawing-room comedy.

"She goes to school with me," I added. "She's in my class."

"He has four daughters," my father said. "Which one is this?"

"The youngest one."

"The pretty one?"

"Yeah, she's pretty."

My father laughed dryly. "You get into Columbia on a scholarship and then you let some brainless little local hussy get you into bed so she can tie you down and ruin your life?"

This time I laughed, probably just about as warmly as my father had. "Hussy?" That's a pretty peculiar word, if you come to think of it. "I never said I'd marry her and I never will. She knows that."

"Oh, come on, when those girls see a chance to break out of the kind of life that's in store for them, they take it. Believe me. You haven't got a chance, boy. You haven't got one chance in hell."

Please don't let me strangle my father. My life is complicated enough right now without a manslaughter charge. "Dad, could you at least get the facts straight? Cheryl wants to give the baby up for adoption. I'm the one who wants the child."

"What for? You're eighteen! Your whole goddamn life is ahead of you. You're going to be a doctor, you're going to make something of yourself. Look at the way I am with you. Hopeless! I don't know anything about how to do it. I've been a total failure. Men don't have the genes for it. And you're going to raise a baby? While you're in college?"

I sighed. "You're not hopeless." I hate playing into that with him, but I wanted to get away from the topic of Cheryl.

My father looked enraged. "I *am* hopeless! I'm telling you. You hate me. You never talk to me. Here you have some girlfriend, you knock her up, you're going to try and adopt her child, and what do I know about it? Nothing!''

I didn't say anything. I looked at my father's pipe rack, his five carefully arranged meerschaums. ''It wasn't a big deal. We made love a couple of times. If she'd been . . .''

I stopped. I'd been going to say, ''If she'd been someone I was serious about, I might have told you.'' I accuse my father of being a social snob, but I guess I'm one too, in a way. It's the way our town is, the way most small college towns are. At my high school maybe 80 percent of the kids live on farms. Then there are the kids of the college professors, like me, who are envied, pitied, hated. I knew when Cheryl started playing up to me that there was maybe some element of unconscious social climbing in it for her, that I was a catch in a way a football captain wouldn't be. Not that intellectual matters play a great role in her life, but to ''catch'' me probably was a big deal for her. Was she thinking of marriage, of my being her savior? I don't think so. I really believe, even now, that the pregnancy was a mistake, that if I'd offered to marry her she might've said yes out of expediency but felt no deep love and affection for me. She never sent her father after me with a shotgun. True, all this year she's looked at me with a cold, angry stare when I pass by, but that's understandable.

I wonder if it would've been easier if my mother were alive. Would I have told her right from the beginning? Maybe. There was no part of me that wanted to marry Cheryl, but I did feel like a shit a lot of the time, and I have the feeling my mother would've found some way of making me feel better about the whole situation. These things happen, no one's to blame, that kind of thing.

''You don't want to marry her, then?'' my father asked.

I shook my head.

''Don't you love her?''

"No, not really."

"So, it was just—what? A warm body? A pretty face? A chance for some quick experience? You know, Henry Banks may be a garbage collector, but he's a fine, honest man. How am I going to face him after this? I'm amazed he's continued to pick up our garbage and never said a word. That shows a lot about his character."

This is what I hate about small towns, why I'm never going to live in one when I graduate college. Not that there's any employment here in Haysburg, other than the college and a few small stores, but I hate that sense of everyone minding everyone else's business, the dumb little social hierarchy, the petty squabbles among the faculty. My mother was the head college librarian, so she wasn't as involved in all that as my father, but I think it used to bother her too, having to be polite to wretched people just because they came from old families that had lived here hundreds of years, having to join the Tuesday Club, where she had to sit around and listen to some woman she hardly knew give a paper on local history.

"Aren't you happy I'm not marrying her? I thought you'd totally flip out if I did that."

"If you don't love her . . . but that's not the point. I just don't see why you want to sabotage your future. That's what you're doing, whether you know it or not. You may talk yourself into believing it's some kind of tomfool honor thing, God knows what, but when the dust is cleared, you'll see. Try getting through classes and coming home to a baby. Try having a social life. Try all that and in one month, *less* than a month, you'll come whimpering to me with diaper pins sticking out of your ears, screaming, 'lemme out'!"

"Diapers don't have pins anymore."

"You think Columbia's going to care if you flunk out because the kid has colic or whatever? You'll be out, scholarship gone, on the street."

He was clearly enjoying this. Give my father something gloomy to sink his teeth into and he's in seventh heaven. "Dad, could you get your scenarios straight? Which is it? I'm going to flunk out after a month or I'm going to leave the baby in a basket on someone's doorstep?"

He threw up his hands. "Both, for all I know. What I *can* tell you is, if your mother were alive, this would never have happened. Since her death, we've been under an unlucky cloud, both of us. And for all I know, it's never going to lift. That baby'll be born with a cleft palate or worse."

I repressed a nervous laugh. "What wouldn't have happened? I never would have dated Cheryl? She never would have gotten pregnant? I mean, Mom was terrific, but even she never claimed to have magical powers."

My father's hand clenched around a pencil, his eyes blazed. "Don't you say a word about your mother, do you hear me? Not one word!"

Finally I lost my temper. "Why not? She was *my* mother, for Christ's sake! Do you think *I* don't miss her? Do you think the last six years have been fun and games for me?"

At that unexpected outburst my father fell silent. Sometimes I wish I blew up at him more often. It seems easier not to, just to let it pass, make little inner comments, calculate how much longer I have to do time here. Sometimes I think of it like that: doing time, like I'm in prison. "Why couldn't it have been a girl you loved?" my father said more softly. "How about Joely Moore? You're pretty buddy-buddy with her. Why not her?"

"We're just friends. That's all it is. There's no sexual attraction."

My father shook his head. "You love someone and sexual attraction follows. You don't just follow your pecker wherever it leads. It's love that counts."

"You never made it with anyone you didn't love?" I asked sarcastically. "Not in forty years?"

"Well, I never . . . There was always some degree of . . . I never *used* anyone," he said disdainfully.

"Neither did I. I felt exactly what Cheryl felt. It felt good, we had fun together, we—"

"That's what I'm saying," my father interrupted, his voice rising. "You kids today. Fun and games, fun and games. That's all you think about. How about responsibility? Abiding values? You think fun and games and you end up where you are now: up to your ears in trouble."

"Dad, listen. Cheryl's willing to give the baby up for adoption. No one's forcing me to do anything. In fact, I've had to hire a lawyer because the baby's already promised to some couple in Wilmington, and they insist they have a right to him or her, as the case may be."

"You're going to *court*? You're paying some damn-fool lawyer who'll charge you an arm and a leg to harass some couple who've been waiting for this baby for almost a year?"

"I went to Charles Moore." Charlie is my father's best friend, if he has one, and has managed my mother's estate since her death. He's the only lawyer I know.

"I can't believe that. You mean Charlie has known about this all along and never mentioned it to me?"

"It was confidential. I told him I wouldn't have him handle the case unless he was able to keep it that way."

My father's mouth tightened, as though he'd bitten into something bitter. "I always knew there was something slippery about Charlie. Your mother used to say that. She never put it quite that way, but she sensed it. 'I don't trust that man,' she'd say."

"Then why did she make him executor of her estate?"

"Too trusting. Never really thought there was any chance—" He stopped, choked up.

Suddenly I felt not only worn out emotionally but like a heel. My father is self-pitying, and God knows I don't understand why my mother married him, but he is pathetically cut off from life and people. True, it's his own fault, but he just never learned. My mother was his Seeing Eye dog. She connected him to life. He just doesn't know how to reconnect. "I think Charles is doing . . . is going to do a good job," I said. "I don't think he's a crook. If you want to come to the hearing, you can."

"When is it?" my father asked.

"Next week."

He sighed. "I'll see. . . . You don't need me to testify or anything?"

"No, nothing like that." I stood there awkwardly. "Well, I have some studying to do. See you at dinner?"

"Right." He looked abstracted. In front of him on the desk were some papers he was correcting. "What are we having tonight?"

"Lamb chops." I do all the cooking—otherwise we'd be eating corned beef hash or TV dinners every night.

My father tried to smile. "One of my favorites."

CHAPTER 2

There's a word I came across the other day that made me think of my father. *Anhedonia:* the inability to experience pleasure. Maybe that was some kind of challenge to my mother. Or maybe her chances in a small town like this just weren't that great. Most of the professors her age were married; those who weren't were gay. Also, I have to admit my mother's beauty was more the inner kind than the outer. When she smiled, her teeth protruded slightly. She had thin, brownish-blond hair, which she wore parted in the middle, flat to her head. Maybe it was her eyes, a warmer, brighter blue than my father's, or her smile, but I think many people didn't stop to think of her as plain, though technically that was what she was.

Whereas my father, whatever the defects in his character, is handsome. He's always had that thin little mustache that

13

to me makes him look a little like a Nazi general (his German heritage), but is evidently considered dashing by some. He has chiseled features, high cheekbones, a good profile. When he was younger, he rode horses a lot. He has good posture. He even, before my mother's death, anyway, could be witty in a dry kind of way. In a college town that, and a few good tweed jackets, can carry you far; extra men are always needed at dinner parties or for bridge. My father is a whiz at bridge— he used to play in national tournaments.

Each year, for as long as I can remember, there've been anxious discussions among my father's colleagues about whether Taylor will survive. It's a small women's college in Massachusetts, extremely isolated, though in beautiful country. Still, most girls nowadays want a coed college, and if they're feminist enough to want a women's college they pick someplace more prestigious or closer to a big city: Mount Holyoke or Barnard. Taylor hovers somewhere around the edges of the Seven Sisters. If you teach there, you'd say only location makes it miss. Frankly, I think most of the faculty is as dull and lackluster as the town. The ones who got tenure while they were still giving it, like my father, thank their lucky stars. The others do time for a while, then head elsewhere.

I do like the beauty of the country. I'm not much into sports, except for bike riding, but I like taking long walks, especially in the fall. Even though I chose Columbia deliberately because I wanted to try out life in a big city, I'm a little wary. I suppose you can develop them, but I haven't exactly grown up with street smarts. We don't even have a traffic light here. In some ways Haysburg is like some 1940s movie with Jimmy Stewart. It's the kind of place where people don't lock their doors, where Mr. Remer, who's eighty-seven and runs the local hardware store, will tell people, if he's leaving on a vacation, "The key's under the front mat.

Just take whatever you need and let me know about it when I get back.'' Elderly people here, like our next-door neighbor, Mrs. Galper, who's blind and almost ninety, live at home; neighbors stop in with her mail, Meals on Wheels come every evening to bring her dinner. In short, there are enough virtues to living here that even though I'm convinced everyone feels some degree of the discomfort I feel, they might not move, even given the chance. For the tenured faculty, like my father, that's a moot point; they make do, maybe travel on vacations, if they can afford it.

But you are watched. That's the fly in the ointment, a kind of vague, uneasy sense that there isn't really such a thing as private life. Not that anyone's phone is tapped; there's no local secret police, but there's the feeling that if you do anything even mildly untoward, that fact will communicate itself almost faster than the speed of light, while it's *happening*, almost. I am gigantically relieved that so far, I think, not many people know about Cheryl and me. Of course at school, where her condition has been pretty evident for a while, everyone knows. They used to not let pregnant girls graduate, but a few years back someone took the school to court over it. It is kind of brave for Cheryl to face it out. I see her with her friends, chatting in the hall, her face still pretty and young looking, with this thing in front of her, as though someone had stuffed a pillow under her skirt. She hasn't gotten humongously large; she's built on the petite side, and as I say, it's more like one part of her grew while the rest stayed pretty much the same.

I told my father Cheryl was pretty. She is—soft, curly black hair, dark eyes, smooth olive skin. But it wasn't her looks that made the difference. It was her setting her sights on me, making a point of coming up to chat after class, stopping me in the hall to ask some useless question like did I know when Thanksgiving vacation began. For a guy like me it's great, not only having a girl show that kind of interest but making the whole thing so easy. I could say, "All I did was stand there," but that would make me sound more passive than I was. Eventually, obviously, it takes two to tango. But way before any tangoing was in sight, I got a distinct message: you will not be rejected. Also, Cheryl is a talker, a babbler, when she's nervous. Even though our interests and world views were pretty far apart, she managed to fill in any potential gaps or silences with chatter about this or that, managed to listen or appear to listen to whatever I said with admiration and interest. If I sound like I was never sure how genuine all this was, that could be because that's how I feel even now. But she could just as easily say the same—that I was feigning interest to get her into bed.

Let's just say there was probably a touch of playacting on both sides: neither of us really deep down feeling we were "in love," but no one had to have his or her arm twisted to end up doing it. An elaborate way of saying I think the sexual attraction between us was genuine, if the rest was a bit contrived. My father may be right: that could be defined as using someone, but I'd say not, not if both are enjoying it for what it's worth. I'd call it sexist to assume any girl is deep down expecting the guy in question to marry her. It seems to me Cheryl was after a little fun; I think she got it just as much as I did.

I lied to my father about one thing, or rather didn't lie, but neglected to give the full facts. I discovered, through a friend at school, that Cheryl wasn't just giving our kid up for adoption; she was selling him (or her). So what, you might say? There are plenty of couples desperate for babies, and Cheryl comes from a poor family. I'm not a moralist; I don't begrudge her the chance to turn a misfortune into a small windfall for the Banks family. But it was around that time, a few months ago, that the idea implanted itself in my head about contesting the case, about adopting the kid myself. Now that I've gone ahead with it, hired Charlie to represent me, I feel like there's no turning back. On the days when I wake up and think, "What the hell am I doing?" I realize that this is not the point to start questioning my motives. I'll do my best in court and will abide by whatever the judge says. Charlie thinks our chances are about fifty-fifty. Clearly, as a potential provider I leave something to be desired compared to this couple who want to adopt the baby, the Sidels, who are married, settled, and own a home.

The hearing took place in Wilmington, which is about seventy miles from Haysburg. I was relieved at that. I was also relieved that my father chose not to come. He'd called Charlie and chewed him out a little, but Charlie just told me with a grin, "Abner'll settle down. He was always a little quick off the mark. Give him time."

In the judge's chambers with me were Cheryl, her mother, the couple who were planning on adopting the baby, the Sidels, and our lawyers. Charlie is a shortish, plump guy with snow-white hair, though he's no older than my father—late fifties. He looks solid, but has a genial air. Cheryl's lawyer, Mr. Forlenza, looked only a couple of years out of law school: handsome, thin, with carefully groomed black hair and glasses.

Mr. Forlenza called Cheryl to the witness stand first. "Miss Banks, could you tell us a little about the circumstances leading up to your present condition, your relationship with Mr. Weber?"

Cheryl was wearing a pretty blue maternity dress with a flower embroidered over the pocket. She looked fetching and a little girlish, but that's simply the way she looks most of the time; it didn't seem especially premeditated. "Well, we just kind of dated and, you know . . . went out, and I guess one thing kind of led to another." She was nervous, looked straight at Mr. Forlenza as though he were a teacher questioning her about a paper handed in late.

"Was this your first sexual experience?"

"Yes."

"How did it come about?"

"Pardon me?"

"Could you, without going into any details that make you uncomfortable, describe your first sexual encounter with Mr. Weber. Had you planned it? Did it 'just happen'? "

Cheryl swallowed. She pursed her lips. "We never really, um, planned it exactly. I mean, we'd been doing other things and . . . I suppose it was on our minds, but it's more like you said, it just kind of happened. My parents were out that night and one thing led to another."

"Was any form of birth control used?"

"No, not then."

"That was because of the unplanned nature of the event?"

"Yes."

"Was this the first of several sexual encounters between Mr. Weber and yourself?"

"Yes."

"And on these other occasions was some form of contraception practiced by you and Mr. Weber?"

Cheryl glanced at me furtively. "By him . . . Condoms."

"And did Mr. Weber assure you that these were safe?"

"I guess he thought they were."

"Did you ever discuss what might happen in the event of an unforeseen pregnancy?"

"No."

"Did you and Mr. Weber ever discuss marriage?"

"You mean like, as a topic? Or about us?"

"Either."

Cheryl pursed her lips again. "Well, this girl in our class

got married—had to get married her junior year—and we talked about that once.''

''What was Mr. Weber's feeling about this situation?''

''That they were both kind of stuck, basically.''

''He never seemed envious, or eager to be in that situation himself, to be the father of a child at that age?''

Cheryl laughed, ''Are you kidding? No way!''

''Why was that?''

''Well, the guy, like Tim, I mean Mr. Weber, he was going to college and now it looked like maybe he wouldn't be able to.''

''So, as you remember it, Mr. Weber mainly expressed the feeling that parenthood would be a burden to both these young people, that they simply weren't prepared at that age to be responsible parents?''

Charlie got to his feet. ''Your Honor, I object. Mr. Forlenza is putting words in his client's mouth.''

''Sustained,'' said the judge.

Mr. Forlenza touched his mustache self-consciously. ''At any point in your relationship with Mr. Weber, did he express a desire either to get married or to father a child?''

Cheryl frowned. ''He said he wasn't sure he was ever getting married. He said . . . not till, like, when he was thirty at the earliest.''

''Did Mr. Weber ever say, in relation to the young couple we've been discussing, that he thought they should have just offered the child up for adoption?''

''Yeah, he did.''

''He felt the baby would be better off raised by a married couple with a stable family situation?''

''Right.''

I wished Cheryl were lying. The fact is, I can't remember saying exactly that, but I can imagine I might've, if only to set the record straight on where I stood. Mr. Forlenza looked over at the judge. "That's all for the moment, Your Honor."

Charlie stood up. He marched over to the stand in his self-confident, hearty way. "Miss Banks, when did you first discover you were pregnant?"

"December sixteenth."

"And when did you inform Mr. Weber of the pregnancy?"

"Late in January."

"What made you wait so long?"

"It wasn't *that* long," Cheryl said indignantly. "Only six weeks."

"What made you wait six weeks, then?"

"I thought maybe . . . well, sometimes people, girls, miscarry in the first months."

"You were hoping that might happen?"

"Not exactly hoping, but . . . Well, I knew I didn't believe in abortion." She looked nervous, as though uncertain what to say.

"You've testified that in your sexual relations with Mr. Weber, he always took responsibility for contraception. Why was that?"

"Well, he had them. He had the condoms. So, why not?"

"It never occurred to you to take precautions yourself?"

"Not if he was."

"Was there ever any occasion, other than the first time, when Mr. Weber did not use condoms?"

"No," Cheryl said. "That's what's so weird."

"You were not having sexual relations with any other young man at the time?"

"No!" Cheryl looked horrified.

Charlie has a nice, relaxed manner. I could see that he was setting Cheryl at her ease. Oddly, she seemed less nervous than she had with her own lawyer. "When you and Mr.

Weber first discussed your pregnancy, did you ever discuss the possibility of marriage?"

"Not really . . . I mean, he never, like, proposed."

"Did he offer to pay for an abortion if you wanted one?"

"Yes, he did."

"And did you accept that offer?"

Cheryl hesitated. "Well, once I did, but then I thought about it and I decided no."

"You were ambivalent?"

"Pardon me?"

"You weren't really sure where you stood on the issue of abortion?"

"No, I said that I didn't think it was a good idea," Cheryl said. "Only I thought maybe I should do it anyway. But then I, like, thought there might be some nice couple who really wanted a baby and it wouldn't be fair."

"How did you find this nice couple? Through an adoption agency?"

Cheryl started biting her lip. "No, my sister knew someone from work, and she told that woman and her husband and they called me up."

"So the adoption was privately arranged?"

"Right."

"Did the Sidels, the couple in question, offer to pay for your hospital costs?"

"Yes."

Charlie paused. "Did they offer any other form of recompense?"

"Pardon me?"

"Are you receiving any other form of payment from the Sidels?"

Cheryl really looked torn. I could see she hadn't known we knew about the payment. "No," she whispered.

"Just the hospital costs?"

"Right."

"How much are the Sidels paying you for hospital costs, Miss Banks?"

"Ten thousand dollars." This was barely audible.

Charlie smiled. "Ten thousand dollars! Well, that's a very generous amount of money. Do you have any idea what an average stay in a hospital to have a child usually costs?"

"No," Cheryl said.

Charlie took a sheet of paper from his pocket. "Well, I happen to have checked with several local hospitals in this area. The most expensive postpartum hospital stay, including costs to the gynecologist and anesthesiologist, comes to two thousand dollars." He looked at Cheryl. "Doesn't there seem to be a slight discrepancy here?"

By this point Cheryl looked like she was in shock. I felt sorry for her, so overwhelmed by the occasion, by this sudden move, though of course it was one of our main strong points. "What does that mean?" she squeaked.

"It means that there appears to be some indication that you are, in effect, selling your baby to the Sidels, that 'hospital costs' is a euphemism for money received under the table."

"Oh, no," Cheryl said, terrified. "I thought it was for the hospital."

"You're aware that you're under oath, Miss Banks."

"Yes, I just thought—" She stumbled. "They seemed to want the baby so much. And they have the money, I mean, why is that so bad?"

Charlie smiled gently. "That'll be all, Miss Banks."

CHAPTER 3

Charlie sat down next to me and drew a little smiling face on a piece of paper, his sign that he felt things were going well. I was beginning to feel like a heel. Cheryl's ingenuousness, her not understanding half the words Charlie used, is part of her appeal, though I think beneath it there's also a certain calculating streak. But as I watched her walk gingerly back to her seat I felt my heart sink. Let them win. Let her have the baby or sell the baby, or whatever. I wished I were a millionaire and could just say to Cheryl: "Here's ten thousand dollars. Take it for having to go through this whole thing, and I'll take the baby." I didn't care much about the Sidels.

Mr. Forlenza called Mr. Sidel to the stand. He was a tall, husky man, broad shouldered, who looked like he might have played football in college. His wife was plump, with boyishly short blond hair and round glasses.

"Mr. Sidel, could you tell us how long you and your wife, Patricia, have been married?"

"Eight years."

"And how long have you been trying to have a child?"

"Five years." He spoke too loudly, as though he were giving a speech and was afraid someone in the back row might not hear.

"Could you give us your reasons for waiting that long to try and conceive a child?"

"We wanted to make sure our marriage would last."

"In other words, you didn't want to bring a child into an unstable marital situation where there was a possibility that the child would end up suffering the damaging effects of being in a single-parent home?"

Charlie stood up. "Objection, Your Honor. He's putting words in his client's mouth."

The judge waved his hand. "Sustained. We get the point, Mr. Forlenza. No need to repeat your client's testimony."

"Yes, sir. . . . Mr. Sidel, what is your profession?"

"I'm an engineer. I work for Tyson, McGrath, and Coro."

"How long have you been employed at that particular firm?"

"Six years."

"Does your wife work?"

"She teaches nursery school."

"In the event of your adopting a child, would your wife continue to work?"

"No, sir."

"Why is that?"

"We both feel a child needs the undivided care and attention of a mother in its early years."

Mr. Forlenza beamed with approval, glanced at the judge

to make sure that it had sunk in, and then proceeded. "How large is your home, Mr. Sidel?"

"It's a three bedroom ranch-style house on an acre and a half of land, with a twenty-year mortgage. I'd say we've paid off about half."

"Do you have a separate room set aside for a child, should you succeed in adopting one?"

"Yes, sir."

"Have you and your wife been looking forward to adopting a child for some time?"

Sidel nodded. "Yes, we have, once we realized we couldn't have one ourselves."

"You have no reservations about your ability to give this child a happy, stable home environment in which you would both share in its care and development?" Mr. Forlenza leaned forward as though apprehensive about the answer.

"That's right."

Mr. Forlenza looked up at the judge. "No further questions."

Charlie got slowly to his feet, glanced at some papers, then said, "Mr. Sidel, you and your wife have tried adopting a child through several adoption agencies, have you not?"

"Yes, we have."

"And what was the result of these efforts?"

"Nothing . . . A couple of close calls, but no baby."

"So you were both beginning to feel a little desperate?"

Sidel frowned. He had his broad hands interlocked, as though to prevent himself from making any unintentional gestures. "No, not desperate, just disappointed."

"How did you happen to hear of Miss Banks's pregnancy and the possibility that she might be willing to offer her child to you for adoption?"

"Her sister knows my wife."

"And what made you decide to use this rather idiosyncratic means of adoption rather than the traditional one?"

"We wanted a baby." Slight irritation, concealed by a well-practiced amiability.

"How much did you want a baby, Mr. Sidel?"

"Very much . . . We both love children." He glanced warmly at his wife.

This guy was like a rock. I didn't see how Charlie would ever get past him. "Did you want a baby enough so that you were willing to pay for one?"

"No, sir."

"You never, at any time, offered to pay Miss Banks, as a reward or recompense, for giving up her child to you?"

"Never."

Charlie moved closer to the witness stand. "Mr. Sidel, what would you call the ten thousand dollars that you did agree to pay Miss Banks, if *not* recompense?"

"It was to cover hospital expenses."

"You've heard the hospital costs I quoted a short time ago. Were you aware that there was such a discrepancy between what you agreed to pay and the actual costs of a postpartum hospital stay?"

Sidel hesitated. He glanced at his wife again, as though for moral support. "There can be complications," he said slowly.

"How frequently do you think such complications occur, complications which would enable a hospital to charge ten thousand dollars?"

"I don't know, exactly." He was nervous but determined to hold his own.

"You just wanted to be on the safe side?"

"That's right."

"Are you aware, Mr. Sidel, of the economic situation in Miss Banks's home?"

"Yes, sir."

"What is her father's occupation?"

"He's a garbage collector."

"Does her mother work?"

"No."

"How did you become apprised of these facts?"

"Through her sister."

"Did it ever occur to you that, given these slightly difficult economic facts, a cash offer might induce Miss Banks to part with her baby?"

Sidel hesitated. "I knew she'd been through a lot. I didn't want to make things hard for her."

"Did you offer to buy this baby, Mr. Sidel, using 'hospital costs' as a euphemism for such a purchase?"

"No, sir. It was in case of complications."

"Thank you, Mr. Sidel."

For some reason Mrs. Sidel wasn't going to take the stand. It was strange. Even though I cared about the outcome of the hearing, part of me was watching it the way you'd watch a Perry Mason show on TV. I'd never want to be a lawyer, but it was interesting watching Charlie and Forlenza playing around with the same facts, twisting them here, tugging them there. It was a game. The best player would win, not necessarily the person on the side of justice. But then the judge must have known that. Maybe in his mind it was a balance between justice and game playing. He had a lean, implacable face; it was impossible to read anything into any of his expressions except occasional impatience or boredom.

"Mr. Timothy Weber, would you please take the stand?"

Now that I was being a participant, I shifted in record time from a kind of interested detachment to heart-thumping anxiety. I swore to tell the whole truth and nothing but the truth. Then I looked into Mr. Forlenza's thick, black-rimmed glasses with as honest and cool an expression as I could muster.

"Mr. Weber, you're an only child, are you not?"

"I am."

"So you grew up without ever observing your mother, who was a librarian, caring for babies or small children."

"That's correct."

"Did your family live near any relatives with small children or babies? Cousins, perhaps?"

"No, sir."

"Did you ever baby-sit in your high school years?"

"No, sir."

"So it would be fair to say that your experience caring for babies or small children is next to nil?"

"Right."

I glanced at Charlie. I'd clearly lost that one, but he had said, "Don't lie about facts, it'll only cause trouble," so I hadn't.

"Mr. Weber, when you first discovered your girlfriend, Miss Banks, was pregnant, you suggested that she have an abortion, did you not?"

"Yes, I did."

"Why was that?"

"I knew we didn't want to get married, and I thought she might consider the baby a burden."

"So you believe in abortion when a couple is not ready to have a child or, for whatever personal reason, chooses not to?"

"Yes, I do."

"Did you consider Miss Banks's pregnancy a burden?"

"I was sorry it happened, but I wasn't the one who was going to have the baby."

"Did you at that time consider the possibility of adopting and raising the child yourself?"

28

"No, sir."

Suddenly I felt like we were going to lose. I didn't feel I was answering wrong, but it seemed like any judge on earth would award the baby to the Sidels. Hell, I would've.

"Mr. Weber, this fall you intend to enroll in a premed program at Columbia University toward a B.A. degree, do you not?"

"I do."

"You will be on scholarship at Columbia?"

"Yes, I will."

"Is one of the conditions of this scholarship that you maintain a B average in all your courses?"

"Yes, it is."

"And you believe that, while caring for a small baby, you can do that?"

"I hope I can, yes."

"Where do you intend to live while at college, Mr. Weber?"

"I'm going to rent an apartment."

"Do you have any idea of the costs of apartments in the Columbia area?"

"About one thousand dollars a month for a studio, fifteen hundred dollars for a one bedroom." Thank God, Charlie had looked into that.

"That's a pretty steep amount of money for a boy on scholarship to spend. Where will you get that money?"

"Well, I have some saved from summer jobs, and I have an inheritance from my mother."

"Will that inheritance also cover the costs of child care?"

"Yes."

"What do you intend to do with this child, if you should raise it, during the day?"

"I'm going to find a day-care center."

29

"So during the day the baby will be in the care of a stranger?"

"A well-trained, caring stranger with some experience in child care," I said. Suddenly I felt determined to at least put up a good fight. It was like a chess game where you know your opponent is a better player, but you can still try to out-psyche him.

"Mr. Weber, do you personally feel that the care of a stranger is equal to the care of a baby's mother?"

"If it's supplemented by the care of a father in the evenings and on weekends, yes."

"In short, you feel a father can be as good a mother as a mother?"

"I feel a father can be as good a *parent* as a mother." Great. I figured that was a good answer. Don't be smug. Stay on your toes.

"You feel a part-time, teenage father can be as good a parent as a trained, responsible, full-time mother?"

"Yes, I do."

"Thank you, Mr. Weber."

As Charlie came up for questioning, I felt a bit down: *Shit, I blew it.* The whole thing seemed ludicrous. I just wanted to say "Forget it, let's go home, this is a farce." I wondered if my father was right about Charlie—that he just took on the case to get some extra dough, that he'd never thought we had a chance in hell to win.

"Mr. Weber, it's been stated that you are an only child. Did you ever, as you were growing up, think about the possibility of one day having a family of your own?"

"Yes, sir."

"Did you want your child to be an only child, like yourself?"

"No, I wanted to have at least two children."

"Your mother died six years ago, Mr. Weber. Until that

30

time, did you feel your parents executed their role as parents well? Did you consider them role models?''

''Yes.'' Naturally, that was a lie in relation to my father, but Charlie had said lies about feelings are allowed, since the judge can't open you up and see what's inside you.

''So, on the basis of the way your parents raised you, you feel you derived a feeling of how you yourself would raise a child?''

''Yes, sir.''

''As Mr. Forlenza has stated, you will be pursuing your college education while raising your child. If it should become necessary to go to college part time in order to provide your child with greater care, would you be willing to do this?''

''Yes, I would.'' Hypothetical, but still true.

''Mr. Weber, your grades in school have been consistently excellent. Your teachers describe you as responsible and hardworking. Do you feel these characteristics will enable you to shoulder the responsibility of caring for your child?''

''Yes, I do.'' I tried to look responsible and hardworking.

''Does the fact that this is your child, who will, of course, carry your genes, matter to you?''

''Yes, very much.''

''Does it also matter to your father, who is, as we have stated, a widower?''

''Yes, it matters to him.'' Okay, I'm not hooked up to a lie detector, thank God.

''In short, you feel that the fact that this is your child will give you a tie, a connection and sense of caring that a stranger cannot give?''

''Yes, I do.''

Charlie moved closer; he became stern. ''What was your reaction, Mr. Weber, on discovering that Miss Banks would receive ten thousand dollars as a payment for giving up your child?''

''I felt she should have discussed it with me.'' I didn't really want to play that up too much. It seemed to me Charlie had gone over it pretty thoroughly.

''Why did you feel that?''

''Well, it's our child, not just hers. I feel its future should depend on me as much as on her.''

When I sat down and listened or half listened to Forlenza and Charlie replay their main points, I felt neither elated nor discouraged. Charlie seemed to me a better lawyer, less seemingly eager, more mature and relaxed. Maybe it was one of Forlenza's first cases, but he overdid it, made points too often, hyped things where it wasn't really necessary. If I were the judge, I'd have thought he was acting like the whole thing had to be spelled out, whereas Charlie's attitude was: Let's be grownups about this. When they had both finished summing up—Forlenza went last—Charlie and I filed out.

CHAPTER 4

Charlie didn't say anything until we were in his car. "So how did you think it went?" I asked.

"You were good, kid. Kept your cool. Nice going." He started the motor.

"Yeah, but how did you think it went? I mean, who won?"

Charlie laughed. "That's a tough one. Pretty even-steven. I wouldn't want to bet my life on either side."

I glanced out the window. It was a cool March evening, soft air, trees beginning to turn green. "If you were the judge, who would *you* give the baby to?"

"Hey, Tim, let's go for a beer, okay? I can't take any more grilling on an empty stomach."

We drove to a pub near Charlie's office. "The usual," he said to the bartender, "and a ginger ale for my client, here."

My father would have hit the ceiling if he knew I was out

drinking with Charlie, but I liked the man-to-man feeling about it, the fact that he'd referred to me as his client, not just some kid. I would have preferred beer to ginger ale, but I knew Charlie wouldn't risk that. Boy, if I was a lawyer, I'd probably become an alcoholic. I don't know how they handle the pressure day after day. I guess they must get a kick out of it. And the pay is good.

"So who would *you* award the baby to, if you were the judge?" I asked again.

Charlie made a wry expression. "Jeez . . . well, okay, if you want honesty, probably to the Sidels."

"Because you think they'd do a better job of raising it?"

"That, and I don't really think you know what you're getting into."

"But—" I began.

"Not you, as an individual, Tim. I think no one, at your age, can imagine what being a parent is like. It changes your life in a thousand ways, ones you can't even begin to imagine."

He was probably right. I felt morose. "Maybe I should just forget it, then?"

"Well, do you want the kid or don't you? I thought you told me you'd really thought it through."

"I have. No, I did . . . I do want it. I just feel sorry for Cheryl."

Charlie drank some beer. "Why? Because she'll be out a little dough?"

I thought of her big round eyes during the questioning. "It must have been kind of humiliating for her, having that brought up in court."

He shrugged. "How would we have a chance to win, otherwise?"

"I don't know."

Charlie put his hand on my shoulder. "She'll survive. Let me bet you, within a year, two years maximum, she'll be married, raising a kid of her own. You'll be a dim memory, the whole *case* will be a dim memory.''

"What makes you so sure of that?''

"She's pretty.'' He grinned. "She got you. She'll nab someone else.''

I tried to smile. "She didn't exactly 'get' me.''

"She tried. . . . Her aim was off, that's all. Next time she'll take fire at someone within her reach and it'll all have a happy ending.''

I thought of what my father had said the other day. "I really don't think she was *aiming* for me. I think it was just, you know, mutual attraction.''

"Maybe.''

"It's pretty cynical to think any time a girl goes to bed with a guy, she's hoping to get him to marry her, don't you think?''

Charlie smiled. "Well, Tim, at my age maybe you've earned the right to be just a little cynical. I'm not saying anything against Cheryl Banks. I have three daughters myself. I know a little something about the female species. I'm just saying that if you had said 'Cheryl, marry me,' she'd have said yes so fast you wouldn't have had time to finish the sentence.''

I shook my head. "I don't think so. Don't you think we'd have been a pretty mismatched couple?''

Charlie laughed. "Are you asking me: would you have been happy together, or would she have said yes?''

"Well . . .''

"Look, like I say, we'll never know. You liked each other for a while, this happened, no villains, the Sidels will find another baby.''

"God, he was such a jerk,'' I said with unexpected vehemence.

"Really? How so? I thought he seemed like a nice guy.''

"I don't know. I just hate guys like that who seem so sure of themselves about everything.''

Charlie shook his head and beckoned to the bartender for another beer. "He wasn't sure of himself. He was nervous as hell. . . . No, if I feel sorry for anyone, it's not your ex-girlfriend, it's the Sidels. Maureen and I had trouble in the beginning, when we wanted a baby. It can be a pretty grueling thing. You figure all you have to do is try to have one. No one on either side of our family had ever had trouble. And you *try*, and you *try* . . ."

I stared at him, at his red, shiny face. "I don't get why you took the case, if you basically sympathize with them, *and* you think I'll be a lousy father—"

"Abner's an old friend, you seemed kind of desperate . . ." Charlie paused. "I was convinced if I turned you down, you'd look elsewhere and I knew, no matter what my personal convictions were, that I'd do a darn good job on your behalf."

"I don't see how anyone can be a lawyer," I said. "I mean, you're getting up there saying things you don't mean!"

"You don't believe in our legal system, is that what you're saying?" Charlie looked amused rather than challenged.

"No, I believe in it, I guess. Personally, I just wouldn't want to get up there and pretend things I didn't really believe."

"So you won't be a lawyer. . . . But isn't it good that not everyone feels that way?"

"I suppose."

Charlie just gazed at me. "Well, one thing is certain: I wish your mother were around. Abner's not going to be one whit of good if you get the baby. You're going to do this on your own."

"I know." That was the understatement of the year.

Charlie leaned forward. "Look, Tim, I don't mean to plant ideas in your head. I'm just saying the baby's not due for a few more months. If you change your mind at any time, just give me a call, okay? There are plenty of couples out there who'll be happy as larks to get the baby—this is assuming we win the case. If we don't, chalk it up to experience. And make sure your girlfriend uses some protection next time, not just you."

"Don't worry."

I went home a little depressed. My last thought before I fell asleep was, I hope Cheryl wins.

A week later, Charlie called to tell me that the judge had decided in my favor. "Obviously the ten thousand dollars swung it," he said. "Which is a pity because, between you and me, who cares who pays what, if they think it's worth it. But congratulations."

"Thanks." Suddenly I felt peculiarly triumphant. I was glad I'd gone to court and glad the baby would be mine. I was determined to prove everyone wrong. I would do a good job, and I would get through college without letting my average slip.

I didn't see Cheryl at school that day. We don't have any classes together this year, but sometimes I run into her in the hall or see her during lunch hour. But as I was leaving at the end of the day, I saw her by herself, walking away from the school building. Impulsively I ran over and caught up with her. "Hey, listen, Cheryl. I'm sorry. I mean, well, I'm glad, but I'm sorry that it had to happen this way."

She just looked at me, her face frozen in anger. "Yeah, you're really sorry? I'll bet!"

"I am." I swallowed. "I'm not sorry I'll be raising the baby, I'm just sorry that, well, on top of having to be pregnant you had to go through all this stuff with the court case and—"

Cheryl's eyes had narrowed into slits. "You are *such* a liar, you know that? I can't *believe* this! You're so sorry, you're so sorry . . ." She paused, breathless. "If you're so sorry, why'd you make me *do* it? What was the point? What do *you* care if some couple with money to spend want to spend it on a baby that they're going to love and take care of?"

"I don't— That didn't make any difference to me."

"Then why'd you bring it up in court?"

"Because Charlie thought it would help us win the case."

Cheryl's mouth was shut tight, bitterly. "You just don't know anything about anything, do you? To you, money is nothing, big deal. You can't imagine what that money would've meant to my family. To you it's like peanuts. Ten thousand dollars—big deal."

The fact is, my mother's inheritance isn't that great. I had tried to make it sound larger so that the judge would think I could definitely make it on my own. But still, everything's relative. To Cheryl, I'm rich. To a lot of people I'm just middle class, at best. "Look, if I really *was* rich, I'd just give you the ten thousand dollars. I wish I could. I wish I *was* that rich."

She snorted derisively. "Thanks a lot. I love imaginary presents."

Suddenly I felt frustrated. At least I'd been trying to be nice. "Don't you think you should've at least discussed it with me?"

"What for?" She looked bewildered.

"Just to give me a chance—to see how I felt about it." I felt awkward, the words seemed to jump out unevenly.

"I *know* how you feel about it! You feel like you're the king of the whole goddamn world, like you can do anything; get a scholarship to college, raise a baby. You can do anything a girl can do, anything! So, good! Go do it."

This is probably crazy, but still, even in the middle of this ugly, stupid argument, I felt attracted to Cheryl. Maybe it's that she has this intense kind of honesty that can lash out, but at least it isn't pretending. Or maybe it's just that she's so pretty, even with this big lump under her dress. "I'm going to try," I said stiffly, fighting back this other feeling, afraid she would sense it.

She stared at me with her black eyes. "You know what I wish? I wish I could go out and have the baby aborted right this afternoon. I wouldn't care if it was alive or what; I wish

38

I could kill it to spite you, just so you couldn't get it. Because I think you're a mean, selfish person who doesn't deserve a dog, or a cat, even, much less a baby.''

"Thanks." My mouth tried to curl up into a smile. "You didn't act like you felt that way when we going around together.''

"*You* didn't act that way then. You acted nice, just so you could sweet-talk me into bed. And I fell for it because I'm just a jerk! My sister said, 'I can't *believe* you'd be that stupid. A professor's son, and you actually believe he *loves* you, he *cares* for you. You've got to be kidding,' she said.'' Cheryl was talking so fast and breathing so hard that if I hadn't been used to her way of speaking, I wouldn't have been able to understand what she was saying.

"I did . . . care for you," I heard myself saying. "I wasn't just pretending. Your sister's wrong."

"But you never even—" Her voice broke, she half turned away. "When you heard I was pregnant, you never even *once* said, you never even *once*—" It was like she was caught in that sentence and couldn't get out, perhaps because at the end of it the word "marriage" loomed.

I lowered my voice. "I didn't want to get married. I didn't think I was ready. It wasn't a matter of loving you or not."

"You're not ready for marriage, but you're ready to raise a baby alone?" She snorted, her sarcasm and self-possession returning.

"Maybe I'm not. Maybe I'll do a lousy job."

"Yeah, maybe you'll wreck some baby's life as well as mine and the Sidels'. Then you can *really* be happy."

Finally I felt angry. "I *haven't* wrecked your life."

"Well, you sure haven't made my senior year a piece of cake.''

"I told you I was sorry about that."

"Why don't you stop being so sorry?" Cheryl yelled. "If

39

you had to carry this baby around in your stomach for nine months, you'd have an abortion in less than one second!''

"The baby's in your womb, not your stomach," I said coolly.

"Thanks so *much* for the information, Tim. Now why don't you just go to hell and leave me alone, okay?'' She marched off, almost at a run, her body a little unsteady.

I stood there, stunned. It wasn't like I felt I really was in the wrong, but this was the first time in my life that I'd ever felt someone hated me. Not just disliked or envied or was irritated by, but *hated*. That the feeling could come out of what was once something resembling or simulating love was stupefying. *I'd have an abortion this afternoon.*

Cheryl disappeared, and I was still standing there, staring into space, waiting for a feeling of numbness to take over. Just then Cheryl's best friend, Beth Williams, sidled up out of nowhere and said softly, "Don't feel bad, Tim."

I looked at her. Beth is chunky and freckled, with a friendly face. We used to be pals when we were in fourth and fifth grade, and we still are on the school newspaper together. "Cheryl just feels bad," she said.

"I know," I said.

"She really kind of, well, loved you so—"

"Yeah, sure." I didn't feel like talking about this with anyone else. Beth looked up at me. Was she flirting? It was hard for me to tell.

"Maybe you just weren't suited. Your personalities, I mean," she said.

I realized that Beth didn't know about the court decision. I suppose I could have gotten a big dose of feminine sympathy if I'd told her about it, but I didn't want to. "Listen, I'll see you around," I said abruptly, and walked to my car.

I wish that Howie Robinson hadn't moved away when we were in seventh grade. He was the only really close friend I've ever had. His father taught physics at Taylor, and after he'd been at Taylor only two years he took a job at Los Alamos. Neither of us write, so I don't know much about what's been happening with him since he left. The thing is, we never exactly talked about personal things, but he had all the same interests I did. He was as sure he wanted to go into physics as I was sure I wanted to go into medicine. With him I didn't feel I had to hide whatever I was reading, to pretend I was interested in sports. We were so much alike that we could just sit around all afternoon doing nothing and have a really excellent time. If I was in a bad mood about something—this was the year after my mother died—he understood right away. I didn't ever have to say anything. He just somehow knew. I wonder if you can have that kind of rapport with a girl. When things were at their best, Cheryl and I had some good times together, a feeling of warmth and horsing around, but there was always some game playing. We never really trusted each other.

Think how lucky I am I didn't offer to marry her! Imagine someone you were married to lashing out at you like that! My parents fought, but never that way, never like they wanted to kill each other. But then, in spite of myself, I thought of Cheryl lumbering off, having to lug the baby, whom she wouldn't even raise, around for another four months. I wished I had said something to her like if she ever wanted to see the baby, or visit it, she could just write me or call me. Maybe I should write her a letter about that, just friendly, nothing to get her started again.

But why should she want to see a baby she'd had with someone she hated? And maybe by then, like Charlie said, she'd be married, or engaged, and she would hardly remember who I was. I hope the baby is a boy. I never thought of that until now, but what if it's a girl and looks exactly like Cheryl, and she starts screaming at me about things in that same way?

CHAPTER 5

I took a long walk before supper. That's what I do when I want to get away from it all: just disappear into the fields or the woods. The farms around here are small and spread far apart. You can walk without running into a soul. It's probably typical of me that when I was little, my favorite fantasy, the one I used to play around with before I fell asleep, was of being alone on a desert island and how I would cope. I never even ended it with people coming to rescue me. The whole thing was just the idea of me being there, taming the animals, fishing. My favorite book was *Island of the Blue Dolphins*, probably because it was about someone surviving completely on her own. I never liked as much the books where a whole family or a group of friends was shipwrecked.

Once Cheryl and I saw this movie together, *The Blue Lagoon*, in which Brooke Shields and some idiot blond guy get shipwrecked as kids, gradually grow up, "discover" sex, and have a baby. They made it seem like an idyll, away from everything, just the two of them. Cheryl was crazy about that movie. She went to see it two more times with her friend Beth, and once, when it was on cable, she wanted me to come over and watch it with her again. Maybe that shows the difference between our fantasies. Mine certainly wasn't being stuck on a desert island with a girl and having to take care of her *and* her baby. Even if it was Brooke Shields, who's never struck me as that sexy anyway.

Walking along, I thought of that weird moment, when Cheryl was lashing out at me and I'd suddenly started feeling attracted to her again; I wish I could figure that out. The part that's easy to figure out is that some girls are pretty or flirt with you or seem to like you, and—whammo—there's some inner explosion that makes you temporarily act or feel a little like a maniac. What's strange to me is that there'd be some nights both of us had looked forward to, when everything would be just about perfect, and I'd feel like I was just going through the motions, like mentally I was at home playing chess with my father. And then there were other times when, out of nowhere, even during a fight, there'd be this feeling that was so strong I almost felt physically sick. Like, right now I know as definitely as I know anything on earth that my relationship with Cheryl is over. I don't even want to sleep with her again. And not just because she's pregnant. Because she wasn't honest, she lied to me, I don't respect her anymore. But just the same, for that moment there, the attraction I felt for her came back, like someone had thrown a black hood over my head and I could hardly breathe.

I wonder if girls really feel that, or feel it so intensely. I certainly think that unless Cheryl was bluffing her way through the whole thing, unless I'm just devoid of any ability to judge people's behavior, that part of the time, even most of the time,

43

she was enjoying the sex. But I wonder if it's the same kind of enjoyment, where part of you wants to run toward it and part of you wants to run away. Or maybe it's just me. If Howie was here, maybe we'd talk about it. Certainly my father is about the last person on earth I'd talk to about sex or girls, or anything like that. Once, after my mother died, I found a bunch of poems he'd written. I glanced through them. They all seemed to be love poems to my mother. They were the kind of poems I'd expect him to write, though I hadn't known he wrote poetry at all. "Alone, alone, alone . . ." started one. A few had lines about "white breasts glimmering softly in the moonlight."

At dinner, shoveling a slice of ham steak onto his plate, I said, "Well, I won the case."

He looked up at me dryly. "Does this call for some sort of celebration? Should we open the champagne?"

"Not necessarily." I sat down and tried to concentrate on my food. When I was little, no matter how well I did in school, my father always managed to take the edge off the triumph by using that dry, sardonic tone. Maybe he felt he was keeping me from getting a swelled head, that my mother spoiled me. Anyway, though I'm used to it by now, I still hate it.

"So I'm going to be a grandfather, am I?" he said.

"Right."

"A grandfather at fifty-eight . . . sooner than I might have expected, but late by American standards. Mrs. Worley has five grandchildren and she's just turned forty." Mrs. Worley is our cleaning lady who comes in once a week.

"Does it make you feel old?"

He was trimming the fat off his ham. "Old? Well, I *am* old, so of course I *feel* old."

"You're middle-aged," I corrected him.

"Depends on how you look at it. In the old days, people died before my age . . . and of course it depends on how you feel. I feel like I'm just sitting around, taking up space."

44

At certain remarks of my father's, like that one, I hear imaginary violins sounding in the background. I didn't respond.

"When did you say the baby was due?"

"In July."

"And they're allowing her to graduate?"

"Why shouldn't they allow her to graduate?"

"Well, in *my* day, if a girl was pregnant, the family shipped her off to a home somewhere, to avoid disgrace, to keep the neighbors from talking. Even teachers weren't allowed to go on teaching if they were pregnant, even *married* teachers."

"I guess things have progressed slightly since then," I said wryly.

My father tilted his head to one side. "Progressed? You call it progress, do you? Flaunting something like that in front of the entire student body?"

It seemed ironical to be defending Cheryl, but I said, "She didn't do anything wrong. Half the girls in the class are having sex with their boyfriends. She just got caught, that's all. It's not a crime."

He clenched his jaw. "Yes, it is."

I smiled. "What is? Sex? Having babies?"

"Babies having babies. What does a girl that age know about babies? If you aren't ready to be a parent, you shouldn't indulge."

"You didn't, when you were my age?"

"Absolutely not. Of course, I was attracted, I had impulses, but I reined them in. That's what civilization is all about: reining in our impulses. Otherwise we'd all be running around like wild beasts, fornicating, robbing banks . . ."

I picked away at some lima beans heaped on one side of my plate. "So you and Mom were virgins when you got married?"

My father flushed. "No, we weren't virgins. We were . . . we'd had a few experiences, but they were *love* experiences. We were old enough to know what we were doing."

"So how come you never married any of them?"

My father was getting annoyed, but trying, as he would put it, to "rein it in." "Not everyone is suitable, not everyone has the same life plan. Some people change. Any number of things can happen. But at least you start with someone of the same social background, someone who shares your ideals and views of the world."

"I thought you were a socialist," I couldn't help pointing out.

"I believe in the socialist ideal," my father admitted. "But *only* as an ideal. I'm a realist when it comes to life as it is now. You, who will one day be a doctor, could *not* have been happy with a garbage collector's daughter. That's all there is to it. And if you were old enough to know what you were doing, you would have thought of that."

I tried to mentally count to ten. "Dad, you know it's pretty insulting and stupid to keep calling Cheryl 'the garbage collector's daughter.' Her sister works in a bank. Why not call her 'the bank manager's sister'? Your father was a farmer. So have you gone through life calling yourself a farmer's son?"

My father pushed his plate aside. "You always feel that if you win an argument by semantics, you've got me," he said angrily. "Well, life *isn't* semantics. You live in a small town. A girl went after you, whom you should have known was not a suitable life's companion. You acted stupidly, and you got her *and* yourself into a great deal of needless trouble. Why not accept the responsibility for that?"

I felt like smashing the plate in his face. "Look, I don't give a damn *who* her father is! I don't care who *she* is! Maybe I'll marry a girl who's a garbage collector herself. How about that? If I marry, I'll marry a person, and I won't sit around staring at their pedigree as if I were buying a show dog!"

I knew my father was really riled. "Marry whoever you want! Make as big a mess of your life as you feel like! Throw your mother's inheritance down the drain! If you're bent on self-destruction, I won't do a thing to stop you."

My father used to act in amateur theater productions at the college. He has an excellent singing voice, and he played the male lead in *South Pacific* and the hero in *Hedda Gabler*, opposite Professor Ramsey, the art historian who really acted up a storm as Hedda. Maybe he ought to go back to acting. Then I thought, In six months I'll be at college. "Do you want me to move out when the baby arrives?" I asked. "I can get a room somewhere, if you want."

"Of course not," he snapped. "We're in this together. Is that understood?"

"I guess."

As I tried to do my homework I thought of what it must be like for Cheryl at home. One of her older sisters still lives with them. It's a weird, crowded little house that started out as a mobile home. They added on a few rooms, so you can't really tell until it's pointed out to you. When we were going together, we came to my house a lot more often than we went to Cheryl's, because it's bigger and because my father's schedule is pretty set, what with office hours and committee meetings. He prides himself on the fact that the day after my mother's death, he put in a whole afternoon of classes. I have a lock on my bedroom door. I installed it myself when I was ten. That might seem like a strange thing for a kid to do. I just wanted my room to be private, and my mother understood. She said that as long as she could inspect the room once a month, and I was willing to change the sheets, it was okay.

Cheryl always said there was something spooky about our house. Maybe it was her knowing about my mother's death. Maybe it's that everything is neat but sort of airless, unlike her house, which was always a mess, but noisy with everyone yelling from room to room. She thought my putting a lock on my door was strange. "Why would you do that at ten?" she asked.

"For privacy." "But what's there to be private about, at ten? You didn't even have brothers or sisters to bother you."

Even though I knew my father's schedule, and Cheryl always left a good hour before he came home, I still always locked the door when we were in there together. And even with the door locked I felt uneasy, not as though someone might come in, since obviously it wasn't possible unless someone scaled the walls outside the house and climbed through the window. I just used to feel watched somehow. Maybe it was a feeling that my mother, if she were alive, wouldn't approve, or that if she were alive, I certainly wouldn't have been bringing Cheryl back to our house. I remember once we did it when Cheryl had her period. I put a towel under her, but she bled through anyway, and it gave me a kind of sick feeling, as though I'd literally committed a crime. She insisted it didn't hurt at all to do it then, and either I couldn't believe her or the idea made me too nervous, but that time I just couldn't come. We did it for what seemed like hours, and all I could think of was the blood seeping into the towel; finally we just gave up. I wonder if that's when she got pregnant. All the books say it's incredibly rare for a girl to get pregnant when she has her period, but still there's an infinitesimal chance of some sperm hanging on and just waiting for its chance. But if I didn't even come? Well, who knows?

But this is typical. Even thinking of that slightly gruesome experience I'm starting to feel horny again. I hate to even admit this, but sometimes, late at night, when I'm in bed, I wonder what Cheryl's body looks like now. My fantasy, which probably *is* somewhat sick, is that I become invisible and sneak (though I guess if you're invisible, you don't have to sneak) into her room at night when she's getting ready for bed. She takes a bath every night, and I sit in the bathroom (again, I don't know if invisible people "sit" or just drift around) watching her bathe herself. I watch her soap herself up and lie there.

Maybe it's because I imagine Cheryl in a warm tub as feeling peaceful and content, the way she occasionally seemed after we made love. And I want to think that at such moments, if she feels the baby move or kick, she has some pleasant memories of our times together, not just rage and hostility, but some . . . Oh, who am I kidding? I'll never know, anyway.

But my fantasy continues with her getting out of the tub, drying herself off, slipping into her nightgown, and getting into bed. I guess the next part is even stranger, but our psychology textbook said that any fantasy, no matter how strange, has been felt by millions of people, even presumably normal people. At this point it's like I'm a combination of invisible and not, in that I get into bed with her and stroke her body and kiss her, and even make love to her, but she doesn't exactly know I'm there. I touch her belly and feel the baby move slightly, but the fact that she's pregnant doesn't make it hard to make love, in fact it's easier. It just all happens with no one saying anything, both of us feeling satisfied and good when it's over. And then I kind of melt away, and even though Cheryl is asleep by then, she has happy, peaceful dreams.

The only trouble with this fantasy is that it can boomerang. Sometimes it really literally puts me to sleep. Anyway, it's all so fuzzy that I don't have to figure out any real details the way I might if I was fantasizing about an event that might actually happen, the way I used to imagine ahead of time Cheryl and me making love. But other times I'll sit up in bed feeling ferociously horny, almost wishing I was still a virgin. Not that I didn't get horny then, but it was all comparatively easy. I just regarded it as an urge, I masturbated, and that was that. I never had any desire to do it with a girl or—no, to be accurate, let's just say that the possibility seemed too remote. I figured the guys in my class who actually did it were the hunks, the jocks, not the brains like me. I still masturbate, for lack of any other outlet, but it doesn't seem quite as enjoyable as it once was. That is, it's quick and easy, no problems, no need for conversation or any of the amenities. But let's face it, it's a pretty pathetic substitute for the real thing, even at its less than best.

Here's another possibly sick thing: I feel glad I was the first guy with Cheryl. I even, in what may be a sadistic way, like to imagine her future husband, assuming she marries the next guy she does it with, feeling jealous of me. Because they say girls always remember the first guy they have sex with. I'm not quite sadistic enough to hope he's a lousy lover, but yeah, at times I even imagine that. I imagine Cheryl lying there, lawfully wed to this jerk, this tall, good-looking dumbo, like most of the guys in our class, who works her over in around ten seconds and then falls asleep. Don't get the wrong idea. I wasn't a great lover. I think I wasn't the worst, but there were times when it was less than excellent like most other things in life. I hadn't been exactly prepared for that. You spend so many years wondering if or when it's going to happen, that it's hard to believe you might be in bed with a pretty, willing girl and even if both of you come, even if nothing goes wrong, it doesn't necessarily make for a great experience. Maybe that's good. If it was always great, it might get dull. You'd think, Big deal, it was great, so what.

But the few times it *was* great, it was always slightly mysterious. There never seemed to be any special reason, either that we'd waited a long time or were in the right mood. It was more the way it is when I take one of my favorite walks. Some days it's just a walk and I enjoy it. And other days, even though I'm walking past barns or stone fences or fields I've seen a hundred times, there'll be something about the way the light falls or the quality of the air that makes me just stop and look around and wish I could take a mental photo, not to capture literally the way it looked but to capture the way I felt at that exact second.

50

CHAPTER 6

Charlie and his wife, Maureen, always invite my father and me for dinner on Easter Sunday. It started after my mother's death. I guess they figured, correctly, that holidays were kind of morbid and lonely for just the two of us. Even though Charlie and my father went to parochial school together, my father is a lapsed Catholic, and Charlie and his wife are fairly conventionally religious. Also, Charlie's a Republican, and my father, as I mentioned, is usually voting for someone who doesn't stand a chance, at least in this part of the country. My father's an academic and pretty dry and detached in his manner whereas Charlie is warm and ebullient and often starts singing popular songs at the piano when he's had a little too much to drink. In short, you wouldn't figure them as two men whose friendship would have lasted throughout

51

all these years, but for some reason it has. They argue, they josh each other, but there's a kind of good will behind it.

This Easter I was feeling more uncomfortable than usual. I figured that probably my father, if he'd mentioned it at all, had talked to Charlie privately about the court case. He hates "scenes." But still, until this year, Charlie had just been a good-natured guy, kind of like an uncle, with whom I got along in a low-key way. This year, seeing him, I thought of the whole business with the Sidels, about our going to the bar and his admitting that if he were the judge, he would have given the baby to a married couple. It didn't make me dislike him. I like Charlie's frankness; it's a lot easier to deal with than my father's deviousness, but I would have liked this to be just another dinner like all the others. I also wondered who else in the family he'd told. His wife, probably. I hoped that was it. He had arranged for the court case to be far enough away from Haysburg geographically so that no one would know. The fact that the Sidels were from Wilmington also made it easier.

Charlie has one married daughter, Peg, who always seems to be pregnant. I don't think I've ever seen her in anything except a maternity dress. She has three young kids who are usually running around yelling and getting underfoot. Then there's the middle daughter, Sylvia, who works the cash register at the IGA and still lives at home. I guess she must be about twenty-three. She's the homeliest of the three daughters; she has terribly crooked teeth, and I've always wondered, since Charlie obviously makes a decent living, why she doesn't have something done about them. She has a boyfriend, Mack Levant, who lives in the next town. They've been "courting" for four or five years, supposedly waiting to get married when he can support her. He's a spry little man a couple of inches shorter than Sylvia, and seems to dote on her. The youngest daughter, Joely, is a year younger than me; she's a junior at my school. I guess I'd call her pretty. She's bouncy and looks like Charlie's wife—ginger hair, freckles. She's on the gymnastics team at school. For years I got the feeling that both my parents and Charlie and his wife would have been delighted if I had liked Joely or asked her out. That kind of double parental pressure can put the whammy on anything, but even if it hadn't existed, Joely's just not my type. She's a nice girl, fairly intelligent, but more like a sister than a girlfriend. I'm sure she's a virgin, not that that matters one way or another; all I mean is, she doesn't exude any special awareness of the opposite sex.

Maureen's a good cook. She always serves a big ham, mashed sweet potatoes, an array of vegetables. "Almost as good as yours, Tim?" she asked with a smile. I've had all of them over for dinner once or twice to reciprocate.

"Not quite," I said, "but almost."

Mack reached for the rolls. "You'll make some lucky girl a good wife one of these days, Tom."

He's made that joke a hundred times. "It's Tim, not Tom," Sylvia corrected him.

"It's just that you look like this guy Tom, someone I used to go to school with," Mack said, unperturbed. He looked around at the rest of the family. "So, did Sylvia mention? We set the date!"

There was so much screaming and hugging and running around in the next five minutes that you'd have thought they'd won the lottery. For some reason I glanced over at my father. He was staring straight ahead, lost in thought, but he looked pained. Maybe an overdose of family happiness or togetherness gets to him. Not that the three of us ever had feasts like this—my mother was an only child, and my father's relatives all live in Germany, with the exception of his parents, who aren't living.

Once all the din had died down, my father said, "Congratulations, Sylvia. Congratulations, Mack. That's wonderful news.'' Then, after a pause, he said, "Tim and I have news, too. I'm going to be a grandfather.''

This time, instead of a commotion there was dead silence. I had the feeling that my father, in some perverse way, was enjoying everyone's discomfort, including mine. "You've heard of unwed mothers, haven't you?'' he said. "Well, Tim here is about to be an unwed father. What do you think of that?''

Mack, who clearly had no idea what my father was talking about and thought it might be a joke, said, "He doesn't look pregnant to *me*.''

"His girlfriend does,'' my father said. I wondered if he'd had too much to drink, which he does occasionally, or was just doing this to provoke me. "Cheryl Banks, Henry Banks's daughter.''

Mack still looked confused. He looked over at me; I was sitting opposite him. "You're getting married?'' he said, still trying to piece it together.

I shook my head.

"This is the modern age, Mack,'' my father said. "You don't get married, you do it, you have fun, and then . . . let the best man win.''

God, I hate my father. Maureen looked over at me sympathetically. "Tim has decided he wants to raise the baby himself,'' she said in her gentle voice. "Cheryl intended to give it up for adoption.''

Still looking confused, Mack said, "You mean you're not marrying her?''

"Why should he marry her?'' my father said. "He's not in love with her. She's the garbage collector's daughter. He's going to Columbia on a scholarship. You don't expect him to marry a girl like *that*, do you?''

54

Mack looked flustered. "Well, I don't know. I guess not, if . . ."

Once again Maureen tried to intervene. "Cheryl's a lovely girl, Tim. But I can understand. At your age it's a big commitment."

Mack was still looking from me to my father. "I guess maybe I've had a little too much to drink. I thought you said he was having a baby. Did I hear that wrong?"

"No, you heard it *right*," my father shouted. "The way it goes is this: *She* has the baby, *he* brings up the baby."

At that Charlie reached over and put his hand on my father's shoulder. "It's going to be fine," he said. "It's going to work out just fine."

My father looked indignant. He shrugged off Charlie's attempt at sympathy. "Do you hear me complaining? Sure, it'll be fine. We should drink a toast. A toast to Sylvia and Mack, and a toast to Tim and his baby and to me, because I'm going to be a grandfather."

Everyone toasted and drank.

"It hit me hard when I became a grandfather for the first time," Charlie said. "I was only fifty-two. A mere kid. And then I figured, heck, relax, enjoy . . . And that's just what I've been doing."

"Just what *I* intend to do," my father said. "Relax and enjoy. That's the key."

After that my father piped down, but my appetite had completely gone away. I couldn't even eat Maureen's lemon meringue pie, which is one of my favorites. I stood up while everyone was still finishing dessert. "I'm going to take a walk," I mumbled, and left.

It was raining slightly, a faint, misty spring rain. I heard footsteps running after me. It was Joely. "Hey, Tim, wait up, okay?"

I stopped. I really wanted to be by myself, but I didn't want to be rude. "I feel like taking a walk, too," she said.

"Okay," I said, not especially graciously.

We walked in silence, Joely trying to match her steps to mine. "I knew about Cheryl," she said. "I mean, just that she was . . . I didn't know . . ."

"Well, it doesn't matter," I said curtly.

"Your father was acting strange," she said. "I guess he's real upset about it, huh? Does he think you should have married her?"

"I don't know. He just enjoys getting my goat."

She hesitated. "I think it's really, like, courageous of you to do it. I wouldn't have that kind of courage. I'm a coward."

"It isn't a matter of courage," I said, sighing. "I'm just doing it. Maybe it'll turn out to be a big mistake."

"Yeah, but you're *doing* it," she insisted. "That's what counts. There're so many things I'd like to do, but don't because of my parents, of what they might think or say, not wanting to rock the boat . . . I *hate* that in myself, I just *hate* it!"

She was so vehement I stared down at her in surprise. "What kind of things?" I asked.

Suddenly she looked away. "Just . . . things," she said evasively.

I didn't say anything. We kept on walking. We were getting near the part of town where Cheryl lives; something inside of me tightened. "Promise you won't tell, ever, ever?" Joely said suddenly.

"What?" I was somewhere else, lost in a flash-memory of Cheryl and me making love outdoors one spring evening like this, when it started to rain in the middle, and we laughed and tried to find a tree with leaves thick enough to shield us.

Joely took my hand. "I'll only tell you if you swear to never tell anyone, not in your whole life."

"I never tell secrets." I wasn't sure I felt like listening, but I didn't feel like I had a choice.

"I'm gay," she said. She let go of my hand. "I'm in love with someone and nobody knows about it. And my parents would die. I mean, they'd literally die! They'd be worse than your father."

I was really amazed. Not that there aren't gay students at Haysburg High, but Joely never struck me as the type, though I'm not even sure what I meant by that. "Don't tell them, then."

She laughed. "I won't! Are you kidding? But I keep being so afraid they'll find out. We're extra, *extra* careful, but you know what Haysburg is like. You sneeze and someone two houses down says 'God bless you.' "

"That's why I can't wait to get out of here," I said.

"Me too!" She sighed. "There are times I think I just can't make it. I even used to think of dropping out of school and just moving off somewhere with . . . my friend."

"Don't," I advised.

"No, I won't. But I hate this whole pretense. This whole happy family, everything is fine crap. Did you know Mack has had his license taken away twice for drunk driving? He's a *criminal* practically and yet they're so glad Sylvia's finally marrying someone, *anyone*. . . . He could be Jack the Ripper, for all they care! . . . What's so great about marriage? Who says it's the only solution to everything?"

I looked down at her. It was strange, our families having been friends since we were babies, and yet our never really having talked about anything until this night, her not really knowing anything about me, me not knowing anything about her. That's the thing about Haysburg: You know people, by which you mean, "He works at the bank" or "She has red hair," and that's it. That's all you ever know. "Your parents seem happy, though," I said. Truthfully, I'd always slightly envied the Moores. The relaxed noisiness of their family appealed to me, having come from a home with such quiet, repressed parents.

Joely shrugged. "Yeah, I guess they're happy. . . . It's all so surface, but it's what they want. It would kill *me* in a day, I can tell you. I guess what gets me is anything Daddy says, Mom just flattens herself to the ground. She doesn't have *one* opinion that he doesn't have. She wouldn't know how! It's like she's 'wife of,' period, end of sentence, end of life. Your mother had so much more spunk."

"Really?" I always thought of my mother as shy, compared to Maureen. "She was so quiet."

"Yes, but she had her own opinions. She'd say what she felt, even when your father disagreed. I always remembered that, how I admired her for doing it. Not in a belligerent way, but she would just quietly say what she had to say. She never seemed to let your father boss her around. Maybe she did at home, but never at our house."

"No, she didn't at home, either," I said. That made me feel good, having someone else's memory of my mother as a real person, not just a fuzzy, vague icon.

Suddenly Joely put her hand up. "It's really raining," she said. "We're going to get soaked."

It was true that the mist had gradually changed into a real rain. I hadn't even noticed. "We *are* soaked," I said.

Then both of us laughed, as though I'd said something incomparably witty.

As we neared the house Joely smiled at me. "Bet anything they're all sitting around planning our marriage."

I smiled at her. "Right."

She imitated her mother's voice. "Oh, wouldn't they be a sweet couple, Charlie? And they've known each other all their lives."

"He's a fine boy," I said, lowering my voice, imitating Charlie. "Hardworking, responsible."

"They'll have some problems with the baby," Joely went on in her mother's voice, "but frankly I think this is *just* what Joely needs—to settle down, enough of this career nonsense. Raise a family, learn what life's about."

I shook my head. "Jesus," I said, but I felt a lot better.

When we walked into the living room and everyone looked up at us, we couldn't help smiling, knowing they would misinterpret the happy looks on our face. I went over to Maureen and told her I was hungry and would have the pie I hadn't had at dinner.

She took me into the kitchen. "Now, I'm *so* glad you said that, Tim. I wondered: am I losing my touch? That boy usually puts away three slices and tonight he barely ate a bite." She set down a mammoth piece in front of me.

"Well, my father—" I began.

She patted my hand. "I know," she said. "You just eat up. He'll settle down. He needs someone to talk to. He's too alone."

"Maybe he ought to start dating," I said sarcastically.

"Well, there are many women in town who would like nothing better than to keep company with your father," Maureen said. "But he knows that. I have the feeling he'd still rather nurse his memories."

"Right." I liked Maureen. Since my mother's death I've had fantasies of her as a mother, or maybe just as an aunt, as a kindly, down-to-earth older woman who has some instinct about life.

We got ready to leave about half an hour later. As we walked toward the car my father turned to me. "You drive, Tim. I'm feeling a little unsteady."

My father has a disease which affects, or can affect, his balance. Frankly, I feel he uses it to get out of things he doesn't feel like doing anyway, like dancing at faculty parties. "Okay, I'll drive," I said.

I got into the car and placed the pie Maureen had given us on the backseat. "Drive carefully," my father said. "It's raining."

I clenched my hands around the steering wheel. "Oh, it is, really? That's funny. I just thought that was some wet funny stuff coming down out of the sky. I was planning to careen home at my usual ninety miles an hour."

"There is a lot of drunk driving in this town," my father said angrily, "and most of it done by teenage males."

"I didn't have anything to drink."

"How am I supposed to know that?"

"Because you were right there, all during dinner."

"You went off with that girl. How do *I* know what you did? You could've both taken half a pint of scotch and finished it behind the barn, God knows what."

"No, that was *before* dinner," I said. "After dinner we just smoked a couple of joints and took a little LSD."

"Don't be such a smart ass!" my father said.

I turned on him, furious. "You're such a jerk. I ought to just let you walk home! Why did you act like that at dinner? You didn't just humiliate me, you wrecked the whole damn party. Don't you ever think of anyone other than yourself?"

"Charlie and Maureen are my best friends," my father said stiffly. "They know what I'm going through. They are completely sympathetic. They said so when you and that girl disappeared."

"Dad, that girl is Joely, remember? Christ, Charlie's your best friend, you've known him fifty years. Can't you even remember the names of his kids?"

For some reason my father got flustered. "I never took it in," he muttered, closing his eyes. "I'm bad about remembering names, always was. Your mother . . ."

60

I started the car, glanced over at him, and thought, Forget it. That's another of my father's little tricks, just closing his eyes. You never know if he's asleep or just trying to get beyond the point where he has to communicate. When we arrived home, he opened his eyes immediately and got out of the car, then silently marched to the front door and disappeared upstairs without saying good night.

I turned off the rest of the lights and went upstairs. Lying in bed, I thought of Joely's confession, her vehemence about her family, how to her it all seemed pretense, Mack being a drunk driver, Maureen's passivity. I wondered if every family in town had at least one family member who felt that life here was a charade that you had to use all your energy to perpetuate, to convince yourself as much as your neighbors. But I realized the conversation with her was one of the only ones I've had in the time since Howie moved away, where I've felt I was doing more than making my lips move—except when I was arguing with my father.

I've been reading up on babies. I'll be a parent in three months. It seems far off, but it isn't. I know that's typical of me, wanting to know all the facts about something, all the theories before I embark on it. Some people just do it, plunge in, learn as they go. I'm not like that. I'm not convinced that theoretical learning is the key to everything, but I don't trust my instincts that much. There are three libraries in town. The school library is pretty pathetic. I ran through most of what interested me there when I was in junior high. Then there's the town library, which is tiny and has peculiar hours. It's only open twice a week from six to nine in the evening. The one I usually go to is the college library. Normally I wouldn't be allowed to check books out, but they've always let me use my father's card. Of course, when my mother was alive there was no problem, since she was the head librarian.

That may have something to do with why I love the college library. It happens to be a beautiful building. Someone gave money for it about a decade ago. It's big and modern, with comfortable chairs, little desks, a photocopy machine, every magazine you could ever want to read, and rooms and rooms of stacks. Sometimes I go there to do my homework, even if there isn't any special book I need, just because it's such a peaceful, beautiful, calm place. And maybe I do feel something of my mother's spirit there, if that doesn't sound corny or weird. I know some people think of librarians as little uptight women with steel-rimmed glasses who are always hushing people, but my mother wasn't like that.

Her replacement is a woman named Margaret Hansen. She's small and plump, with frizzy graying hair and a friendly smile. I guess, like Maureen, she's one of various older women whom, on some fantasy level, I connect with my mother. If there's any special book I want that I've read about somewhere, she'll order it for me. She always asks me how I've liked a particular book when I return it, seeming really interested, and sometimes, if I recommend a book, she'll read it herself. She's always trying to get me to read more fiction, but somehow fiction just doesn't interest me that much. I'd rather read about history or science, something where I feel I'm learning something. "You can learn about people from fiction," she'll say. But I figure I can learn about people just from living; I don't see how I need to get that from books.

I didn't want to take the baby books home. I decided to just go there every day and read one book an afternoon, starting with Dr. Spock and going through some of the other supposed experts. I was interested in the section about childhood diseases. Sometimes I've thought of going into pediatrics, though I'm not sure. Of course I hope my baby is fine, but it can't hurt to know all the symptoms and how to deal with them when they arise. But the line that really got me was the opening line in Spock: 'You know more than you think you do.' That's just about exactly the opposite of what I believe to be true, not just about babies, but about everything. Of course, maybe that's why the book was, or is, a bestseller. He was just trying to make everyone feel like an automatic expert, just to give them confidence. How many copies would sell of a book that began 'You know less than you think you do.' But really, I think that it's true. I don't think anyone really knows much of anything about anything. And I'm talking about myself, someone who reads a lot and thinks a lot. If you take half the kids in my class, forget it.

I guess I went off on a private extension in my mind about that because I was startled when Margaret came by and tapped me gently on the shoulder. "It's almost six, Tim. I have to close up now."

"Oh, okay."

"Would you like to check any of those out?"

I hesitated. "No, but maybe you could put them aside. I might come back tomorrow to look at some sections again."

She gathered up the books. "Doing a paper on child development for school?"

So, I guess not everyone in town does know. "Right." I stood up and followed her to the checkout counter.

"Boy, it's so different in reality from the way it seems in those books!" she said. Margaret has three kids, but she's divorced. Her husband was a history professor here who ran off with one of his students.

"In what way?" I asked.

"Well, they try to make it seem like kids all go through these stages, like peas in a pod, the terrible twos, what have you . . . But with my three, they were all as different as could be. What was true of one was the opposite with the next. I figured by the time Max was in nursery school, I knew less than when I started. Of course, I was raising them pretty much alone. Maybe that makes it harder.''

I looked at her a moment. She's never struck me as a self-pitying person, like my father. ''I don't really know,'' I said, not wanting to add ''yet.''

After a second Margaret said, ''It must have been hard for your father, raising you alone—not that you seem like a difficult kid.''

''I'm a breeze,'' I said with a grin. ''*He's* the one who can be a pain.''

''I think he tries his best,'' Margaret said. ''He's just a . . . well, a very private person, that's all.''

As I walked home I wondered if Margaret was one of the droves of women who, according to Maureen, would give their eyeteeth if my father asked them out. They ought to thank their lucky stars that he doesn't. But then I wondered if some woman could bring my father back to some kind of life, the way he seemed when my mother was alive. Frankly, I wouldn't bet on it.

CHAPTER 7

$\mathbf{F}$riday night I usually go to the movies. Now that I have my driver's license, my father lets me take the car into Cardoba, which is about twenty miles away. The shopping mall there has six movie theaters, so there's a fairly wide choice. Even though it's not allowed, some kids go from movie to movie and spend all night in there. I never feel like doing that; one's enough. If it's a good movie, I like to think about it afterward, and if it's bad, I get restless and definitely don't want to see another one.

I think I have fairly catholic tastes. I do like horror movies if they're well done, not the gory kind where people disintegrate into globs of snot, but the kind that play on your sense of psychological horror. And there are some decent thrillers. Cheryl and I had about as different taste in movies as two people could have. She hated anything even mildly scary. I don't even mean special effects. I mean, if someone with a sheet over his head jumped out and said "Boo!" she'd be under the seat, practically. If the music started getting ominous sounding, she'd scrunch her eyes shut, hunch down in her seat, and then ask, loudly, right in the middle, "Did they kill him? Did they kill anyone?" Or we'd walk out after the movie was over and she'd ask, "So what happened at the end? Did he kill *her*, or did she kill *him*?" It's pretty hard to concentrate under those circumstances, especially when she'd grab my hand and squeeze it so hard I thought it might fall off.

The movies she liked best were romantic comedies with a plot so transparent a child of two could figure it out by the time the opening credits were done. I sat through a lot of those, mentally writing my history papers or rewriting the script in my head, or just looking forward to what we might be doing after the show was over.

Just to be polite, I usually ask my father if he feels like going with me, but he always says no. This Friday he asked, "What movie is it?"

"*Kramer vs. Kramer* . . . It's a revival."

"What's it about?"

"Some guy whose wife runs off, leaving him with a kid. It won a lot of Academy Awards."

"Sounds educational," my father said dryly. "Well, why not? My connection to popular culture is tenuous at best, and this, so you say, won awards? Maybe I'll enjoy it."

"I kind of doubt it," I said, sorry I'd asked him.

"Why?"

"Well, you never go to the movies. Why go to this one especially?"

"I thought you said it was supposed to be well acted. Who's in it?"

"Meryl Streep, Dustin Hoffman . . ."

66

My father looked blank. "Are they people I should have heard of?"

"Well, most people have, but—"

"You consider them to be good actors?"

I started getting impatient. "Dad, look, I wouldn't be going if I thought they were terrible. It got good reviews, I never saw it before, I don't feel like doing my homework right now. If you want to come, come. Okay?"

"Okay," my father said with surprising mildness. "I'll come."

He let me drive. My father dislikes driving. He does it as seldom as possible, and when he does he goes so slowly he's probably more of a menace on the road than most speed demons. We have an excellent tape deck in the car. He hates rock music, so I stuck in a Vivaldi trio. I can put up with classical music a lot better than he can put up with rock. And he was acting so docile, I didn't want to spoil the mood.

The movie theater was surprisingly crowded, given that it was a revival. I think on Friday a lot of people come in and, if the movie they want to see is all sold out, buy tickets for another one and either see it or sneak to their original choice, if they can find a spare seat. We got good seats, somewhere in the middle. The theater was dimly lit, and they were playing some garbage on the Muzak. Then, as I was looking around, wondering if I'd run into anyone from my class, I saw Cheryl and her sister, Henrietta, the bank manager. They were sitting off to one side, ahead of us. *Don't let them turn around.* Luckily we were in the middle, with a lot of heads around us. Also, Cheryl is totally near-sighted but almost never wears glasses except during a movie. Still, I wished I hadn't seen her until after the show.

Kramer vs. Kramer was okay. I guess I'd rate it a B minus. They made the kid overly adorable, the way they always do in Hollywood movies, and Dustin Hoffman gets on my nerves, the kind of short, supposedly funny-looking guy who you know, deep down, thinks he's a hotshot with women. Meryl Streep is beautiful, but she's not my type exactly. She acts like you'd have to break your neck to get her attention, and I don't mean just her part in this movie. There's just this air she has, kind of cool and condescending. The only sexy point in the movie, as far as I was concerned, is when some woman Dustin Hoffman brings home for the night runs into his son as she's coming out of the bathroom. She's naked, and the scene only lasts a second or two, but I knew it was going to be replayed in my mind long after I'd forgotten the rest of the plot.

Surreptitiously I glanced over at my father. I wonder how he feels during a scene like that, seeing a woman's body, a beautiful body. Obviously, middle-aged men don't think about sex as much as teenagers, but he must've had some kind of sex life with my mother, and unless he's been leading some secret life no one knows about, he hasn't had anything since. Is it just like: Oh, a body. Like: Oh, a truck or a bunch of flowers. Whereas for me it was as though, suddenly, a whole montage of scenes with Cheryl and me started playing themselves over the movie, a mixture of the way she looked, the way it felt. Once there was a real-life scene slightly like that: I'd stayed over at Cheryl's pretty late because she thought her parents were away for the weekend and Henrietta would be out late with her boyfriend. I went to the bathroom, and just as I was unlocking the door I heard Henrietta's voice saying, "Oh, hi, did I wake you?" At that point Cheryl hadn't told her anything about our relationship. I relocked the door and prayed that Henrietta wouldn't go to the bathroom right away. She didn't. I wrapped a towel around me, raced back to Cheryl's room, and got dressed in record time. I doubt Henrietta would've gotten much of a thrill out of seeing me naked. It wouldn't have been a memory to treasure throughout the years.

When the movie ended and the theater lights started coming up, I gave my father a nudge. He was just sitting there in a seeming daze. "Hey, Dad, it's over. Let's go, okay?"

"Relax. There are plenty of people trying to get out of the theater. What's the hurry?"

Shit. Should I pretend I needed to go to the bathroom? Instead I just scrunched down in my seat and looked away from the side of the theater where Cheryl was. Then I glanced quickly over to where she'd been sitting and saw her walking up the aisle. There always seems to be something pathetic and accusing about the way she looks pregnant, though I know this is probably all in my mind. I couldn't tell if she saw me. I just continued to look preoccupied.

My father elbowed me in the ribs. "There's your girlfriend," he said.

"Okay," I muttered. "I saw her. Could you just pretend you don't see her?"

But as I said that I couldn't resist looking over in Cheryl's direction. She was looking right at me. Her expression wasn't vindictive; it was more sorrowful, which was almost worse. Suddenly my father jumped to his feet. He walked down the aisle and over to her. I followed a few feet behind. "Enjoy the show?" he asked.

Cheryl, for some reason, looked petrified. "Um . . . yes . . . Did you?"

"Very much. I rarely get to the movies, and I wasn't familiar with this one, but Tim assured me it was highly recommended."

"I've—I've seen it before," Cheryl stammered.

"Yes, well, I would say it's what one might call a woman's picture, but charming, nonetheless. . . . How did *you* like it, Tim?"

I didn't get this. My father, the least sociable man on earth, for no comprehensible reason decides to charm my pregnant ex-girlfriend. Maybe *he* should marry her. There are a lot of professors his age who run off with young wives.

"Did *you* like the movie?" Cheryl asked, looking timorously at me.

I realized I'd been standing there, immobilized. "Yeah, pretty much."

"You don't usually like movies like this."

"It was okay."

"He likes horror movies," she told my father. "Or science fiction."

"Yes, well, when I was that age . . ."

Cheryl's sister said, "Cheryl, you're blocking the aisle. Move!"

The four of us moved, one ahead of the other, up the aisle. When we finally emerged from the theater, my father said, "Could we offer you young ladies some refreshment before you start home?"

"I don't think so," Henrietta said crisply. She looked like he was overdrawn on his account.

But Cheryl smiled at my father. "*I'd* like to." She glanced at her sister. "I'm really thirsty," she said pleadingly.

God almighty. What is this about? Maybe Henrietta and I can drive home together and let my father treat Cheryl to an ice-cream soda. But the four of us moved inexorably toward the Sweet Shoppe, a few doors down from the theater.

Henrietta and Cheryl sat side by side. I sat next to my father. I gave him a quick look that said: This is your fucking show. You handle it. I don't think he noticed.

The waitress came by, set down four glasses of water, and asked what we wanted. She was the same waitress who had waited on Cheryl and me lots of times last year, but she didn't act like she remembered.

70

"I'll have a Coke," Henrietta said. She has Cheryl's looks, but on her they seem severe and a little forbidding. Unlike Cheryl, she always wears glasses, not contacts, and you have the feeling she can see right through you. But I'm willing to admit this could be projection.

Cheryl looked up at the waitress. "I'd like a vanilla ice-cream soda," she said.

"You can't," Henrietta said, as though she were Cheryl's mother.

"I can if I want," Cheryl said, sticking out her lower lip with that pout which can be endearing or irritating, depending on your mood. "I'm *dying* of thirst!"

"So drink your water." To my father and me, Henrietta explained: "The doctor said she's gaining too much weight. It's a myth to think you can eat for two. That way, you'll never lose it. You'll be a tub all your life like Mary Ellen Posner."

My father smiled gently. "Well, one ice-cream soda can't hurt, can it? I think I'll have one myself, now that you mention it."

Cheryl looked triumphantly at her sister. "No whipped cream," she said to the waitress, as a concession.

Henrietta rolled her eyes. "Whipped cream is about thirty calories. It's the ice cream that does you in."

"Vanilla is less fattening than chocolate," Cheryl said hopefully.

"Look, it's *your* body," Henrietta said. "If you want to have varicose veins and look like some kind of blimp on the beach this summer, fine."

It's funny—the thought of Cheryl on the beach this summer, looking like she had the summer before, had somehow never occurred to me. Meanwhile the waitress was staring at me impatiently. "Sir?"

"I'll have a cup of coffee and—do you have any home-made apple pie?"

"Do you mean made here in the store?"

"Yes."

"Well, we may have one piece left. I'm not sure."

"Okay, well if you do, I'd like one piece, with three slices of lemon on the side."

"And more water all around," my father said.

The waitress looked relieved to be rid of us.

"My wife gained a lot of weight during pregnancy," my father said, "but then she simply did exercises and went on some kind of diet, and within three months, less perhaps, she was her old weight again. So I wouldn't worry."

"Oh, I'm not," Cheryl said, gulping down her water. "*She's* worried, not me. And you happen to be wrong, Henrietta. Thin mothers produce undernourished babies. And they can have birth defects and everything."

I remembered that horrible fight we'd had in the school-yard, when Cheryl said she wished the baby was aborted. Our glances caught and then both of us looked away.

My father reached over and patted Cheryl's hand. "My dear, the baby will be fine. Nature takes care of these things. I think it's very brave of you to go through all this."

Cheryl stared at my father with her big dark eyes, which were filled with tears. "Well, I . . . I wasn't sure I was doing the right thing. I'm still not sure."

"Of course you are. You're a wonderful, brave girl." He beamed at her.

At that, Cheryl gave way and laid her head on the table and sobbed. Henrietta, looking bewildered, put her arm around her. I kicked my father under the table. Just then the waitress appeared with our orders. My father pushed one ice-cream soda toward Cheryl and took the other one for himself. "This will make you feel a lot better," he said.

Silently, with red eyes, still snuffling, Cheryl began to sip her ice-cream soda. "You're a very nice man," she said almost in a whisper to my father.

"Thank you," my father said softly. He looked over at me. "Why did you order lemon with coffee?" he asked. "Is that some new fad?"

"No, see, he thinks most apple pie made in stores is too sweet," Cheryl explained, "so he always orders lemon and squeezes it over the apples to give it the right taste."

This was, in fact, just what I was doing, peeling back the crust, then replacing it.

"Well, there's no accounting for taste," my father said. "I myself like a sweet apple pie. But then I'm not much of a cook. In fact, you know which scene really got to me in the movie? The one where Dustin Hoffman, the young man whom I gather played the lead, tried to make French toast for his son. After my wife died six years ago, I tried to carry on some of our family traditions, and she used to make the most wonderful French toast you can imagine. I even had her recipe. I followed it to the letter, and the result was the most inedible French toast you've ever tasted. Didn't have a woman's touch, that's all there is to it."

Cheryl was spooning up the ice cream from her soda. "Tim is a good cook," she said.

"Yes, he is," my father agreed. "He's had to be, I guess. If he'd relied on me, he would have wasted away by now."

"He thinks he can do anything," Cheryl said tightly, chin up. "Anything a man can do, *and* anything a woman can do."

My father looked vague. Was it possible he hadn't picked up on that? "He's a bright boy, no doubt of it. But of course without a mother it's been hard. A father tries his best, but

73

he can't take a mother's place. I don't pretend I have. I've done my best, but sometimes I wonder."

For the first time in my life, my father's self-pity came to the rescue. Cheryl and Henrietta were both looking at him with that expression women always get when confronted by his pathetic widower's story.

When we were all finished and had walked out to the parking lot adjoining the theater, my father shook Cheryl's and Henrietta's hands. "Now, if there's anything you need, any help, just give us a call. And afterward, any time you want to come around and see the baby, you just come."

"That's very nice of you, Mr. Weber," Henrietta said, as warmly as I've ever heard her say anything.

Suddenly Cheryl reached over and threw her arms around my father and kissed him. He stood there, startled, and then she and Henrietta walked away.

We found our car and got in. "Well, well, well," my father said.

"Well, well, well, what?" I asked dryly.

"It's been a long time since I've been kissed by such a pretty young girl," my father said with a bemused expression.

"She's a good kisser," I said. I started the motor.

My father was glaring at me. "Did I do the wrong thing? You saw how pleased they were to be treated civilly. What's wrong with you? You knocked her up, you're taking her baby. Where are your manners?"

"Look, Dad, you know nothing about it, so—"

"Nothing about it? Whose fault is that? I know what I've been told, period. And I can tell you one thing, my boy. That girl would marry you tomorrow if you looked at her cross-eyed. She admires you and respects you. She's proud to be carrying your child."

I stared at him. "Are you crazy? She was going to sell the

kid, for Christ's sake, to some couple she didn't even *know*! When I won the court case, she told me she'd rather have an abortion than let me have it.''

My father was silent a moment. ''Well, women are like that, *if* provoked. 'Hell hath no fury like a woman scorned.' And of course all of us, at the best of times, have ambivalent feelings.''

The apple pie lay like a rock in my stomach. I opened the window so a cool breeze could come in. ''Sometimes I think you get some perverse kick out of torturing me,'' I said.

''Perverse?'' My father looked indignant. ''Where is the perversion, may I ask, in being kind to this poor, forlorn, sweet girl, showing her that we care, that we empathize with what she's going through?''

''Maybe she'd rather no one paid attention to it,'' I said. ''Maybe she'd like some privacy.''

My father snorted. ''It's a little late for that, isn't it?''

''It's between the two of us. It has nothing to do with you.''

''Really? I was under the impression this infant had some genetic tie to yours truly . . . and I haven't had the feeling you've been going out of your way to make the situation any easier for her.''

''Marry her yourself, then. She'd probably rather marry *you* than me,'' I said.

''You know, you really have a cold streak to your personality,'' my father said thoughtfully. ''I've never realized that so clearly before tonight.''

''I wonder where I got it from.''

We drove in silence back to the house.

CHAPTER 8

I doubt that even if there weren't "Cheryl's condition," I would be whooping it up for graduation. Basically, ever since I got my acceptance letter from Columbia, I've just been marking time in my classes, not goofing off exactly, but mainly taking up space. There's a prom, and I suppose if things were otherwise I'd be going with Cheryl, even though I'm not much of a dancer. But as it is, she'll sit home, and I'll just go to bed early. At least that was my plan until Joely called.

"Tim . . . are you alone?"

"Yeah, hi. What's up?" I see Joely now and then at school, but we never talk much and haven't said anything since that Easter dinner.

"Well, I want to ask you this favor, and of course feel free to say no. No hard feelings if you don't. . . . It's just—my friend—you remember I mentioned I had a friend in my class, someone I love who no one in the family knows about?"

"I remember."

"Well, my friend and I would really like to go to the prom together, as a couple, but I know the school wouldn't let us, and Mom and Daddy would have a fit. But it seems stupid for us just to have to sit home. . . . So, what I was wondering was—would you be willing to invite me, I mean, pretend to invite me?" She took a deep breath. "What I'm saying is, we could go as a couple, but once we got there we could just separate and do whatever we want. That'll give me a kind of cover. Mom and Daddy like you so much."

I thought about it. "But—what are you going to do at the dance? Be together?"

"Yeah, we'll handle it. Don't worry about that part. We'll be discreet. We just figure we have a right to come to this dance, but we don't want to create any scandal or anything." She laughed. "I told you, we're cowards."

"Sure, that's fine with me," I said finally.

"I figured you might not be planning on going at all—"

"I wasn't."

"I'll pay for the flowers and whatever, the gas for the car—"

"We can split it. No problem."

"Tim, this is so great of you. I really appreciate it."

"I'm glad to do it."

Hanging up, I wondered. I debated various ways of handling the evening. I could just bring Joely to the dance, go home, and then return at the end of the evening. But then I realized that it might look odd. Well, I'd figure something out.

When I told my father I was taking Joely to the prom, he was almost as ecstatic as Joely's parents probably were. "Now, for once in your life, you're using common sense," he said. "Joely is as nice a girl as you'll find anywhere in the world. Smart, thoughtful. Your mother often said, 'If only Tim and Joely would get together some time when they grow up.' And of course Charlie and Maureen feel the same way. This is on me. I'll pay for everything—flowers, tuxedo, if you need to rent one, a limousine . . .''

Given my father's tightness about money, this was pretty amazing. "Thanks, Dad, I think we can handle it.''

I hadn't even thought about all that shit of renting a tux. A limo was out. There are limits, after all. Some kids really do it up and go to Cardoba, hit the clubs, and end up on the beach, reliving the highlights. I think I'll just turn into a pumpkin at midnight and drive Joely home.

Joely and I may have to dance together more than she had bargained for. I'm not clumsy, really. I just never feel especially carried away, the way I think you should be. I did rent a tux, which looked somewhat ridiculous. There are probably guys who can fill these things out, carry it off or whatever. I'm not one of them.

When I arrived at the Moores' house, Maureen and Charlie were in the living room, just like always. He was reading the paper and she was knitting something. "Joely'll be right down,'' Maureen said with a warm smile.

What made me feel less hypocritical than I might have was that I figured both of them knew there wasn't any great romance between Joely and me. We'd never even been out on a date, so how could there be? I imagined they thought we both wanted to go to the prom and didn't have regular dates, and so were going as good friends.

"Well, I never thought I'd see Joely going to a prom,'' Charlie said. "Never thought I'd see her in a dress. Come to think of it, have I *ever* seen her in a dress?''

"Don't be silly,'' Maureen said. "Of course you have.

Girls just don't wear dresses much anymore. Until they get jobs.''

"Not even then," Charlie said. "I hired a new secretary. She came to the interview in a dress, and that's the last one I've seen her in. Slacks every day!"

"Well, so what?" Maureen said in amiable annoyance.

"Her figure!" Charlie exclaimed. "There are women in slacks and women in slacks. Now, you don't need to be an expert to know the ones who should and the ones who shouldn't.''

"She probably just wants to be comfortable," Maureen said. "And she knows that in a skirt, all you men would be gaping at her legs and making her uncomfortable.''

Charlie winked at me and roared with laughter. "Making her uncomfortable? Looking at legs? Honey, we've got *work* to do in that office. And from what I saw at the interview, you've got nothing to be nervous about.''

Maureen gave him a wry look. "I didn't *say* I was nervous.'' To me she said, "He's just old-fashioned.''

Charlie stood up and went over to the piano. He sat down and started singing. "The girl that I marry will have to be as soft and as pink as a nursery . . . the girl I call my own.'' He beckoned to Maureen, who reluctantly got to her feet. They began singing together. "Will wear satins and laces and smell of cologne . . .''

Right in the middle of this Joely came bouncing down the stairs. She was wearing black velvet slacks and a gold lamé top. Charlie stopped singing. "Ready, Tim?" Joely said with a mischievous smile.

"Young lady, I assume this is some kind of joke," Charlie said, turning red.

"What is, Daddy?" Joely said innocently.

"Where is your prom dress?"

"I don't have one.''

Charlie looked at Maureen. "I thought I gave you two hundred dollars to buy the nicest dress in the store!"

"There weren't any she liked."

"You mean to tell me that in the entire store there wasn't one dress, one single dress, you liked?"

Joely sighed. "Daddy, calm down, okay? Tim's taking me, and he doesn't care at all. Do you, Tim?"

I got to my feet. "I think you look terrific," I said. "Here's your corsage."

I'd gotten her gardenias, like she'd asked for. Joely pinned them on her lamé top. Then she went over to Charlie, who was standing there in stunned silence. "Forgive? Wish us a good time?"

"I just don't get it," Charlie said half to himself, half to Maureen and me. "The highlight of high school, all those beautiful dresses . . . I simply don't get it. Your mother, when we went to our high school prom, looked like Miss America."

Joely gave him a quick kiss on the top of his nose. "Times have changed."

As we walked to my car Joely took my arm, I guess so we'd look like a normal couple going to a prom. "Families, families!" she said.

"Yeah," I agreed.

When we were in the car, she glanced at me. "You're such a sweetie to do this. I really, truly appreciate it."

"It's nothing," I said. "Only I may as well warn you. I'm a lousy dancer."

"Oh, me too. Who cares?" She looked down at her outfit. "You know, I really think I look nice. I mean, I really *like* this outfit. I hate pastel colors, and I look sick in them. Sometimes I think Daddy's caught in some time warp. Who *wants* to look like Miss America? Anyway, if I was in one of those dresses, I sure as heck wouldn't. What it is, is no one in the family ever really rebelled against him except me. Usually it's the oldest who does, and by the time the youngest comes along, it's a lot easier.'' She looked at me. ''I guess you never had any of that.''

''Any of what?''

''Rebelling, not rebelling . . . It must be so different, being an only child.''

I hesitated. ''It's been hell since my mother died. My father and I just aren't . . . suited. He's up to his ears in self-pity, and half the time I don't think he knows I'm alive.'' Then I realized I must sound pretty self-pitying myself.

''Still, it must have been such a blow for him,'' Joely said.

Despite myself I was getting riled up. ''Yeah, it's hard, but it's like he's making a lifestyle out of its being hard. He doesn't even *try*.''

''I know what you mean,'' Joely said. ''It's just—'' she stopped.

''Just what?''

''Well, you seem kind of a loner yourself. In that way I'd think you two would have a lot in common.''

''I hope not.'' That thought had crossed my mind, but it's more something I see as a possible danger, not a character trait that's glued into place irrevocably.

''It's why I was so surprised when you started going around with Cheryl. I didn't figure that would be your kind of thing.''

''What do you mean—'your kind of thing'?'' I asked warily.

''Well, using her, kind of . . . Wasn't that it, basically? I hate to be crude, but apart from sex it didn't look like there was much in it for you.''

I tried not to get angry since we were, technically, going to spend the evening together. ''It was mutual, the using part, if it existed,'' I said defensively.

''It never is,'' Joely said. ''She must have wanted more.''

"How do you know?" I said, exasperated. "Do you know her at all?"

"Girls are just different," Joely said. "Especially girls like that. Sex is a hook to get guys. Pregnancy is a hook. . . ."

"I don't see it that way," I said. "That sounds kind of sexist. Can't girls enjoy sex for its own sake?"

Joely was silent. "Well, I *hope* she got something out of it. It must have been hell this year, going through all her classes looking the way she did. Like a scarlet *A* around her neck."

I felt annoyed with Joely. Here I was doing her a favor by taking her to the prom, and this hardly seemed fair play. Why do women always think they can understand everyone else's relationships? I certainly don't go along with the image of myself in relation to Cheryl as the cold-blooded seducer just in it for sex, anymore than I can go along with the image of Cheryl as this pathetic creature trying to "hook" any passing guy. By the time we got to the prom I was almost wishing I'd just told Joely to go by herself. Talk about using people!

The gym was decorated with streamers and balloons and soft lights. It was pretty crowded already, and the music was going full blast. "Listen, let's just go our separate ways," Joely said. "Maybe at the end we can—"

"Sure, I'll be around," I said, probably a little curtly. It occurred to me again that I could go home now and return at the very end, but that didn't seem like it would be fulfilling my part of the bargain. I went over to get something to drink. They always spike the punch, since officially liquor isn't allowed. Being a little high seemed one way to soften the effect of being here. I took my drink over to one side of the gym, where Nate Rafalsky, a guy from my chem class, was slouching, drink in hand. "I don't even know why I'm here," he said. "I can't dance, and there's no girl in our class who'd dance with me, even if I could."

Nate is short, five two, maybe, and not fantastic looking. "Look at Dustin Hoffman," I said.

"Where? Is he here?" He looked around excitedly.

"No, I mean look at him figuratively. He's short, like you, and he's done all right."

"That's just in the movies," Nate said gloomily. "That doesn't count."

"No, in real life too," I said, though I wasn't really sure. "He's married, he has kids."

Nate looked impressed. "No kidding. Hey, want some more punch?"

"Sure." I handed him my glass since there was a mob scene over there. By the time he returned I was already feeling mildly buzzed. Nate and I stood gazing out at the dancing couples. "Remember when we studied the Middle Ages?" he asked dreamily.

"What?" I didn't get the connection.

"Remember what Hawkins said about courtly love, how couples used to never . . . how nothing was ever really consummated. It was the feeling that counted. That's how I feel about Amelinda."

Amelinda Lamers is a tall, statuesque redhead who's been going steady throughout high school with the president of our class, a loud, husky guy named Ray Altshuler. "That's a nice . . . sentiment," I said.

"Ten years from now, Ray whatshisface won't remember who she was," Nate said. "She'll just be some girl he fucked in high school. Whereas *I'll* remember her all my life. Forever. She doesn't even know that, but there it is . . . Do you know what I mean?" He gazed at me drunkenly.

"I think I comprehend what you're trying to say," I said stiffly. "But if she never knows—"

"That's the point!" Nate shouted. "It's what you *feel*. These guys are like animals. They just pounce on girls. They don't care or know anything about what love is all about. If they did, they'd—"

Suddenly a girl appeared in front of us. She took Nate by the hand. "Come on, Nate, let's dance," she said. "You can pretend I'm Amelinda." It was Ketti Drennan. She's plump and blond, with granny glasses, and just an inch taller than Nate.

He looked bewildered. "What?" he said.

"Come on, let's go. . . . If you don't say yes, I'm going to ask Tim."

Nate looked at me. "Is it okay?"

I laughed. "Sure." Watching them, I thought they made a much better couple than he and Amelinda would have made. Evidently everyone in the world thought Cheryl and I were a ridiculous couple. But who cares? What do people know, really? They were right in some ways, in some superficial ways, but deep down, they didn't know anything about it. I looked around to see if I could find Joely. She was standing in a corner with a girl I knew slightly, Courtney. I guessed that Courtney must be her secret "friend," since they were dressed exactly alike.

After the second glass of punch I was high enough so that just standing there letting my thoughts wander seemed a not unpleasant thing to do. Time seemed to pass quickly. I started mentally working on a chess problem I'd had on my desk for the past two weeks. Then Ketti materialized in front of me, without Nate.

"Where'd Nate go?" I asked.

"Oh, he's impossible. He'd rather drool over someone imaginary than dance with someone real. A pox on him! How about you? Or are you and Cheryl still—"

"No, we—" I followed her onto the dance floor. The music changed to a slow number. Ketti is a foot shorter than me, shorter than Cheryl, even, but she has a nice, rounded body. She glanced up at me. "Did you come with anyone?"

I hesitated. I didn't want to betray Joely. "Technically, as a favor to a friend," I said.

"Oh . . ." She hesitated. "I'm sorry about you and Cheryl . . ."

I let her sentence drift off. I don't really know Ketti very well, but in the dark, with her body pressed that closely against me, it was hard not to feel some kind of attraction. "I had such a crush on you all through high school," she said, almost to herself. "I never got why you ended up with Cheryl."

"That seems to be the general consensus," I said. I was surprised by her confession, which sounded genuine. Ketti hardly spoke a word to me that I can remember. Maybe I was her courtly love, like Amelinda was for Nate.

"I used to have these fantasies that I'd suddenly grow in my senior year, and you'd notice me."

"That doesn't—"

"But then I figured Cheryl wasn't that much taller than I was, so maybe you just wanted someone who—"

"Listen, Ketti, could we not talk about Cheryl? I'd just rather not, if you don't mind."

"Sure."

After the song was over, we went over and got some more punch. The music was getting wild again. A few of the best dancers were in the middle, doing their stuff. "Want to go outside?" Ketti asked. "It's so noisy in here."

"Yeah, I'd love to." A second after I said that, I realized she could interpret that as my wanting to be alone with her, rather than just a desire to escape the room.

"Want to sit in my car?" she suggested once we were outside.

"Okay." The cool air felt good. I reminded myself to keep track of the time.

Ketti had a beat-up old Volvo. For a while she sat behind the steering wheel, smoking. "Feel like making out?" she asked with a quizzical glance.

I hesitated. "I don't know . . . I guess I'm not that much in the mood."

"Because it's me?"

"No, because . . ." I thought of Joely's remarks. "It wouldn't be the beginning of anything."

"So? You're not a virgin."

"Aren't you?"

"No. Anyway, I wasn't thinking of . . ." She looked embarrassed. "Oh, forget it. I just thought, for old times' sake. Or whatever."

By then I figured I was acting like a prude, and I didn't exactly see what issue I was trying to uphold. We fooled around for a while, keeping it within certain boundaries. We kept our clothes on but managed to make it worthwhile on both sides. But I felt in a strange kind of fog, like part of me was home sleeping.

"Did you know I was going to Barnard?" Ketti asked after we had pulled apart and settled down. She lit up another cigarette.

"No."

"I wanted to go to Yale, but I only got on the waiting list. It'll be a relief to be somewhere where everyone is smart—or at least where it isn't some kind of stigma. Maybe guys don't feel it here the way girls do, but if you are even college bound, it's like you're some kind of freak."

"I didn't feel it that strongly, but I felt it," I said. Ketti's parents aren't connected with Taylor—her father's a contractor who lives in a big house at one end of town.

I don't smoke, so I just waited until she finished, then we

walked back into the gym. *Girls are just different . . . Sex is a hook . . . Courtly love . . . I hate to be crude, but apart from sex . . .* Suddenly I felt really awkward with Ketti, not certain if I'd been doing what Joely had talked about earlier or not. "Thanks," I said stiffly. "I . . . It was—"

She touched my shoulder. "Take care, Tim," she said easily, and walked off.

Look, *she* approached *you*, I defended myself. And we didn't actually . . . I looked around for Joely. The band was doing a slow number again, and she and Courtney were swaying in place, not really dancing, eyes closed. They were going as far as you could go without anyone noticing. So was everyone else, but I didn't see any other same-sex couples besides them. I waited until the last dance was finished, then walked over to the part of the room where the two of them were standing. "Have a good time?" Joely asked.

"Yeah, I survived." I looked over at Courtney, a little embarrassed. "Hi. Do you want a lift home?"

"That's okay. I have my own car." She has a very soft voice. "Thanks, Tim. We appreciated it. . . . Maybe we were paranoid about the whole thing. Maybe we could've come as a couple. . . . Who'd you dance with? Anyone?"

"Ketti Drennan. Actually, we sat out most of the dance in her car."

"Sat out?" Joely asked.

"She said she's had a crush on me all through high school. I never knew."

"Don't tell me you fucked her just because—"

"I didn't, but what if I had? God, Joely, don't you think girls ever have minds of their own?"

Joely gave me a steely glance. "You'd better look out, Tim. I mean it."

"Look out for what?"

"Just remember girls have feelings, okay?"

Why had I told her anything? I was ending the evening feeling as angry as I had felt driving to the prom. "I'll try," I said.

Just to round things off, when we got back to Joely's, I got out of the car and went inside, but it seemed like Maureen and Charlie had gone to sleep. The house was quiet. "See you," I said, backing down the steps.

My father was still up when I came in. He was in the living room, reading. He often stays up late, especially on weekends. "Have fun?" he said.

"Yeah, it was good." I tried to sound more enthusiastic than I felt.

"Joely's a nice girl," he said. He sounded like he'd been drinking. "You couldn't find a finer girl in this town."

"True. Only we just went to the prom together. We're not engaged, so relax."

"Of course you're not. I doubt she has any desire to get involved with a young man who's starting out life encumbered with an infant. I would doubt strongly that that is her intention."

"You're right," I said. "You've hit the nail on the head."

He looked at me, as though uncertain how sarcastic I was being. "Well, sleep well. Rest on your laurels."

That's one of my father's favorite expressions. If you say "What laurels?" he just waves his hand vaguely.

It seemed a fittingly fucked-up ending to my high school years; taking a gay girl to the prom, making out with someone who had a crush on me but never let me know it, jerking off while my pregnant ex-girlfriend sat at home with her sister, probably watching *Dallas*.

CHAPTER 9

I had my usual summer job as bellhop in the local fancy hotel in Cardoba, the Stanmore. The pay isn't extraordinary, but you get at least as much again in tips. I worked the same shift I had before, from ten at night to six in the morning. Being a bellhop is a little like what I imagine being a cabdriver is like. You get quick glimpses into people's lives, just impressions, and you can build on them in your mind, fill in the gaps, but you never end up knowing if you are right or totally off the mark. The ones I noticed most that summer were the young couples. The Stanmore doesn't have any honeymoon suites exactly, but some couples pass through on their way to Niagara Falls. There were a few that had what seemed to me a "Just Married" look on their faces, as clearly as if they had rice stuck behind their ears. I remember one couple especially. He was tall and skinny, like me, and maybe

I read this into it, but it seemed to me he had a panicked look in his eyes. Even if he did, it could've been for any number of reasons. Maybe they'd never been to bed together before, and he was scared he'd be lousy. What struck me too was the way his wife, who seemed, like him, in her early twenties at best, walked into the room with a proprietary look on her face and sat smugly on the bed, looking all around. The way I would have interpreted the balloon over her head was: "I finally made it!"

Having a schedule like that pretty much took care of my social life. That is, if I'd had a social life, I would have had to work hard to arrange to see anyone, but I didn't. I saw Ketti around town a few times, and it occurred to me I could've asked her out, but I felt the way I had at the prom, that she would have interpreted it as a beginning, something to be continued in the fall at college, and I didn't want that. I figured I'd have enough to handle with "the kid."

That's what I called him in my mind: "the kid." I never thought of him as "the baby," and I wasn't sure about the name. Until he appeared, he seemed anonymous. There were whole days when I didn't think of him at all. How can you think of something that's totally new, unimaginable? I'd gone through all the baby books in the library. I figured I knew as much as you can know from books and that hopefully, some instinct would take over once he was actually here.

Even though there was no girl in my life, I thought of them occasionally, but it was more like in the pre-Cheryl days, a vague female person who floated around in my fantasies and took different shapes and forms. Or sometimes I'd just take out a mental tape of some really good time Cheryl and I had had together and replay it slowly, leaving out the dialogue, the way I'll sometimes turn off the sound on the TV. There are times when a fantasy just doesn't work for me unless it's rooted in reality. When I thought of Cheryl, I could remember tiny details—a certain soap she used, the way her hair smelled, the fact that one of her breasts was slightly larger than the other, the way she hated me to see her naked from behind, because she thought her ass was too big, her habit of nipping on the lobes of my ears just to tease me. I'd like to think that what I had with Cheryl was just a preview of coming attractions. It would be weird and pathetic to think of myself spending the rest of my life looking back on the times with her as some kind of highlight, the way my father looks back on his life with my mother.

In early June I bought a few baby things: a crib that you could carry around, a few sleep suits, some diapers in the smallest size. I'd asked Maureen for advice. I didn't want to involve my father, nor did I really have the feeling he'd know anything about it. Buying them I felt the way I did when my mother once sent me to the drugstore to buy some sanitary napkins for her, embarrassed, hoping no questions would be asked. Not that I think people who work in drugstores even hear what you ask for half the time, but in any case I'm sure they thought I was buying the diapers for my mother, who'd just had a new baby. I bought everything in Cardoba, where no one would recognize me, or care; that made it easier. I just put the stuff in my room. I figured the kid could sleep in there with me until we went off to college together.

Still, just the simple act of buying those things suddenly made what was happening real. I walked out of the store with a sudden sinking feeling, not quite panic, but acute apprehension. *I don't know what I'm doing. I'm doing something lethally stupid. It's not too late to call it off. Call Charlie, call the Sidels.*

But it seemed so cowardly to back off just at the thought. And I didn't think I could face my father's quiet gloating ''I told you so'' or ''Thank God you finally came to your senses.'' Plus there was, which may be totally insane, some

91

kind of excitement, even pride. How many guys my age could even *think* of handling this? And always that feeling that my mother, were she alive, would have approved, understood.

One thing which was a surprising help was a course—Family Life—they'd forced us to take freshman year. It was just one semester, but they had us all pair off and pretend we were married couples about to have babies. We had to plan everything, rent apartments, figure out a budget. And then, at the end, a few mothers came in with actual babies and we all had to do the whole procedure: change diapers, give them a bath, feed them a bottle. Then, I thought it was the biggest waste of time on earth. I couldn't believe what a struggle it was trying to wash the baby's hair and not get soap in its eyes. Actually, most of the class thought the course was stupid, especially the guys. What I'll always remember was Mrs. Burns, the teacher, saying at the end, "This will be more helpful than you know . . . someday." As I walked out Joe Bentley laughed grimly and said, "I'm marrying someone who'll do it all . . . period," and silently we probably all agreed with him. Cheryl's due date was July 27. I know those dates are pretty inaccurate, but that was what the doctor had told her, and it seemed to fit with the one time we'd done it when she had had her period. But July 27 came and went, and nothing happened. The next couple of days I had a jittery, peculiar feeling on the job. I'd told my father to call me the second he heard anything, and he'd promised he would. Every time they called me to the front desk I kept expecting it would be him. I don't know why, but I felt some kind of panic, as though something might go wrong. Maybe it was remembering Cheryl's wish that the baby be born with some kind of defect. I had nightmare-like dreams of his being born dead, or just never being born, disappearing somehow. In one dream I went to the hospital, and Cheryl had checked out and taken the baby with her, and no one knew where she was. Would she do that? I doubted it, but I woke up with a sick kind of dread.

In the end it was Charlie who called me, and I wasn't on the job at all. It was around one in the afternoon, I'd just woken up, and I was staggering into the shower. "Tim? It's Charlie. You've got a boy. Nice, healthy. No problems. It was a quick labor."

"Can I go over to see him?"

Charlie cleared his throat. "Not yet. That was one of the judge's stipulations. Cheryl evidently doesn't want to see you, and he felt her wishes ought to be obeyed in that, if nothing else."

I felt bewildered. "I just want to see *him*, not her."

"Look, Tim, relax. You'll have all you can handle in no time. She'll only be in the hospital a couple of days. There don't seem to be any complications. I've spoken to the doctor."

"Couldn't I just come when she's asleep? I won't try to see her, I promise."

"I said no, damn it!" His voice rose. "This is how she wants it. Give her that, at least."

I felt cowed. "Okay. So you'll let me know when I can come over and get him?"

"Of course I will. Give Abner my congratulations when you see him. Tell him being a grandpa isn't as bad as it sounds."

My father was out, but later in the day a telegram arrived from Charlie saying: COME ON IN. THE WATER'S FINE.

My father raised one eyebrow. "What's *that* supposed to mean?"

"The baby came. Only I'm not allowed to see him yet. Cheryl doesn't want me over there until she checks out."

My father frowned. "I don't get it. You took her to court, didn't you? It's your kid, isn't it?"

"Charlie said those were the stipulations."

"She better not try any monkey business," my father said. He was pouring himself a drink.

"You mean stealing the baby and disappearing?" I said, remembering my dream.

"Anything." His face softened. "Still, the poor kid. She's got to be feeling pretty awful now, don't you think? To have the baby taken away like that—"

"It was her choice."

"She's just a kid. What'd she know? She should've kept it. Her mother could've helped her raise it."

"Her mother's had five already. Maybe she'd had enough."

"Still . . ."

It was frustrating not being able to mark the occasion in any way, as though it had happened but not happened. As if he sensed that, my father said, "Well, what the hell. I'll take you out to dinner. Might as well do *something* to celebrate."

I was surprised he regarded it as a cause for celebration. But I got dressed in a jacket and tie, and we went to an Italian place we both like: Fiorello's.

"What're you going to call him?" my father asked after we'd been seated.

"Mason." That was my mother's maiden name.

My father gazed off into space. "I was hoping for a girl, I have to admit."

I made a wry expression. "I thought you were hoping the whole thing wouldn't happen."

"You mean, rewrite history? That's another matter . . . No, I've come to terms with it, as an idea. *You're* the one who has to handle it."

"I know that."

"The minute you feel it's too much for you to handle, say so. No stupid pride making you hang on with gritted teeth. There are plenty of—"

94

"—young couples who'd be delighted," I finished for him. "Dad, I know all that, okay?"

"You know a lot of things from the books. Let me tell you, life is something different. Even with your mother to do most of it, that first year with you was a nightmare. I thought I wouldn't survive."

Despite my father's propensity to exaggeration, I felt taken aback. "A nightmare?"

"You had one illness after another. I can't even remember most of them now. Some kind of eczema. I remember the doctor said you had to wear gloves, mittens, so you wouldn't scratch yourself. He was afraid of infection. He even wanted to tie your hands down with splints, but your mother said absolutely not. It was tough all around, but especially on your mother. Maybe that's why later—"

I was about to plunge into my shrimp cocktail. "Later? What?"

My father looked around the room, avoiding my glance. "Well, she had a tendency to pamper you. She thought of you as delicate. It was based on that first year, her fear you wouldn't make it. She always worried, the smallest illness she was sure would be something fatal."

All I remember is having what seemed like asthma when I was little, attacks of not being able to breathe. Once I went off to camp, and it got so bad they sent me home. I think I was driving the other kids in my bunk crazy, wheezing at night. "So you wish it had been a girl because it would be like starting off fresh; she'd be healthy?"

"No, it *is* starting off fresh . . . I suppose I just feel . . . well, maybe certain tensions would be, shall we say, less acute. Daughters so often seem to adore their fathers." He looked wistful. "I always envied Charlie. Three! The way they'd sit on his knee, stroking his cheek. He's led a charmed

95

life, no doubt of it.'' My father sighed. His blue eyes looked watery. "But envy is an unprofitable emotion, is it not?"

"Definitely. I'm glad it's a boy."

"So you can identify?"

"Yeah, I figure I'll be able to understand him better."

My father looked grim. "I never felt I understood *you*. Your mother did. I didn't."

I didn't say anything.

"And I never felt *my* father understood *me*. He never tried, for that matter. But we were as unalike as two human beings could be."

My father almost never talks about his childhood, and his parents were dead before I was born. "What was he like?"

"Brutal, drank too much, used the strap on us . . . An unthinking man. I suppose he would have given some extenuating circumstances—born into poverty, wanted to toughen us up. Squashed your grandmother. She was like a deaf-mute. Never spoke. A dreadful marriage. You can't imagine what that's like. Your mother and I—"

"Yeah, I know." But I was interested in what he'd said. I wished I'd asked my mother more about her family too; they're still living, but I hardly ever see them—they live in Oregon. "Was that why you waited so long to get married?"

"Yes, I decided at your age I would never marry. It seemed such an ugly institution to me, two people tied together in fear and loathing. And I saw so many horrendous marriages among my contemporaries, so much bickering, pettiness, quarrels. I still believe that. It has to be the one person, the person without whom life wouldn't be worth it. No other reason."

I had drunk a glass of wine. My mood kept teetering between a kind of high and trying not to react to these morbid confessions. "I may not marry either. I'm not as romantic as you. I'm not sure there's anyone like that out there for me."

"There may not be," my father said flatly. "I was lucky. Most people aren't."

That surprised me. I'd expected he would say some cheerful, optimistic thing about my being too young to form such judgments. It was strange, too, to hear my father say, "I was lucky," when usually he seems to feel exactly the opposite.

"You make your life," he went on. "I made mine, and I don't regret a day of it. Not that I waited so long, not that I'm alone now. People who go around feeling sorry for me don't know what it's all about. I had more than they'll ever have."

It wasn't exactly the most cheerful conversation to have as a celebration dinner, but dinners with my father rarely are. I wished then, so much, that I had Howie, or some other friend my own age, whom I could call up, someone to talk to. My father and I seemed like two little isolated wheels spinning around in their own orbits.

Later, after my shift at work, at six in the morning, I impulsively drove to the hospital on my way home. I didn't even get out of the car. I just sat there, looking up at the building. I wondered if Cheryl had decided to see the baby, or handle him. I'd read that some mothers, if they know they can't keep the baby, don't even want to begin forming any kind of attachment. But it all seemed kind of pathetic and sad, the three of us, me sitting alone in the car, forbidden to enter the hospital. Cheryl asleep in her hospital bed, feeling forlorn, and the baby, not knowing anything.

A day later I was shopping for food in the local supermarket when I ran into Henrietta. We were in the canned fruit section. She gave me a quick, hard glance. "Cheryl's okay?" I asked.

"Yes, she's fine," Henrietta said. "Do you mean physically or psychologically?"

"Both."

Henrietta reached for a can of peaches. "It's going to take her a long time to get over this," she said severely.

I didn't know what to say. I knew she wanted some craven apology, but I didn't feel I had to give her that satisfaction. "I hope she'll be okay. . . . And like my father said, if she feels like coming over sometime and seeing him—"

"That would be the worst possible thing," Henrietta snapped. "She has to pretend it never happened. She has to take up her life again. Do you want her to go on being torn about it all her life?"

"N-no, I just meant if she ever felt like it, she could," I stammered, "not that she should feel any obligation."

"I hope not," Henrietta said. "It's been a terrible year for her. You didn't make it any easier."

I was drumming my fingers on my leg, a habit I have when I'm nervous. "Well, I'm glad she's fine. I'm looking forward to seeing the baby."

"Not until she's out of the hospital," Henrietta said quickly, as though I were about to dash over the second I left the store. "You understand that, don't you?"

I nodded and moved down the aisle, wanting to get away from her. Cheryl used to say that Henrietta had always acted like her mother, that her real mother was too busy with all the other children to do much of that, Cheryl being the youngest. It was Henrietta whom Cheryl used to feel she was rebelling against by going to bed with me, Henrietta whom I always thought of as watching me disapprovingly when I came over, as though in her mind this whole scenario had been written and she was just waiting with some kind of grim satisfaction for it to unfold. Cheryl explained it all, not only by Henrietta's maternal impulse but by her having had a bad romance with some married guy at the bank who promised he was on the verge of divorce, then "discovered" his wife was pregnant and couldn't leave her. So maybe, in addition to giving her a bad feeling about men it made her doubly angry about the pregnancy, something men do to give women a hard time. He still works at the bank, but Cheryl said Henrietta refused to quit once their relationship ended. "She didn't want to give him that satisfaction," she said.

I gave notice at my job. It would've just been a few more weeks, and they handled it well. I gave them the real reason, too, instead of making one up. The hotel manager, Mr. Frings, listened impassively. He's not married, and I don't know if he has ever been. "Well, I wish you the best of luck," he said. "I'm sure you're aware that you'll need it."

It's funny how many people in the world seem to take some kind of delight in the hope of other people's failure or misery. Was there anyone on earth who hoped, or believed, I could really raise this kid? No one I could think of.

CHAPTER 10

Charlie called and said that I could come to the hospital the following morning. I gathered a few things together: some diapers, a stretch suit. My father followed me around, watching my every move. "Is that enough? Just a light suit like that?"

"It's summer. What else do I need?"

"Some kind of blanket. Don't they always need blankets?"

I looked at him and smiled. "Maureen said it wasn't necessary to take one to the hospital."

He looked relieved that I'd consulted Maureen, though I'd never mentioned it before. In fact, I'd been calling her about once a week, partly for moral support.

When he started following me outside to the car, I turned around and said, "Where are you going?"

"Where do you think? To the hospital with you."

"Dad, I can handle this alone."

"What do you mean? One person has to carry the child, the other to drive the car. That's common sense. At any rate, this is my first grandchild. Am I to be denied the privilege of seeing him?"

Actually, now that he mentioned it, I realized he was right about the baby, but I had thought I could just put him in a basket in the backseat and drive carefully. Somehow I didn't feel like sharing this experience with my father, even though there was no one else I could share it with. I'd just assumed he would be totally disinterested.

We took the elevator to the maternity ward on the sixth floor and approached the front desk. A nurse was sitting there, looking through some papers. I waited until she looked up. "I'm Timothy Weber," I said. "I'm here to pick up my son."

"Yes, of course. Come this way. We've been expecting you. I believe Dr. Neilson would like to have a word with you." She glanced inquiringly at my father.

"I'm Tim's father," he said, extending his hand. "Abner Weber. Am I permitted to come along?"

"Of course," the nurse said. "Just follow me."

The baby was in a large room with a lot of other babies. We stood outside, looking through the glass window. A few mothers stood there in white gowns, looking disheveled. There were family groups of different kinds, grandparents, fathers. "They all look pretty much alike," my father said, "at first, anyway."

I didn't think so. Some of them had a lot of hair and looked much older and more mature; others looked skinny and bald and wrinkled. I hoped Mason was one of the decent-looking ones. A different nurse came out of the room, carrying a baby. She was young and friendly seeming. "I'm Sue," she said. "I thought while we're waiting for Dr. Neilson, I might show you a few things about feeding and so forth. I'm assuming this is your first?" She looked uncertainly from my father to me. It was true, technically it could be my father's child, if he'd remarried some much younger woman.

"It is," I said, just to clear up the kid's paternity. I tried to look at him, looking for some resemblance to anyone, Cheryl, me, my father, my mother. Somehow he didn't look that much like anyone, more like some generic baby. He had Cheryl's coloring, a tuft of dark hair, but his eyes were scrunched shut. He wasn't a knockout, but there didn't seem to be anything wrong with him either.

Sue led us into a small sunny room. She had a bottle on a table in the corner. "You're going to bottle feed?" she asked. I laughed nervously. "Well, I don't think I have much choice." She stared at me, puzzled, so I added, "I'm raising him myself."

She didn't seem to react to this, just took the top off the nipple, and said, "Why don't you sit in a chair? I'll hand him to you."

I sat down in a green vinyl chair and looked up expectantly. She handed Mason to me. He seemed incredibly small. I know they grow fast, but you'd figure nature would have had them born twice as big. But maybe then it would be tough on the mothers, carrying them around. She handed me the bottle. "Now, just offer it to him gently, don't force it on him."

I took the bottle. "He looks like he's sleeping. Why should I wake him up?"

"Well, if you were at home, you wouldn't have to. But it's been four hours since he was fed, and we find that for the first month it's important to feed them at least that often. Don't worry. Once he's a little older, he'll let you know when he's hungry. Just put the nipple near his mouth, and you'll see.''

I did. Without opening his eyes, Mason's mouth opened and latched onto the nipple. ''Can they drink and sleep at the same time?'' I asked.

''He may not be sleeping. Their eyes are very weak, and they don't see much at first, even when they're open. There—he's opening them.''

His eyes were blue, like mine. He looked at me; it was a strange moment. Maybe babies can't see, and obviously they don't know what they're seeing since they don't really know anything, but it was like that moment was his first knowledge of who I was. I felt incredibly self-conscious. It's odd to think how everything you do, even with a newborn, is making some kind of impression and you have no idea what it is. Was I holding him differently than Cheryl would have, than any woman would have? Not that he'd ever have any point of comparison, but I felt extremely awkward, as though maybe my father was right, there was no male instinct about how to do it. I just watched his mouth sucking away while his eyes looked at me with that unblinking stare. Then he closed them again and stopped sucking. It didn't seem like he'd had much to drink. The bottle was mostly full. ''What now?'' I asked. I kept thinking the nurse was going to yell at me for doing it wrong.

''He may have had enough,'' she said, taking the bottle from me. ''Their capacity is limited, and you really have to leave it up to them. Some drink the whole bottle, and others seem to prefer little snacks throughout the day.'' She showed us how to burp him and then looked quickly at her watch. ''Let me see if Dr. Neilson has put in an appearance.''

My father had been just standing there, watching me. ''It's amazing,'' he said.

''What?''

"He looks just like you. I can't get over it."

"But I didn't have dark hair."

"Yes, you did. It fell out and when it grew in again, it was blond. But the shape of his face, everything. History repeating itself."

I looked down at Mason. "He doesn't seem very lively, does he?"

"Just wait. In a month he'll be screaming around the clock. They put on their best behavior in the hospital."

Dr. Neilson was a harassed, gray-haired man who looked like he'd been up since dawn. He shook my father's hand. "Mr. Weber?"

"My son is the father," my father said. "*Timothy* Weber."

Neilson looked down at some notes. "Right, the mother checked out yesterday. Okay, well, we don't seem to have any problems. He's eating well, sleeping fine. A little trace of what could be some kind of eczema."

"Where?" my father said, alarmed.

Neilson took Mason and set him on the examining table in the middle of the room. He undid his diaper and showed us a slight reddish patch around his behind. "Nothing to worry about. I'll give you some cream. If it seems to bother him, call me. Otherwise I'll see you in a month."

"I won't be here in a month," I said. "I'll be in New York. I'm going to college there."

Neilson looked at my father. "Well, you bring him in, then."

"The baby's going to New York with *me*," I explained, sure he was going to register some kind of protest.

"Okay, make it in two weeks. I'll find you someone in the city. Once a month for the first year . . . Any questions?"

I had so many questions that they all seemed to come

together and dissolve in my mind. "About the eczema," my father began anxiously.

Neilson patted my father's arm. "Not to worry. It's a mild case, extremely common."

"But it runs in the family," my father said. "What if it gets worse?"

Neilson grinned. "What if it gets better? Relax, Grandpa." He patted me on the shoulder. "He's doing fine," he said, and rushed out of the room.

My father looked indignant. "What kind of doctor *is* that? *I* know about eczema. It could cover his whole body by nightfall! Is this what they call medical attention?"

"Dad, he said it was a mild case."

"They said it was mild with *you*!" my father exclaimed. "Those were their very words. 'A mild case.' You had to wear mittens! You were suffering! It was horrible."

Jesus, here I'd expected he wouldn't even notice the baby's existence. "Why don't we not worry unless something happens?" I said. "He may be fine."

My father was pacing up and down. "I hate doctors!" he said. "Why are they all like that? This is a newborn child, his first week of life."

"The doctor's very busy," I said, though I knew what my father meant.

"He just says, 'I'll give you some cream.' What cream? What kind of cream? Are there side effects?"

"It didn't look that serious to me," I said.

My father fumed. "You've had this baby, what—forty minutes, and you're an expert? I'm telling you, this is *exactly* how it started with you. I have photos somewhere. I'll show you. It determined your whole personality."

Maybe I should leave for New York next week. I thought the baby would be my main problem; I hadn't thought what it would be like with my father. "Dad, look, I'm kind of nervous about this, okay? And somehow, what would help, if you *want* to be helpful, is to try and act relaxed. Even if you don't feel it. I can get hysterical on my own.''

"Who's hysterical?'' my father said. "This is concern, legitimate concern.''

I just stood, looking at him.

He wiped his brow. "No, you're right. I *am* hysterical. I was a terrible father. I'm going to be a terrible grandfather. Babies make me feel that way. That's why I didn't want one. I knew. If your mother hadn't been so insistent . . . But I'll be good. I'll take a few Valium.''

I was amazed. "I thought you didn't believe in drugs of any kind.''

My father looked chagrined. "I don't want to be a bad influence. You handle it. I shouldn't even have come here. I knew it would be like this. Hospitals, doctors. It's like the time your mother—''

Just then Sue, the nurse, reappeared. "Well,'' she said cheerfully. "Everything okay? I have the cream and a box of free bottles. We usually start out with the smaller size, but once he's taking more than four ounces at a feeding, you can move right on to the larger.'' She glanced at my father. "Are you all right, sir?''

My father was sitting down, looking like he was going to pass out. "Could I have a glass of water?'' he asked very quietly.

"Of course.'' She brought the water and my father took a sip, then struggled to his feet.

I was holding Mason. He was wearing the stretch suit I'd bought, which seemed way too big. My father took the package with the bottles and cream. As we were waiting for the elevator, another couple was leaving with their baby. The man smiled at me. "How'd it go?'' he said.

"Pardon me?''

"Weren't you and your wife in our Lamaze class?" he asked. "Jeremy Walker?"

"No, he's an unwed father," my father said.

The man looked startled. "Oh, I'm sorry. I didn't— Your face just looked familiar." When we got out of the elevator a few moments later, he waved at us. "Good luck!"

"Same to you," my father said sarcastically. Once the man and his wife were out of sight, he muttered to me, "What business is it of *his* how the childbirth went? Why do people do that with total strangers?"

"He thought I was someone he knew."

"You weren't," my father said. "He didn't know you from Adam."

Outside, the sun was blazing. It must have been nearly ninety degrees. My father pulled out his sunglasses. He has very weak eyes and can hardly look into the sun. "Do you want me to drive?"

"Sure." I waited while he opened the car door and then slid in, carrying the baby. My joints felt stiff, even though he was so light. I guess I must have been more nervous than I realized.

My father drove at his usual snail's pace, ignoring all the honking of impatient drivers in back of us. "What is their hurry?" he said to himself. "What use will they make of their time if they go sixty, seventy miles an hour, risk their lives, risk other people's lives?"

I sighed. Mason's eyes were starting to open. He looked at me with that unnerving steady gaze, and that's all he did the rest of the way home. A couple of times I looked away, but when I looked down again, he was still staring up at me.

I was sure that if he knew the setup he was getting into, he would've opened his mouth and let out the loudest howl on earth. Maybe I would've, too.

CHAPTER 11

August, or what remained of it until I was due to leave for college, was the longest and shortest month of my life. In a way, nothing happened that would've made the local paper. Mason's eczema cleared up, he began eating pretty regularly, I became adept at changing diapers.

But it was like being in jail or in a mental hospital. My life disappeared. Every waking moment seemed to be spent tending Mason, worrying about him, even dreaming about him. One night I actually dreamed he died. In the dream I went in to give him his bottle and he was lying there, stiff as a board. I felt one moment of enormous relief and calmly began thinking, Now, what kind of coffin should I order? I woke up bathed in sweat, feeling guilty as hell. Mason was crying. I tried to smile at him ingratiatingly as I changed his diaper.

What's weird with babies is their total, monstrous egotism. You exist to satisfy their needs, period. I could have been a thirty-year-old woman, a ninety-year-old man—Mason couldn't have cared less. The thought never crossed his mind that maybe, on a beautiful summer's day, I would have liked to be somewhere else, just off somewhere, free, unencumbered. Say thank you, you fucker, I thought as he burped and lolled sleepily against my shoulder.

You can get out of this any time you want. Once, at three in the morning, I actually reached for the phone to call Charlie. It was pitch black in the house, I felt bone-tired, actually sick with fatigue, and looking at Mason in the crib, I thought of him as a time bomb. *He'll be up again in four hours!* And he wasn't even a bad baby, according to the books. He didn't have colic. This was what a *normal* baby was like! Some of them were twins! But pride, twisted and indomitable as that emotion is, prevented me from dialing. *You'll get through this. You'll show them.* But who was them?

Finally, my father, who'd been amazingly discreet, noticed. I think it was because one morning when he came down for breakfast, he found Mason asleep in his cot and me asleep, head in my arms, at the breakfast table. "It isn't that this is a problem, you understand," he said. "But what we need here is some kind of schedule. Look, once you're at school, you'll get some kind of sitter, right? Or some kind of day-care center. But right now you need your sleep. So I've worked out a plan which enables both of us to sleep six hours at a stretch and still have some time to leave the house at least once a day."

I looked at the schedule. He'd printed it up on his computer. According to it, he took the first night shift, I took the second, he took the third. "I can handle it," I said. "Seriously, I don't want you to get all . . . upset, like you said. I don't think it'd be good for him."

109

"Forget the hospital," my father said. "I was just . . . a lot of things. Something came over me. That's not what I'm usually like. Give me a chance. Don't always assume I'm a failure."

I was stunned. "I don't. God, when did I ever say that?"

"I can read your thoughts," my father said. "You don't have to speak. And you're right. I have failed in many things. I failed your mother. I am frankly not certain to this day that I was a good husband. That's the truth. I was moody, peculiar, I wasn't used to the day-to-day give and take. My students look at me sometimes like they think I'm crazy. I'm too rigid. Some of them drop out after a week, two weeks. I found a note once: 'He's driving me crazy.' I do that. I drive people crazy."

Somehow I had a sudden longing for my father as he seemed to have been before Mason was born—laconic, spaced out, detached. I tried to grin. "We're in this together," I said.

My father tried to smile. This is not easy for him. "That's—thank you," he said.

For that month my father and I probably were more of a family, in however peculiar a way, than we had ever been in the six years since my mother died. I saw that he was right. Both sides of my father can drive you crazy. Either he's not there, or he's so much there you want to put a pillow over his head. Sometimes at night I'd hear him get up to feed Mason. I'd have an impulse to get up and do it myself, even if I'd just been up a few hours earlier. Then I'd repress the impulse and try to go back to sleep. But I never quite could. I'd hear my father shuffling around, muttering to himself (we had Mason's crib out in the hall during the night so both of us could hear him wake up), sometimes even talking out loud. It was eerie, hearing my father's voice in the still house. The way he talked to Mason wasn't the way he talked to me.

110

It was like someone thinking to himself, or at any rate, saying everything that entered his head. "That's right. . . . Good boy. I know you feel wet, that rash still bothers you, doesn't it? Well, let's just see how this cream feels. Is that good? Is that better? Maybe it doesn't feel better now, but give it a few minutes. . . . Hungry, huh? Well, there's plenty more where that came from. We have twenty-seven bottles down there in the kitchen. I counted them. Just drink up. . . . That's all? That's not even a meal! . . ."

I would listen and not listen, the way in high school I used to watch TV while I was doing my homework.

One day Nate Rafalsky called to ask if I wanted to go on a picnic at the beach with him and his best friend, Andy. I looked longingly out the window. It was the middle of a heat wave. I could almost feel how cool the lake water would be. I love swimming, but I hadn't even been down there all summer. "I don't think I can," I said after a long, agonizing moment. "I have the baby now and it may be difficult to get away. Thanks for asking me, though."

I hung up, smothered my feeling of resentment, and went downstairs.

My father was reading the paper at the kitchen table. "Who was that?"

"Nate Rafalsky, a guy from my chem class at school."

"What'd he want?"

"Some guys are going on a picnic down at the lake. He wondered if I could join them. I said I couldn't." What I felt probably was written all over my face.

My father looked up. "Go!" he said. "I can handle Mason."

"Yeah, but—"

"Do you have doubts I can handle him?"

"No, it's not that. I just—"

111

"Will you go to the goddamn beach!" my father exclaimed. "You're getting on my nerves, hanging around the house all day. It isn't healthy. Even mothers get out occasionally, go bowling or whatever. From the day you were born, I always gave your mother a night out. She'd go over to Anne's house, or Maureen's, or go play bridge with friends. 'Go!' I'd say. 'Take the night off.' "

It was too damn tempting. A break! Freedom! I grinned. "Okay. Well, thanks."

My father just waved his hand. "Call him back."

I arranged to meet them at the beach. I brought along some beer and potato chips. Nate said he and Andy would bring sandwiches. The lake is gigantic, twenty miles long, two miles across. There are a lot of summer cottages along the edge, but this particular area, Stony Point, was set aside by the town as a local gathering place. "Beach" is a bit of a misnomer, since there isn't a lot of sand. But there are picnic tables, and you can cook out at various stone fireplaces. It's not built up in any other way, which I like. You have to bring your own food, for instance—there aren't any stands selling hot dogs or cold drinks.

Andy is Nate's sidekick, a tall, shy boy with hair that stands up in a wedge. I don't know him that well, though he's been in some of my classes. "Maybe Amelinda will be here," he said jokingly, giving Nate a nudge.

"Oh, quit it," Nate said, but he looked eagerly up and down the beach. "Anyhow, that's over. That was high school. Now I'm on to bigger and better things."

"I thought you said you'd remember her forever," I said, recalling the prom. The sun near the beach was just as hot as it was in town, but offset by the cool breezes blowing off the lake. It felt terrific.

"I will," Nate said, unwrapping a sandwich. "But I'm not going to be celibate or anything."

112

"Great," Andy said. "You had us all worried there." He looked over at me. "How come you went to the prom? I thought your girlfriend got knocked up."

"I took a friend," I said.

"Who?" He looked surprised.

"Joely Moore."

"That was fast. Christ, here we didn't see any action in all four years, and you—"

"She's just a friend," I said quickly. "She didn't have anyone to go with, so I just did it as a favor."

Nate was rubbing sun cream on his white, pulpy skin. "I thought she was gay."

Andy looked at him in amazement. "Are you kidding? How *can* she be?"

Nate shrugged. "What do you mean—how *can* she be? She just *is*, that's all."

"How do you know?" Andy asked. I was relieved he wasn't asking me.

"I keep my fucking eyes open, that's all," Nate said. "She and Courtney used to go around holding hands in the halls."

Andy sat there with a beer can in his hand. "Boy, that's weird. I didn't know we had any of those in our class. That is *truly* weird. She's even pretty. I don't get it."

"I don't think that has much to do with it," I put in finally. "She just prefers women."

Andy shook his head. "Why? That doesn't make sense to me."

"Nothing makes sense to you," Nate said good-naturedly.

Andy was munching on a large turkey sandwich. "No, but I mean, like, you have men and you have women. That makes sense. They fit. Women're one way, we're another. . . . But two women?"

"How about two men?" Nate said. "Or didn't you ever hear of that either?"

"Sure, I've *heard* of it," Andy said irritably. "I've read about it in the papers and all, but in our town? In our school? That's pretty far out. . . . Well, what do *I* know?"

"Nothing," Nate said.

Andy sighed. He gazed off at the lake. "It's true. I really know nothing, at least about women. You two are light-years ahead of me."

Nate laughed. "Count me out."

I just shrugged.

"Cheryl Banks is so pretty," Andy said. "Why didn't anyone like that ever make a play for me?"

"You're ugly and you're dumb, for starters," Nate said.

All this was clearly said in jest, but Andy looked gloomy. "Yeah, right." Then he looked at me. "But you're not that— I mean, I don't mean this in an insulting way, but you're not like the guy Amelinda went with. You never went out for sports."

"Blind passion, I guess," I said wryly.

"Yeah," he said sadly. "I've heard about that."

To cheer him up, I said, "It wasn't all that great . . . *and* she got pregnant."

"How come that happened?" Nate asked. "Didn't you—"

"Yeah, we did. But it just happened."

Andy was looking bewildered again. "What just happened? You mean, doing it?"

Nate sighed. "No, he means her getting pregnant 'just happened.' They used protection, but it didn't work."

"Boy," Andy said. "That must be tough. Still, I guess it's worth it."

Nate took a swig of his beer. "God, I wish I'd brought my tape recorder. This is getting profound here. 'I guess it's worth it.' "

This appeared to go over Andy's head. "I wonder how

114

many people in our class are still virgins," he said, "other than me."

"Guys or girls?" Nate asked.

"Either."

Nate considered. "Guys—forty-five percent; girls—fifty-five."

"Really?" Andy looked surprised. "That many?"

"That many which way?" Andy said. "That sounds like a lot, especially for the girls. . . . What do you think?" he asked me.

"That sounds pretty accurate," I said.

"How many did you think?" Nate asked him.

"Well, I *didn't* really think," Andy admitted, "but I guess maybe I would've said twenty-five percent of the guys had done it and maybe five percent of the girls."

Nate roared with laughter. "Five percent! So who are the twenty percent of the guys doing it *with*?"

Andy was chewing methodically on his sandwich. "Yeah, that's true. I hadn't thought about that. Maybe girls who live somewhere else? Older women?"

"There was a rumor about Paul O'Neill and that English teacher, Ms. Matthews. Remember her? The one with the long blond hair?"

Andy sighed. "Yeah, sure, the one who liked Emily Dickinson. Gosh, wasn't she married, though?"

Nate gazed at him. "You are terminally naive, you know that? You really are."

"Will I die?" Andy said, feigning anxiety. "Is it fatal?"

"It can be." Nate turned over on his towel, stomach down. "I'm going to sleep. Wake me up when you say something profound again."

I stood up, stretching. "I think I'll swim."

"You just ate," Andy warned me.

"Not much . . . See you."

115

I walked slowly into the water. The lake stays cold, even in the summer. In my opinion it's a perfect temperature, around 70 degrees, cool enough to make it a shock when you first dive in off the dock, then great once you're used to it. I started doing the crawl out to the raft. There was only one person sunbathing on it. Most of the sunbathers were either on the beach or on the dock, listening to their radios. I took note of some cute suntanned bodies as I passed by. The person on the raft was a boy I didn't know. I lay there a while, getting incredible pleasure out of what a year ago would have been a normal summer's day: the cool air, the sun, being alone, away from my father, away from Mason. Was this what college would be like, feeling giddy with excitement just because once every month, maybe, I could tune out and not worry about the baby? I crushed that thought before it could balloon into full-scale anxiety.

Opening my eyes, I looked across the lake. When it's clear, like today, you can see across not only to the other side but also to all the small houses and farms. I thought about how much I would miss this. I know New York has Central Park, but that's not the same. When I took a walk in it the weekend I went down for my interview, it seemed pretty crowded. I wondered where you went when you wanted to get away from it all.

I deliberately chose a city college; I wanted a total change, but suddenly an unexpected nostalgia came over me about my childhood which, obviously, was over. It seemed to have ended when my mother died; just the sense that things could be, in their own limited way, perfect. I remember when I was little, six or seven, I used to make a funny sound that bothered my parents. I did it because I had some feeling that if I didn't, things would change. I felt like I was protecting what was, the way some kids step on cracks in the sidewalk. Then my mother died, and I realized what I guess I would

116

have realized eventually anyway, that you can step on all the cracks in the world, or go through all the self-created rituals you want, and still never protect yourself from horrible, life-altering, insane changes. That stood my childhood world on its head.

But leaving Haysburg would carry that further. Not just the change from country to city. But in New York, or at Columbia, I would be no one, I would know no one, wouldn't know where anything was, would have no one to call in an emergency. I wanted that, both as a challenge and because I found Haysburg claustrophobic at times, but a faint trace of fear swept over me, wondering if dealing with Mason on top of everything else was going to be too much for me to handle.

I stood up, stretched, and dove back into the water. My body had heated up from the sun; the water felt cold again. I swam about a dozen laps back and forth, then climbed up the dock ladder. As I stood there shaking water off my head, I looked up and saw Cheryl.

She was standing about five feet away in a bikini. There was no way on earth you could ever have known she'd been pregnant a month ago. Her belly was as flat as a board. I just stared at her. I thought it took women months, even years, to get back in shape. She must have sensed me staring at her, because she turned and caught sight of me. I saw her hesitate. She could've just turned back and walked away. Instead she came over. "Hi," she said in a flat, slightly challenging way.

"Hi," I said, feeling peculiarly nervous. "How's it going?"

"Okay. It's a beautiful day, isn't it?"

"Yeah, it really is." It was one of those moments when anything you think of saying sounds so absurd or inappropriate that you're struck dumb. "You look good," I finally blurted, unable not to glance furtively at her figure again.

Cheryl smiled that flirtatious, knowing smile. "Right. *I*

think I do. I was scared it would take forever to get back in shape, but here I am."

It suddenly struck me as ironical. Usually you think of the woman who ends up getting stuck, one way or another. But instead it was the opposite. Cheryl was fine, looked terrific, I was the one wondering how long I could stay at the beach because of the baby. "He's doing well," I said finally. I still wasn't sure if Mason was a taboo subject. "He's really cute."

Cheryl smiled. "Great," she said, but in the same way she would have responded if I'd been talking about a baby that had nothing to do with the two of us. "I'm glad."

I cleared my throat. "If you ever want to—" I began.

"No, that's okay," Cheryl said. "Good luck, though."

I could have said a lot of things, but what I found myself saying was, "I think I'm going to need it."

I walked back to where Nate and Andy were, feeling strangely stirred up. *Okay, so she looked good, so you're attracted, why not? It's over.* Probably if I'd seen Cheryl for the first time on the dock, I would have thought she looked appealing also, but it was the memories of other things that made even that brief conversation tense and uncomfortable.

Andy looked up. "Where were you?" he asked.

"I was on the raft."

"Your girlfriend's over there," he said. "On the dock."

"Yeah, I know. I saw her."

"She's really pretty," he said wistfully. "Did she have her baby yet?"

Nate sat up. "Andy, sometimes I wonder about you. Did she look nine months pregnant to you?"

"How am I supposed to know how many months pregnant she was?"

"Because she's been pregnant all year at school! She looked like she was going to give birth in the hall."

118

Andy gazed over toward the dock. "She sure doesn't look pregnant now."

Nate rolled his eyes. "She is no more pregnant than you or me." To me he said, "It must be weird for you, isn't it, seeing her—"

"Yeah," I said briefly. "Kind of."

"Some people have all the luck," Andy said gloomily.

"Meaning?" Nate asked.

"Him," Andy said. "They did it. Sure, she got pregnant, but now she's fine—"

"And he's got a kid to raise alone," Nate said. "That's luck?"

Andy looked at me. "You're raising the kid? Didn't she give it up for adoption?"

I shook my head.

"Andy," Nate said, exasperated, "what'd I say to you this morning? I said, 'I'm going to invite Tim, if he can get away.'"

"So?" Andy said. "How am I supposed to know what that means? Christ, I'm not a mind reader."

Nate glanced over at me. He looked like he would be badly sunburned by the end of the day. "How's fatherhood?"

I hesitated. Andy and Nate were just casual buddies, but even if they hadn't been, I didn't want to mar the day by thinking about all of that. I wanted to act cool, relaxed, everything I hadn't felt for months.

"Okay, so far." From a distance I saw Cheryl talking to some guy on the dock, probably flirting; I was too far away to see her expression. An involuntary twinge of something resembling jealousy shot through me.

When I returned home, I found my father asleep on the couch and Mason asleep in his crib right next to him. Both of them kept right on sleeping, even when I came into the room. I looked from one of them to the other. My father had his arm over his eyes, his shoes off. Mason was on his stomach, his face turned toward me. I had a brief fantasy of my father begging me to leave Mason with him, offering to raise Mason himself. I thought of the Sidels, who probably still didn't have a baby, but had a room full of bassinets, toys, wallpaper with clowns and balloons.

Then, as though on cue, Mason opened his eyes and let out a cry, and my father leaped in one motion to his feet. "I'm back," I said, going to get a bottle from the kitchen. "I can handle it."

PART TWO

CHAPTER 12

This is what the sign said: THREE GIRLS IN FOUR-BEDROOM APARTMENT ON 115TH AND RIVERSIDE SEEKING ONE ROOMMATE. PERSONS OF EITHER SEX MAY APPLY AS LONG AS YOU ARE QUIET, RESPONSIBLE, AND ABLE TO PAY THE RENT. CALL 555-7162.

In the two weeks I'd been in the city, I'd looked at what seemed like hundreds of apartments. I knew they'd be expensive, but it still amazed me what they were offering for one thousand to fifteen hundred a month. I didn't think I could get away with a studio, but the supposedly one-bedroom apartments were so small that the "bedrooms" were often the size of closets. Some were walk-ups, no doorman, garbage stacked outside on the street. Maybe these were bargains, maybe I hadn't lived in New York long enough to appreciate them, but every place I saw seemed impossible, not worth sacrificing that amount of money. The dorm was obviously out, but I began noticing a lot of signs for "roommate needed." Evidently it was fairly common for a group of students to rent one large apartment in which each person had a bedroom. Clearly you'd have more room than in the places I'd looked at, because some of the time they'd be out. There'd be a real kitchen, not just an alcove tucked into the living room.

When I finally gave up on the idea of having my own apartment, I went to Student Housing. It was strange. I had Mason in a backpack and he was wide awake, but the woman behind the desk either didn't notice him or somehow didn't connect him to me. Maybe it was the same as some people feeling it's rude to mention anything about your being blind or having a hunchback. If she'd said, "Well, finding an apartment with other students who will want a baby on the premises will be pretty darn impossible," I might've started thinking along those lines myself. But she didn't say anything one way or the other and neither did I. It wasn't as though I was ashamed of Mason. It was just that I didn't want to start going into a song and dance and getting amazed or horrified glances from everyone. To top it off I was exhausted.

It wasn't just the newness of being in a strange city, it was having to take Mason literally everywhere I went. I read in the newspaper once that they had some high school kids "experiment" with the idea of having a baby by having to carry a two-pound sack of grain wherever they went. At the end of a week they were all amazed at how much trouble it was. A two-pound sack of grain! They've got to be kidding! Does a sack of grain scream, kick, yell, demand to be fed! Actually, Mason still struck me as a good kid, cheerful, lively, even ingratiating, not that I'd had any basis for comparison. It's funny, at times, just when he seemed to sense by some in-

124

tuitive thing that I was getting at the end of my tether, he'd grin up at me with this irresistibly engaging smile.

We were living in what, for lack of a better term, you'd have to call a fleabag hotel. Real hotels were like real apartments—out of sight financially. There were a few around Columbia that weren't exactly hovels or dens for drug pushers, but they'd clearly seen better days. There were roaches in the rooms, the tap water was rusty, the blankets thin and threadbare, the wallpaper peeling. I'm not a maniac about cleanliness and I've read babies are pretty resilient, but I couldn't wait to get out of there.

What I quickly learned was that honesty was not the best policy. The second they heard the word "baby," everyone I called started mumbling and muttering like I'd said I had a three-hundred-pound mongoloid sister with whom I wanted to share my quarters. Maybe this wasn't unexpected from students, guys especially, but I got just as many responses like that from elderly couples who I'd imagined might go all soft and mushy at the idea of a cute little baby. I wondered if it was New York. In Haysburg it seems to me there would've been some widow, some divorced kindly woman like Margaret who would've been eager to help me out. Here, with a million more people, there didn't seem to be anyone. Sink or swim.

And, of course, Mason didn't care. He didn't know, how *could* he care? He had gotten himself onto a weird schedule—essentially he slept all day and was up all night. Great for him, rotten for me. It made it easy taking him places during the day, since he was sacked out anytime, anyplace, but at night, just as I was ready to sink, exhausted, into bed, he started stirring and going through his repertoire of sounds, which all translated into: pay attention to me. I tried ignoring him. He seemed pretty intuitive about some things. Maybe if he saw I needed sleep, just *couldn't* be woken up, he'd give up. Nope. He just upped the decibel level and kept on until I realized if I didn't take care of him, the person in the next room would begin banging on the wall and yell, "Shut up in there, will ya?"

The only trick that worked was putting him in bed next to me. I put him on the side near the wall so he couldn't roll off. The first couple of times I worried I might roll over and squash him, but once we got through a few nights all right, I figured: The hell with it. It wasn't as though once he was in bed with me, he'd shut up and go to sleep. He kept up his muttering and squeals off and on all night, or so it seemed. But if you're tired enough, you can sleep through anything. Still, it was never sleep in the real sense, the kind where you wake up and all the problems that seemed gigantic the night before turn small and manageable just because you've got your energy back. I would wake up with a start, anxiously, take in where I was, and almost immediately feel worn out. The idea of going through the same fucking motions, making useless calls, rolling the same rock up the same hill, was too much.

Once—this was just a moment, I'm not proud of it—I was sitting in Riverside Park and had laid Mason down on the grass. I saw a water fountain and went over to get a drink. While I was drinking I glanced over at him. He was sleeping. In my fantasy I tiptoed away. Some couple, some couple like the Sidels, would stroll by, find him, be ecstatic, bring him home to a three-bedroom co-op. That it was a crime wasn't what stopped me. Maybe it was just brute stubbornness. I wasn't ready to throw in the towel yet. But as I stood at the water fountain I felt, just from the relief of not having him on my back, literally, as well as figuratively, that feeling of indescribable exhilaration I'd felt at the dock last summer. I'm just a guy taking a drink of water on a beautiful day, with

126

no more problems than what courses to sign up for, how soon I might meet a girl who'll be attracted to me. . . .

Truthfully, I had never thought of living with Mason in an apartment with all girls. But when I saw the ad, it struck me that maybe girls would find my having a baby less of a problem than a bunch of guys would. Maybe some of them would have a maternal streak, or had done a lot of babysitting, or would know something about how to handle babies. I stood there staring at the sign, inventing fantasies in my head, involving some combination of sex, free child care, and various other goodies, before I yanked myself back to reality. *They're in college, they're studying. If they want a guy at all, it's to offer protection of some kind.* Still, what could I lose? I jotted down the phone number and went to a public phone booth.

"Hello?" a girl's voice said.

"Hi," I said, trying to sound responsible, quiet, and hardworking. "I'm Timothy Weber, I'm a freshman at Columbia, and I just saw your ad for a room. I wondered if it was still available."

"This is your first year?" the girl asked.

"Right . . . I came in a little early because I'm . . . looking for a place to stay."

She seemed to hesitate. "Well, we have seen a number of applicants, but if you can come by today, we'd be glad to interview you."

"Interview" sounded a little intimidating. "What, uh, time would be good?" It was eleven in the morning.

"Could you make it at one? Vivian's out now, and we want to interview everyone together."

"That would be fine." I jotted down the address. It was a block from Columbia, one of those huge old buildings I'd passed on my walks in Riverside Park.

I hadn't used any baby-sitters since I'd gotten to the city,

127

but I'd gotten a list of agencies and finally nailed down a girl from Barnard who was available at the time I could look at the apartment. Obviously, I couldn't lie, claim I was just a single, unattached guy, and then show up with Mason. But I wanted to at least get a foot in the door, as it were. Maybe if I acted charming enough, endearing enough, well-behaved, offered to do something extra like cooking, I could ease Mason into the conversation. It was clear to me by now that some kind of shrewdness was going to be necessary just to set up what I would have thought of as the simple amenities of life.

I looked at myself in the mirror to see if I looked the part. I was wearing a blue shirt, a dark blue sweater, khaki slacks, and sneakers. If I were going on a date, I'd say I looked too informal, but I wasn't. Same if it were a job interview. Still, it *was* an interview. I wondered if I should wear or just carry a jacket. A tie would look ridiculous. I took off the sweater and decided to carry the jacket over one arm. It was mild, early fall weather.

The baby-sitter, Janie Lewis, looked younger than I'd expected, almost high school rather than college age. I'd told her to meet me in the lobby. I figured if she kept Mason out in the park, it would go better than having the two of them holed up in my hotel room.

She didn't question any of it, just peered at Mason, who was sound asleep. When I started explaining what to do if he woke up, she said, "Don't worry. I have five younger brothers and sisters. I'm an old hand." They wheeled off together and I felt a funny pang. There was something Haysburgish about her: her freckles, her round unaffected face and smile. *You wanted to get out of there, you felt stifled. Quit the phony nostalgia.*

Walking there, I thought, to calm myself down, that the apartment might be hideous, too small, that the three girls might be impossible, neurotic. You're choosing them, not the other way around, I tried to convince myself.

The building was excellent—a huge, marble-lined lobby, one of the buildings that had clearly been built at a time of economic prosperity for the neighborhood. There was a doorman who asked where I was going. I gave him the apartment number and he called up to give them my name. That seemed like a good sign in terms of safety, though he was just a little elderly man who didn't look like he'd be much use against a gang of teenage hoods with knives.

I rang the doorbell. The girl who answered it was pretty; blond hair to her shoulders, blue eyes, a roundish face, glasses. She looked serious, but friendly. "Tim?" she asked. "I'm Lindsay." She had the same slight Boston accent I'd heard on the phone. "Come right in. Vivian just got back."

She led me down a hall into a large living room decorated in comfortable, student style. There were plants, brightly colored posters, a couch that was beat up but covered at one end by a rug. On one end of the couch was a tiny girl with punk-looking orange hair. She looked around twelve years old. "I'm Fern," she said.

Sitting cross-legged on the floor was a tall girl with straight black hair, a hawklike nose, and a striking, angular face. "Vivian," she said in a voice notably less friendly than the other two. That's the one I'll have trouble with, I thought. I decided to look more at the other two during the interview.

Lindsay indicated a wing chair that was placed diagonally from the couch. "Sorry it's so warm," she said. "We have an air conditioner, but it broke down. We're planning on having it fixed."

"No air conditioner in your room, though," Vivian said. "If you want one, you'll have to buy it yourself and pay for the electricity."

"I can manage," I said. "In my hometown no one had air conditioners."

"Where're you from?" Fern asked.

"Massachusetts, a town called Haysburg. There's a small college there called Taylor."

Everyone looked blank. Fern looked at Lindsay. "You're from Boston."

"I know," Lindsay said. "I just never heard of it. . . . Listen, before we start, would you like to see the room? I could just give you a quick tour, because if this isn't what you want, that would save us the trouble."

I jumped to my feet and followed her down another hall. She pointed to a closed door. "That's Vivian's." The one across from it was open. "Mine." At the end of the hall was another room with a closed door. "Fern." Then she circled back. "What would be your room is really the dining room, but it's closed off, it has doors. It's closest to the living room, just thought you should know that. But it's also closest to the kitchen." She opened the door to what could be my room. It was large, larger than I'd expected, and had a bed and a bureau. We walked out the other door and down toward the kitchen. On the way we passed a tiny room that was jammed full of boxes and books. "That's what they call a maid's room. We use it for storage and stuff. . . . And this is the kitchen. Excuse the mess. We don't have much of a system with cooking. We might work one out this year. We have to decide."

It was a huge kitchen with sunlight streaming through the window, in some ways the nicest room in the house. "Great," I said with genuine enthusiasm.

We returned to the living room, where Fern and Vivian were sitting. "That's a terrific kitchen," I said. Compared to the places I'd seen, it was a palace.

"Do you cook?" Fern asked hopefully. She was wearing

jeans and a huge T-shirt with a face of Bob Dylan silk-screened on it.

"Yes, I'm an excellent cook," I said. I really think this is true, and since it didn't seem a bad credential, I thought I might as well play it up.

"How come?" Vivian said. She had a quick, staccato way of talking. "Didn't your mother cook?"

"My mother died when I was twelve, and my father just, well, he wasn't too good at it, so I more or less took over."

"What are some of your specialties?" She looked slightly ironic.

I decided not to let her daunt me. "Curries, I'm good at Indian food, Italian, I think I'm fairly versatile." I tried to smile ingratiatingly. "I'll make you a trial meal if you want to check me out."

Vivian smiled. "We'll take your word for it," she said dryly.

Fern looked up at me. "*She* can't even boil an egg," she said, pointing at Vivian.

"I like to eat, though," Vivian said.

"*And* she's a slob in the kitchen," Fern went on. "She *never* cleans up."

Vivian laughed. "Hey, listen, we're interviewing *him*, right? Not exposing our all too human foibles."

Lindsay was sitting closest to me. "How did the room seem to you? Is it what you're looking for?"

"It looked fine."

"How about the fact that it's near the living room?"

"Well, I don't think that would be a problem, unless you throw wild parties all the time."

Fern shook her head. "We sometimes watch TV in here, that's all. . . . Lindsay's premed, so she works her head off all the time. You won't even see her. She volunteers in the emergency room twice a week. I'm an art major, but I belong

131

to the Gilbert and Sullivan Club and I'm on the fencing team, and Vivian—"

"—is an English major with a women's studies minor," Vivian said. "*And* I spend every spare moment at the movies. I'm an old-movies freak. I also have a part-time job. So you won't have a noise problem. Will we with you? You don't play bongo drums or anything?"

"No," I hesitated. I didn't want to bring up Mason until the end, until I was sure I had made as good an impression as I could. "I have a stereo, but I play it low."

Vivian was still staring at me with that look that was either hostile or inquisitive. "How about women?"

"What about them?" I said nervously.

"What she means," Lindsay intervened in her gentle voice, "is we're not puritanical, but we don't want some guy who has, like, wall-to-wall girlfriends."

Just as I said "Don't worry," Vivian said, "We haven't decided we want a guy. That's still up in the air."

"What did you mean, 'Don't worry'?" Fern asked. "Are you gay?"

I turned red. "No . . . I just meant, well, I don't think I'm the type you referred to. I did have a girlfriend in high school—"

"And what?" Vivian said quickly. "She's going to commute down here every chance she gets?"

"Hey, Viv, chill out, will you?" Fern said. "He's entitled to have a girlfriend if he wants."

"We broke up senior year," I said. After a second I added, "I'm going to be premed, too, so I don't think I'll have a lot of time for—"

"How about sisters?" Vivian interrupted. "Do you have any? Have you lived around girls much?"

"I'm an only child," I said. "No, I guess I never have, actually."

She smiled her half smile. "Are you what, for lack of a better term, one might loosely call a liberated male?"

"I guess I'm . . . I think I am."

"What Viv means," Lindsay said, "is we need a guy who can coexist with us as people, not get all hysterical if he sees us in pajamas or what have you. Some guys just go into this macho trip without even knowing it, and we can't have that. It just wouldn't work. So, you think, honestly, you could handle this?"

"Definitely."

There was a pause.

"Any other questions?" Lindsay asked. "About us, or anything? We share the phone except for long-distance calls. We kind of pool food, but like I said, we haven't worked that out yet."

My throat was beginning to tighten with anxiety. "It sounds excellent," I said. "For me, I mean . . . I just—there's one thing I ought to mention about my, I guess what you'd call my life situation." I paused, feeling six female eyes staring at me with undivided attention. "I have a baby."

There was a moment of silence.

"*Have* in what sense?" Vivian asked. "What is this, like a morals quiz—you knocked up your high school girlfriend and now she's in a home for unwed mothers?"

I tried to keep my sense of rage under control. *Fuck her. She'll wreck it for me, just to be cruel. I hate girls like that.* "No, it's . . . my girlfriend had a child, our child, that is, but she was going to give it up for adoption, and I've decided to raise him myself."

Lindsay was sitting on the edge of her seat, frowning. "You mean you have a baby right *here*? In New York?"

I nodded.

"How old?" Fern asked.

"Five weeks."

"Where is it?" Vivian asked. "Are you farming the kid out, or what?"

"It's a boy, Mason," I said, trying to sound unperturbed. "We've been living in a hotel till I find day care."

They were all looking at me like I'd just said I was an ex-PLO guerrilla who was planning to concoct bombs in my room. "Now, let me get this straight," Vivian said. "You're not just looking for a room for yourself. You're looking for a room for yourself *and* a five-week-old baby?"

"Right." I looked from one of them to another. "I realize it's not that ideal from your point of view. Obviously, I'll understand if—"

"It's such an unusual situation," Lindsay said thoughtfully. "I think we thought of everything *but* this."

Vivian sighed. "Listen, folks, I hate to be brutal, but I just can't handle a baby. I can't, that's all."

"You wouldn't have to," I said. "He'd just live here."

"You misunderstand me," she said. "I mean I can't handle the *concept*. I don't know what I think about this, but my instant reaction is: No way."

Fern lay back and put a pillow under her head. "I would have thought you'd think it was great, Viv. Here he's, like, taking on all this responsibility himself. I think it's super. I mean, I know what you mean. You weren't thinking of making us baby-sit or anything, were you?"

"Of course not," I said. "He'll be in a day-care center during the day and I'll get baby-sitters if I ever go out. . . . But I doubt that's going to come up very often."

Vivian was shaking her head. "Come on, come clean, Timothy," she said. "I see a classic male fantasy here. Three women. You were counting on our little female, feminine genes to come rushing to the fore. We'd all be scurrying around, doting on this adorable helpless creature? Right? Am I right?"

I didn't answer for a second. *God, she ought to be in law school. She'd make a great criminal lawyer.* "No," I lied. "That never occurred to me." I tried to stare her down.

She turned to the other girls. "Look, we can discuss this later, but I just want it stated right here and now that I am *not* going near this baby, and I don't care if I'm alone with it in the apartment and the place goes up in smoke. Is that clear?"

"You'll never be alone with him," I said, beginning to be irritated. "I'll either have a sitter, or be here myself."

"What if you're sick? What if you're in the shower?" she persisted.

"Viv, give the guy a break, will you?" Fern said. "We all get your point, and I think Tim does, too."

Lindsay smiled suddenly. Somehow she reminded me just slightly of my mother, that slow smile that illuminated her face. "I just had a wonderful idea," she said. "We could use the back room, the spare room, for the baby. How would you like that? You'd be right near him, but—"

"That sounds great," I said, "only I can't afford to pay any more than you're asking."

"Oh, we wouldn't—" Lindsay began, but Vivian interrupted her.

"Hey, what about my books? Where would you put them? I don't want my room filled with any more stuff. It's crowded to the brim as it is."

"We wouldn't have to empty the room out," Lindsay explained quietly. "We could just rearrange it. Babies are tiny, Viv. And I just thought since we're not really using the room now—"

"We are!" Vivian jumped up. "We're using it as a storeroom. Remember—that was one reason we took this apartment."

Trying to nip her hysteria in the bud, I said, "Listen, I

don't really need the spare room. I can manage fine with the room you showed me. Don't let that be a determining factor.''

Fern was looking over at Vivian. "This is *so* typical," she said. "You're so pigheaded about the most minor things. So he puts the baby in the spare room. Isn't a baby more important than a bunch of books?"

"The baby is a symbol," Vivian said emphatically. "It's a first step. Today it's the spare room, tomorrow God knows what. We'll be inundated with baby-sitters, noise, bottles. Who needs this?"

I sat silently, depressed as well as angry, since obviously one person's vehement objections would kill the whole thing. "Yeah, I see what you mean," I said. "I agree. It *is* a big extra. If I were you, I don't know what I'd decide. All I can say is, it's my total intention not to impose the situation on you in any way. But you're right, there's no way to predict, and it could be a problem for all of you, as well as for me."

Lindsay was looking at me with her soft, understanding expression. "We could do it on a trial basis. How about that, Viv? You know, a month, whatever, to see how it goes, and then we could all sit down and decide. If, after a month, you really feel it's too much, we could—" She looked back at me. "How would that strike you?"

"It would be fine with me," I said, trying to look as amiable as possible.

Vivian sighed. "Yeah, but by then the two of you will be all doting and in love with the baby, and if I raise any objections, you'll probably pitch *me* out."

Fern laughed. "Not me, kid. . . . I have no interest in babies whatever."

"I don't have *time* to get interested," Lindsay said.

"Yeah, but you both have kind hearts. Here he'll be, probably struggling, having a hard time. You'll probably end up

136

marrying him by the end of the semester!" She snorted derisively.

Lindsay smiled, glanced at me, and raised one hand. "I solemnly swear not to engage in matrimony with anyone present, *or* anyone not present, for the next four years." She looked at Vivian. "Should I sign in blood?"

"Hey, me too." Fern gave me a mischievous smile. "Don't take it personally, Tim."

"I'm not looking to—"

"That's what they all say," Vivian said, but in a more relaxed way. Then she pinioned me with her unrelenting gaze. "I don't want to be nosy or anything, but how come you're doing this? It's a bit bizarre, isn't it?"

I would have liked to say "Fuck off" or "Mind your own business," but I desperately wanted the apartment. "What strikes you as so bizarre?"

"A guy raising a kid? Why? Have you been taking female hormones, or what?"

"He's my child," I faltered. "He's my son. I didn't want to give him up to strangers."

"I can understand that," Lindsay said softly.

"Yeah, but you're a woman," Vivian said. "He's a guy."

Lindsay sighed. "Viv, you are so inconsistent. I thought you said it was all societal, that women would never look after their babies at all if society hadn't brainwashed them."

"Yeah, but they have been . . . Who brainwashed *you*?" she asked me.

"No one," I said curtly. "I like to think of myself as an individual."

"So you think we can trust you?"

"Yes." I stared right back at her. "Where I come from, people do that."

"Which is where? The moon?"

Fern giggled. "Look, Viv, it's his problem, right? He likes babies. I know lots of guys who do."

"Yeah, but who wants to raise them on their own?"

"That's Tim's private business," Lindsay interrupted. "I don't think this is fair."

There was a long pause. Then Vivian said offhandedly, "Well, look, why don't we think it over for another day or so? We don't want to leave you hanging for an unconscionable amount of time, but I don't want to make a snap decision . . . and I don't think you guys should either." She looked meaningfully at her roommates.

"Fair enough," I agreed.

I said good-bye and left the apartment. I walked back to the building where the other apartment signs had been posted and began slowly jotting down a few names and phone numbers. Then I decided I wasn't up to any more "interviews" that day. Was this what it was like being black and trying to move into an all-white neighborhood? I realized I was no longer going to be judged as a single person but as a sociological situation: guy with baby—as though Mason and I were Siamese twins. Once again thoughts of the Sidels whisked through my mind. I've heard that chronically depressed people use the thought of suicide as a comforting possible option, which they may never seriously intend to act on. For me the Sidels were like that. I had them frozen in their little white frame house, sitting there, waiting for Mason any time I decided life without him would be better than life with him.

As I walked back to the hotel I thought about the apartment and the three girls. The apartment was as perfect as I could imagine an apartment being, even without the spare room. It was on the twelfth floor, lots of sunlight, quiet. As for the three girls, that would be strange. Cheryl and I had dated, and we'd fucked, to be blunt. We'd never lived together, or even coexisted in the relaxed give-and-take way of friends. Lindsay immediately struck me as a sisterly type, maybe a bit repressed, but always trying to do the right thing. Somehow, of the three, she seemed the most like someone who could have come from Haysburg, maybe because of the slightly slow, inquiring way she spoke. Fern was like some of the girls in my high school classes, the ones I'd never had anything to do with, who had boyfriends who played the electric guitar, and who died their hair various peculiar colors and painted their nails black. She was an unknown known quantity. Vivian struck me as more than just a bitch. As a type she was unfamiliar, yet I had to admit that had I been one of the three of them, I would have felt everything she articulated. I probably wouldn't have been as blunt about saying it right to the face of the person involved, but I would have been feeling it. I had the feeling Lindsay had a soft spot for my "plight" as an unwed father. To Fern, if I'd said I had a two-headed, shocking-pink gorilla I wanted to move in with me, it would have been, "Hey, great." But Vivian was right. They clearly had lots of other options. Why select someone who would only be a problem?

There are two things I've always prided myself on: being able to control my moods and being good with money. The first I think of as a reaction against my father, especially as he's been since my mother's death, moping around so that the whole world will know his plight and feel sorry for him. The second is probably more inherited from him, much as I hate to say that. He's said a million times that no matter how much or how little money he was earning, he always saved a third of his income. My parents, in fact, didn't have a lot of money, but there weren't many families in Haysburg that did, especially among the faculty. We thought of ourselves as better off than the farm people who had to go for handouts to the local church, for instance. But in New York everything

139

seemed skewed way out of proportion. Even on campus I saw girls in leather jackets, girls who looked like they'd walked off the pages of some magazine, who seemed to gleam and glitter. And I saw homeless people begging, sleeping in the subways. I didn't know where I fit in, but suddenly, for the first time in my life, money seemed crucial. Money bought time, peace of mind. With enough money I could have just rented a decent apartment and not had to wait around desperately for the gang of three to decide whether I was an acceptable roommate. With enough money I could just enroll Mason in one of the day-care places I'd looked at, many of which seemed terrific, clean, well organized.

But everything was just beyond reach, just that much too expensive, so I knew I'd have to find other solutions. And it was getting to me. As I walked back to the hotel I felt the familiar exhaustion that wasn't just physical tiredness but more a feeling of hopelessness. People slept in rags on the street and everyone walked by without even noticing, like they were heaps of garbage. So who was going to give a damn about my situation, which I'd chosen, created, gotten into of my own free will? In Haysburg people would have cared. Okay, you're not in Haysburg; forget that.

Janie Lewis was holding Mason as she wheeled the stroller back and forth outside the hotel. He was awake and looked contented. He loves the city. Take him on the subway and he's in seventh heaven. Faces just seem to appeal to him, ugly ones, old ones. He just widens his eyes like it was all some fascinating three-ring circus.

Janie handed him over to me. "Guess he's glad to see his daddy," she said.

"How was he?" I asked.

"Like you said, he slept mostly. But he's good, he's a good baby. You're lucky. My little sister, the one they didn't expect, she just cried nonstop for nine *months*! And the littlest

140

is supposed to be the best." She looked up curiously. "Where's your wife?"

"I, uh, don't have one."

"Oh." She looked nervous, as though wanting to ask more, but afraid it would be indiscreet.

"She's finishing up high school in our hometown," I embroidered, "and so I—I'm looking after him."

I don't know why I lied about that. Maybe it was that after the battery of questions about my motives in being an unwed father, I just wasn't ready to go through it all again. Janie seemed to accept what I said. "What do you do with him during the day?" I'd told her I was about to start at Columbia.

"I'm trying to find a day-care center. . . . They're just so damn expensive."

Janie stood there gazing at me. "You could try my aunt," she said.

"For what?"

She swallowed, shifting from one foot to another. "Well, see, she takes in babies because what happened was, my uncle died and he—well, it was sudden and he didn't leave that much insurance and she never really worked, I mean, worked at a real job. So she figured, why not try this, and now she has two little kids and it gets kind of noisy and crazy at times, but she says she likes it. Sometimes I help out."

I'd gotten a list of family day-care places from Columbia, but I hadn't looked at any. I thought of all the horror stories on TV of unregistered day-care centers, child abuse. You become slightly paranoid when you have a kid. "When you say little kids, how little do you mean?"

"Let's see. Well, Ed is nine months and Martha is, I think, a year. . . . They're all under two because that's the age she likes best. You could come and see. Would you like her number?"

"Sure," I said, moving Mason to my other arm. "I'd appreciate that."

When I had Mason back in our hotel room, I checked on his eczema, which had returned. It looked a little redder, if not any more extreme than it had been before. I remembered my father's panic, his dark memories of me as a baby. Mason was quiet; I moved around the room tentatively. A few times he's woken up unexpectedly, not when he needed to be fed, and just started screaming. There is something profoundly unsettling about that, not just the sound, but the feeling that possibly there's some kind of real anguish going on, which can't be expressed in words. In the psychology course I took junior year, they said some theorists felt the first year of life was crucial, that everything that happened then was ten times more significant than anything that could happen in adult life. Then there were those who felt it was all genes, and that everything was predetermined before the child was even born. I wasn't sure which theory I preferred, if either. Cheryl's genes? Maybe in terms of looks, okay. But otherwise . . .

I gave Mason a bottle, burped him, and then put him in his stroller and went down to get some takeout Chinese food. He was fussing a little, but more like some little old man muttering disconsolately to himself. As I was returning, the second I turned my key in the door, in fact, the phone began ringing. I picked it up, thinking it might be Lindsay, though it seemed a little early for them to have decided. It was my father. He had himself on a "strict schedule," calling me only every other day, though he admitted if I were to call in between, he wouldn't mind. As I lifted up the phone, Mason started to whimper. Since he'd just been fed, I rolled the stroller over near the phone and just pushed it back and forth, hoping to settle him down with the movement. "Oh, hi, Dad."

"Where *were* you? I've been trying you all day!"

"Looking at apartments."

"Oh, right." He sounded relieved. "So, anything decent?"

"A few good leads," I said. "Nothing definite yet."

"You said you were going to look into larger apartments. How did that work out?"

"Well, I saw a great one today, four bedrooms, three girls, it—"

"Take it!" my father yelled. "Are you crazy! That's perfect. Three girls. They can help you with Mason, they can be like mothers."

"Dad, these are college students. They couldn't do any of that, they don't want to, and anyway, they don't know if they want me."

"What do you mean? Why *don't* they want you?"

"Because of Mason! The noise, the potential bother . . . Anyway, they said they'd let me know."

He was silent a moment. "Then the hell with them!"

"Sure, only it was a *perfect* apartment." Just then Mason's cries went up a decibel or two. I reached over and lifted him up with the phone tucked under my chin.

"What's wrong?" my father asked anxiously. "Does he need to be fed?"

"No, I just fed him. I don't know what it is."

"How's his rash? Did you go see a doctor yet?"

"It's okay. I haven't had time. I will."

"Tim, that is top priority, do you hear me? Go see a doctor!"

As though responding to my inner feeling, Mason let out a howl. "I will, okay? Listen, I better tend to him. I'll speak to you in a day or so."

"Let me know," my father said. "I worry."

"I know."

I walked shrieking Mason around the room. Had my father ever done this with me? Or had he left it all to my mother? "Hey, come *on*," I said, exhausted. "Give me a break, okay? You're safe, you're warm, you just had a meal, I swear I'll take you to the doctor tomorrow." I realized I was doing what my father had done, talking out loud. *God, I better stop that*. But it seemed as though hearing my voice, or hearing a voice, made him calmer. Not that he had the foggiest notion what I was saying. And maybe it made me calmer, too. No one was around to hear me. I carried Mason from one end of the room to the other until he finally quieted down. Then, still holding him, I opened the container of Szechuan beef and tried to eat it with my left hand.

CHAPTER 13

"**W**e've decided to give it a try," Lindsay said. "It'll be like I suggested, a trial month to see how we all adjust to it."

"That's wonderful!" I said, unable to hold back my feeling of exhilaration. "I hope it's going to work."

"I'm sure it will," she said. "I'm looking forward to meeting him."

It's funny how with some girls you can so easily imagine them as mothers, like Lindsay, and with others, like Fern or Vivian, it's all but impossible. I guess I'd put Cheryl somewhere in the middle. I could see her doing it, but badly, getting impatient, feeling she ought to be out having fun. With her it wouldn't have been a matter of career goals being postponed, just: I'm not ready. I thought of how I used to say I wouldn't marry until I was thirty. Maybe I still wouldn't, but by then—was this possible?—Mason would almost be a teenager! God, no, I can't imagine. Take it one day at a time.

It was a Saturday. I checked out of the hotel, got my things together, and took a cab the three blocks to the apartment. I'd brought only a minimum of stuff to New York. My father was going to ship everything once I found an apartment. Or maybe drive it down, if I didn't stop him in time. In the cab I looked at Mason. "Be good, okay?" I said. "Just one favor. Make a good first impression."

To my relief only Lindsay was there when I arrived with my suitcase, the folding stroller, the portable crib, and Mason. She looked surprised. "Is that all your belongings?"

"My father's sending the rest. I just brought the minimum . . . until I get settled."

"Well, the room's all ready. If you need to borrow blankets or sheets, just ask."

"I guess I might until everything arrives."

"We do the wash on a rotating basis. One person does the whole load once a week. There's a washer and dryer in the basement." She peered over at Mason, who was, blessedly, silent. "He's so small," she said anxiously.

"Well, yeah . . . Not abnormally. They're just small at this age."

She nodded. "I suppose . . . I never did much baby-sitting in high school, not for babies, anyway. I don't know a whole lot about them."

"Same here."

"I'm not sure I'll ever have children," she said wistfully. "I'd like to, but medical training is so arduous anyway."

"Right." I stood there uncomfortably.

"I'm sure it'll work out just fine," she said in her other, cheerful commonsensical voice. "Don't let Viv's comments bother you. She's really not that different from me and Fern. She just says what she feels more. Which I, personally, think

146

is good. I mean, you never have to go around wondering what she's feeling. My family is much more repressed.''

"Mine, too.''

She handed me two keys. "This is for downstairs. They lock it at night, after midnight. I think it's a safe building. It seems to be, anyway, so far. . . . We all roomed together last year, but in a much smaller place. We're sophomores.''

I sat down tentatively on the bare bed. "Maybe tonight I can cook something.''

"Sure. Don't feel you have to go all out, though. We're really spaghetti, hamburger types at heart.''

After Lindsay left, I lay down on the bed and looked around the room. Mason was asleep. I was afraid I was catching his schedule—exhausted all day, restive all night. Perfect for college. Still, it was great to be in a real room again, after the hotel. A few posters and some things from home, and it might look pretty good.

That night, mainly to ingratiate myself, I fixed supper for all of them. I brought Mason into the kitchen with me. If he's where he can see me, he's usually okay. Be good tonight, okay? I begged him silently. This is your debut. I did my spaghetti sauce, which isn't unduly complicated, and bought a bottle of wine. "Where do you eat, usually?'' I asked Fern, who was opening the wine.

"In our rooms, on the floor in the living room, wherever. We like to keep the living room reasonable, but there are, like, end tables.'' She sniffed. "It smells wonderful. Does it have nutmeg, or what?''

"Right. How'd you know?''

"I used to cook. I don't have time now, but I like it. It can be relaxing after a day of studying, if you have the energy.''

The three of them brought their plates of food into the living room. I brought Mason. Vivian, in a red shirt and jeans, sat with her plate in her lap. "How're you going to eat?"

"With one hand."

"Doesn't he sleep at night?"

"Sometimes," I answered laconically.

"Were you glad it was a boy?" Fern asked. "I mean, did you care?"

I hesitated. I was afraid that if I said yes, Vivian might jump on me. "I thought it might be easier. I mean, I thought I might be able to understand him better when he was older, not having had sisters and all."

"I have a sister," Vivian said, "and I don't understand her one bit. I don't think sex has anything to do with it."

"Oh, come on, Viv," Lindsay said. "Of course it has something to do with it! You're the one who's always saying men are impossibly different."

"True," Vivian admitted. "I guess what I mean is, just because a being is of the same sex, it doesn't mean you necessarily are on the same wavelength." She looked over at me. "What's his name?"

"Mason."

She smiled. "That's weird. That's my father's name. It's sort of unusual. How'd you think of it?"

"It was my mother's maiden name."

"Huh . . . You said she's no longer living?"

"Yeah, she died suddenly; a cerebral hemorrhage. It was ironical because my father is much older. He's never really gotten over it."

Again I had that sense I'd had in the interview of the three of them staring at me solemnly. I wondered if I was doing what my father does so often: using my mother to get extra sympathy.

"My mother died when I was twelve," Lindsay said,

148

"only it was cancer. It went on for years. Maybe the way your mother went is better."

I had lost my appetite, though I didn't want to risk setting Mason down for fear he'd yell his head off. The wine had eased everything slightly. "Only it was so sudden. One day your whole life is different."

"Yeah, I know," Lindsay said. "I have two younger brothers, though, and it was like I stepped into having to look after them. My father just tuned out. And then he married a woman we all couldn't stand."

"I doubt my father's going to do that," I said. "He's pretty much the bachelor type. He didn't even marry until he was forty."

"Were they happy?" Vivian asked. "Your parents?"

I hesitated. "Well, sure. I mean, they thought they were happy. Isn't that what being happy is?"

She laughed. "Search me. My parents were at each other's throats from day one. I'll believe a happy marriage when I see one."

Fern looked over at her affectionately. "She thinks she's so cynical."

"I don't think I'm anything," Vivian protested. "I believe what I see with my own two eyes, okay? I don't believe a lot of women's magazine crap about two people walking off together into the sunset."

"Viv," Lindsay said, "it doesn't have to be one extreme or the other. I think *my* parents were happy, but they weren't . . . demonstrative. I mean, I sensed it, but if you asked me did he bring her flowers or whatever—"

"And he remarried three seconds after she died," Vivian shot back. "So what does *that* prove?"

Lindsay refused to be perturbed. "Maybe it just proves he *was* happy, that he wanted to set it up again."

"But you said your stepmother was a monster, that you all hated her," Vivian said.

"I *didn't* say that." Lindsay's cheeks were flushed. "Viv, you do that so often! You distort things. She wasn't good with my brothers. She's never had kids. I never said monster, I *never* did."

Vivian raised her hand. "Sorry." She glanced at me. "So how come your father isn't remarried yet? Or does he have some live-in . . ."

In the crossfire with Lindsay, I had been appalled by Vivian's way of talking, and glad Lindsay had held her own. "He doesn't want to remarry," I said coolly. "He's pretty self-sufficient, I guess from all those years of being a bachelor."

"So that's how come you got into the baby thing?" she persisted relentlessly. "To prove you're self-sufficient, prove that men can do anything women can do, but better, and alone? That we're obsolete?"

"My father's hardly a role model," I said dryly.

"What does he do about sex?" she went on. "You say your mother died when you were twelve?"

Fern hurled a pillow over at her. "Viv, seriously. He's a guy, he just moved in . . ."

Vivian deftly ducked the pillow. "I am *aware* he's a guy, I am *aware* he just moved in. What, is sex a taboo topic? Do we now have to pretend we're all virgins?"

"Tim may consider his father's sex life a private matter," Lindsay said with her gentle smile.

I looked at Vivian. "I don't think my father *has* a sex life, frankly. He's fifty-eight."

"So? That's hardly over the hill."

"We never discuss it."

"Okay, fair enough. Maybe I should fix him up with my

150

mother. Her latest flame is for the birds. Is he dapper and witty, with a dry sense of humor?"

"Kind of . . . Only what about your father?"

"What *about* him? He's on his third wifelet. The second one took an overdose last year. I am not looking to fix him up with anyone because he can do enough damage unassisted."

I felt like at least this might be a key to Vivian's character—her peculiar-sounding home life. "That sounds . . . strange," I faltered.

"Strange? How so? Which part? My mother? My father?"

"I—just the whole thing," I stammered. "Difficult for you, I meant."

"Not a bit," Vivian said quickly. "It's given me an edge, is all."

Fern looked at her. "It's given you rotten taste in men."

"Speak for yourself, kid. One woman's rotten is another woman's terrific."

"You mean Sandor—"

"Forget him."

There was a silence. I was trying to follow all the rapid-fire names and connections, but felt lost. Lindsay glanced at me sympathetically. "Tim, just to explain a bit, I mean, not that you have to know all the ins and outs of our lives in order to coexist with us, but I have a boyfriend in my hometown—"

At that, Vivian and Fern began playing imaginary violins and singing "Down by the Old Mill Stream."

"His name is Kevin, and we're sort of engaged but free to date other people—"

"But they never do," Fern put in.

"I'm very busy," Lindsay said, flustered. "I'm not ruling anything out."

"And *I* kind of play the field," Fern said. She grinned.

I looked at Vivian.

"What can I say? Okay, they're right. Last year I got involved with a jerk, this year I'm cooling it. I have a mild attraction to jerks, but not a full-blown masochistic thing. It's from my father, it's classic. He's a swine, I'm drawn to swinish types, but—"

"You won't have to worry, Tim," Lindsay said. "Really, we're quiet. There won't be a lot of guys tramping through. Not just for your sake."

Vivian got up and poured herself more wine. "How do we explain the baby?" she asked. "Mason, I mean."

I became aware that Mason needed changing. He was beginning to stink. "What do you mean, explain?" I asked, getting up.

"Well, I don't know. Do we tell the true story, do we invent, elaborate . . ."

"I don't get it," I said. "What's wrong with the true story?"

She smiled enigmatically. "No, I was just thinking it would be a great thing, just to, like, suddenly say, 'Oh, I have to tend to the baby,' without ever explaining whose baby or how—"

"That's how you get into trouble," Fern said sternly. "Playing games with guys. You said you weren't going to do that anymore."

Vivian sighed. "Right. So, how about you, Timothy? How are you going to manage? Re: girls, sex, what have you—"

"I have to maintain a B average to keep my scholarship," I said with a straight face. "I think that's going to be my main concern." I went to change Mason, relieved to get away.

Lying in my room that first night in the apartment, I thought of the three of them, their funny, rapid way of shooting remarks back and forth, alternating between seeming hostility and humor, openness and what could have been called rudeness. I wasn't used to it. I guess the closest I'd come to observing that kind of interaction was Charlie and Maureen's family, but they were much more conventional and small-townish. It was as though I'd inherited three sisters. It felt peculiar.

The next day I checked out Janie Lewis's aunt, Mrs. Peters. She lived ten blocks from the apartment, on a side street that was somewhat rundown and shabby. The building was surrounded by scaffolding. Mrs. Peters was younger looking than I'd expected, more Maureen's age. She was slender and had graying hair, and wore glasses and a preoccupied expression. It wasn't a gigantic apartment, but it was homey and comfortable, with well-worn furniture. She'd turned the living room into a makeshift day-care center. There were cribs and toys, and wall hangings of animals were taped near the windows.

Maybe I looked unusually suspicious, because she said dryly, "What exactly are you looking for?"

"Something I can afford," I said without thinking. Then I added, "I just wondered. Are you licensed?"

"No, I'm not. It's not required when you have fewer than three children, and that's all I can handle. Believe me, even two is a lot."

"I *do* believe you. . . . Would Mason be the only baby?"

"Oh, no. I have two infants. He would be the youngest, though. . . . Tell me about him. What's his personality? What kind of schedule is he on?"

I had never thought of Mason being on trial. "Well, I'd say he's pretty good-natured. He seems to like people, strangers—"

"How do you mean that? Do you leave him with a lot of different sitters?"

153

"No, I just meant he likes looking at people in the subway, that kind of thing. Noise doesn't bother him."

"He's not deaf, is he?" She frowned.

"No! He's just pretty calm, as babies go."

She smiled. "Had a lot of experience with babies, have you?"

I hesitated. "No."

"Janie says you have a girlfriend back home finishing up school. Is she joining you soon?"

I looked out the window. "That was a lie, actually. I just— Actually, I'm raising him myself."

I was sure that would release a barrage of questions, but Mrs. Peters just looked at me with a shrewd but not unkind expression. She held out her arms. "So let's see how we get along."

Mason was wide awake. The second I handed him over, he let out a piercing scream. Shit. Thanks a lot, kid. "You don't like leaving your daddy, huh?" Mrs. Peters said, unperturbed. "I don't blame you. Well, why don't we just walk around and see how you like it around here. Your daddy isn't going anywhere. He's going to be right here where you can see him."

Mason was staring at me with puzzled, aggrieved eyes, but his screams were diminishing. "This is unusual for him," I said hastily. "Basically he sleeps a lot during the day."

"And he's up all night?" Mrs. Peters said. "Well, that won't do, will it? You need your sleep." She looked at Mason. "You don't want your daddy to be a total wreck, do you?"

At that, for reasons best known to him, Mason gave a half smile. "It's not their fault," she said. "You've got to train them. Otherwise they'll run you ragged."

"How?" I asked anxiously.

"I'll keep him up more during the day. He'll get used to

it. It's better for you. A crabby, cranky father's not much use, is he?''

The price she'd quoted me over the phone was well within my range. Did she look like a child molester? Did anyone? I thought of all those kindly, round-faced men and women who were hauled off for doing unspeakable things to little kids. Mrs. Peters turned to me. "You're anxious," she said, not as a question but as a statement. "Is it me? Is it dealing with this fellow here?''

I sighed. "No, it's—Well, it's everything, but I can handle it.''

I wished she'd said, "No doubt about it," but all she said was, "I can't do evenings or weekends. You better call Janie if you need that. I need my free time. You know how it is. And if you find a situation you like better, just let me know as soon as possible. Will you do that?'' She handed Mason back to me. I promised I would.

Sometimes in life you have to take a chance. I'd run out of energy for other alternatives. I wasn't a millionaire and Mrs. Peters seemed well intentioned, forthright and small-townish in her manner. She reminded me of Mrs. Frank, who ran the local post office in Haysburg. When you didn't have money for an extra stamp she'd say, "Oh, bring it by tomorrow." And I'd liked Mrs. Peters for her seeming lack of curiosity as to my motives in raising Mason alone, the straightforward way she'd handled him, even when he'd yelled so unceremoniously. "We've got a deal, Kiddo," I told him. He just eyed me.

CHAPTER 14

The first six weeks at Columbia, I felt like a robot. I've always prided myself on being organized and using my time wisely and well, but that became not just an option but a necessity. The second that classes ended I went to the library. There I did all the work I couldn't do at the apartment. In fact, except for a morning jog back from Mrs. Peters' after dropping off Mason at eight, I hardly got any exercise, and I missed that. My muscles felt stiff. It seemed to me my classes were going all right. Two were huge lectures: Chinese history and psychology, but both were extremely well taught and well organized. I'd had chemistry in high school, so that wasn't as bad as it might have been, given that the professor could hardly speak English. I found a few guys to borrow notes from if I missed class, but by and large I didn't make friends. It just seemed a luxury I didn't have time for, like girls: I didn't even miss it that much.

Still, my first quiz in psychology shocked me. I thought I'd been doing well, keeping up with the reading, but there it was: C. Not even C plus. The only thing that salvaged my pride was that the teacher, a youngish guy named Montgomery, looked at all of us and said, "What's with you kids? This is basic stuff. We've gone over it in class. What's the problem?"

The guy next to me, a big, hulking boy with blond hair, raised his hand. "A lot of us are freshmen," he said. "We have a lot of other classes. You ought to take that into consideration."

"Mr.—what is your name?"

"Hughes," the blond boy said imperturbably.

"Mr. Hughes, I assume, whether you're freshmen or not, that you got into other less demanding colleges than Columbia. If you don't feel you can do acceptable work here, you are doing not only the school but yourself a disservice."

"Aren't you even going to mark us on a curve?" Hughes asked, his voice rising.

"Why should I? The standards I'm applying to you aren't stringent. If you're having trouble here, you're going to have big trouble later on. Do you understand that?"

"Yes, sir," Hughes said. Under his breath he muttered, "Fucker." Then he grinned at me.

After class we walked out together. "All I need is to flunk psychology. My father's a shrink. They figure all you do here is study. That's not what college is all about. How about girls? How about extracurricular stuff?"

I wondered wryly if Mason counted as an extracurricular activity. "I know what you mean," I said guardedly.

"Hey, listen, want to stop by the West End for a beer? I've got glee club rehearsal in an hour, but . . ."

I hesitated. "I'd like to, but, well, I should really study."

"Yeah, so should I. . . . Are your parents after you a lot about grades?"

"Pretty much. I'm on scholarship, so I have to keep up my average."

"Where're you from?"

I told him.

"The boonies, huh? That's pretty impressive, that you got into Columbia from a small town like that. How do you like New York?"

"I haven't really—it's kind of overwhelming."

"Well, listen, if you want to cut out some weekend, I know a few really good clubs. Do you have a girlfriend?"

I shook my head.

"Maybe Mary has a buddy she can fix you up with. She's not my girlfriend, we're just . . . it's . . . you know, we fool around a little. You'll like her. Gimme your number. Here's mine."

I watched him walk off with a pang of pure envy. Glee club. Fooling around. Clubs. That was what college was for, not just trying to keep your head above water in terms of grades. Then a horrible realization pierced me. I'm becoming like my father. I'm using Mason as an excuse. Would I be doing any of that without him? Yeah, maybe I would. You can anyway. Get a sitter one weekend. Don't be so stingy. Cut loose.

At times I felt like two people, or maybe three. At school I told no one about Mason. I just didn't want to get into it. I didn't want to be the campus curiosity, some kind of weirdo everyone would stare at. But to Mrs. Peters I was just a father. Mostly it was mothers who came to pick up their kids. Only once did I see a man, and he looked a good decade older than me.

Mason was in one of his cranky moods that day. Mrs.

Peters thought he was teething. "Wife sick?" the man asked as we went down in the elevator together. His baby was eight months old, a girl, Miranda. I knew his last name: Fosdick.

"I'm divorced," I blurted out.

"Already? You look pretty young for that."

"Well, we just . . . it was a high school marriage."

"Joint custody?"

"Kind of. Well, part of the time. That is, I'm taking him this year, she'll take him next."

He laughed. "You got stuck. The first year's murder."

I shrugged. "Does it get better?"

"It has to. This is our first, actually. We were married ten years before we had her, so maybe we just got used to everything being really quiet and peaceful, meals by candlelight, sleeping through the night. Still, it won't last forever, and she's a cutie, isn't she?"

"Yeah, she is." Candlelight dinners! Sleeping through the night! He was complaining, and he has a wife and, from the way he dressed, some money. An involuntary stab of envy and irritation shot through me.

That same week my Chinese history TA said we'd have to meet at night. Eight thirty. I called Janie. She was busy. I called a few other girls' numbers she gave me. All busy. My roommates were out. I wondered if I could chance leaving Mason alone in the apartment. He was usually asleep by then. What were the statistical chances of his waking up? And if he did? But I realized that even if nothing happened, I'd spend all of class worrying, and I couldn't afford to miss the section. I put him in the stroller. He was looking sleepy, but I was afraid the cold air outside might wake him up, so I muffled him with so many blankets he was almost invisible. I decided to sit toward the back so as few people would see him as possible.

The trouble was, the room was small, and about halfway

159

through the class Mason started grunting, a sign he was getting ready to shit. His face turned red, like someone about to have a heart attack, he emitted one sharp cry, and then fell asleep again, or rather continued sleeping. But the stink was terrible in the overheated room. I hoped the teacher might think someone had farted and ignore it.

For five minutes he seemed to. Then he stopped and said, "There's a terrible smell in this room. What's it from?"

There was silence. Reluctantly I raised my hand. "It's my sister's baby," I said. "I had to bring him to class."

The TA looked at me, bewildered. "Why is that?"

"She . . . I baby-sit for her sometimes and . . . I can take him out and change him, if you like."

"I think that would be a good idea," the TA said.

Mortified, I took Mason out in the hall, changed him, tossed the disposable diaper into a wastebasket, and snuck furtively back into class. I hoped I could just sneak out when it was over, but the TA called to me. "Mr. Weaver?"

"It's Weber."

"Mr. Weber, I think it's very generous of you to undertake these services for your sister, but do you think next time you might refrain?"

"She had tickets for the opera."

"Did she? Well, I assure you, there are many baby-sitting services in the city and although I'm sure your rates are less exorbitant, I would imagine she'd understand how disruptive this is."

Disruptive! Mason hadn't let out a peep. "I'll tell her that."

Outside the class a girl was buttoning her coat. "He's cute," she said casually.

"Thanks," I said, then hoped that hadn't sounded incriminatory.

As I walked off she called after me, "See you in class."

Was that an invitation, a suggestion? Had there been something flirtatious in her voice? *What do you care? You can't do anything about it anyway.* You're wrecking my sex life, my grades are slipping, I told Mason in my head. Are you satisfied? Are you happy, you little jerk? I felt like a Jekyll and Hyde father at times. There were moments when Mason could be so engaging, when he'd suddenly figure something out, like how to turn over, and then he'd look at me with such absolute wonder and delight that it would all seem worth it. And other times I'd wake up, see him screaming in his crib, and want to go over and smother him with a pillow just to get some extra sleep.

The thing that hadn't changed: I was still sleeping badly. It was ironical because all my life, hearing my father complain about insomnia, I had always thought, What's the problem? I used to just get into bed, turn off the light, and be asleep before I even thought about it. Now, even though Mason slept through the night, he made a lot of peculiar noises. One was a kind of gasping sound which at first really terrified me; I thought he was having trouble breathing. It turned out that he would make this noise as though he was still drinking from the bottle, but the air went in and out in a way that sounded like a fish going through its last rites on the bottom of a boat. Another thing he did was to start to cry, give just a few cries, and then, right in the middle, fall back to sleep. Or rather I think he was asleep all the time, but something half woke him up, and then he'd forget it and settle down again. The trouble was, if I woke up even once or twice during the night, I'd find I couldn't fall back to sleep. I'd lie there, even after I was sure he was okay, thinking about a paper that was due or a test I was afraid I hadn't studied for sufficiently.

Days I hadn't gotten enough sleep were like swimming

underwater too long; everything would look hazy and strange. I would force myself to concentrate in class and then suddenly find I wasn't. One day, right in the middle of chem lab, out of the blue, I got an almost paralyzing feeling of anxiety. What was strange was nothing had happened to provoke it. We were doing an experiment I understood, I was just standing there. I gazed down at my hand, and it suddenly looked peculiar. I looked up quickly to get my bearings, and suddenly the whole room seemed strange. It's an old room, it needs a paint job, the windows aren't washed, but for some reason it looked ominous to me. It was nothing I could pinpoint. The only thing I can compare it to is that once I was in an elevator downtown and a big husky black guy suddenly took out some keys and seemed to lock the elevator. For that one second I thought of all the murders I'd heard about in New York, unexplained or drug related. It was that kind of panic, bone chilling. But why now? Why here?

After chem lab I was supposed to go pick up Mason, but not only didn't I feel like it, I wasn't even sure I could make it. I started walking very slowly and there was a funny feeling in my legs, a rubbery feeling. Dan Hughes, the guy in my psych class, had said he'd heard medical students started feeling they were getting every symptom they read about. Maybe I'd been reading too much about neurotic reactions to stress. This is simple, classic, I tried telling myself. You're nervous, part of you doesn't want to go pick up Mason, so your legs seem wobbly. But they're not. It's all in your head. My legs didn't seem to buy that. I still was having immense trouble just moving down the street, so much so that a middle-aged woman came over to me and said, "Are you all right? Can I help you?"

I felt chagrined. She looked thirty years older than me. "No, I just, um, got out of the hospital. I'm a little weak."

"Shall I call you a cab?"

I hesitated. I wanted to prove to myself I could overcome this, but the idea of a cab, while I wouldn't have thought of it on my own, was too appealing. "Thanks a lot," I said.

She actually helped me into the cab. *Jesus. This is absurd. I can't afford a shrink. Just get with it, asshole.* To top it off, when I arrived at Mrs. Peters's, I heard Mason's familiar howl, what I'd come to think of as his teething howl. Mrs. Peters was rocking him back and forth. "Poor thing," she said. "I've tried rubbing his gums. That seemed to help."

I stared at Mason. Lately his hair had been growing in. Where before he was bald in places, now he had tufts which made him look more appealing. Sometimes, teething or not, when he sees me, he relaxes. This time he looked at me and just kept right on howling without missing a beat. "Does he do this all day long?" I asked despairingly.

"Not while he has his bottle. That seems to soothe him. Don't worry, it'll pass."

Sure, and so will life, my scholarship. "Why doesn't anyone tell you it's going to be like this?" I asked, taking him. Mrs. Peters always had him clean and fed when I arrived, which I appreciated.

She grinned. "Then we'd all be celibate." She looked at me, concerned. "Are you all right, Tim? You look a little pale. There's strep going around. How's your throat?"

"I'm okay, just—"

"It must be a lot of work, college, being new in the city, and then this little devil here." She looked at me sympathetically.

"Oh, I can—" I realized I was about to say for the millionth time, "I can handle it." Instead I said, "Yeah, well, it does kind of get to me at times."

"Is there a counseling service? Someone you could talk to? That can help."

"No, no, it's not that bad. There are just some days . . ."

163

Our conversation was being held over Mason's wavering screams, which only seemed to diminish when he ran out of breath. Mrs. Peters gave me some teething beads. "These might help."

I got into the elevator with two other people. Mason kept on full force. They glared at me as though it were my fault. "What's with you?" I asked him. "Shape up, okay? So you're getting a couple of teeth. You think that's a major problem? Want to trade places? Want to try being premed on scholarship?"

It seemed to me I had worked out as many ways to cut corners as I could. Most mornings I showered with him, just to save time. The water pressure was low and he seemed to love it. I'd hold him up high and let the water splash all over him and he'd yelp with pleasure. Then I'd wrap him in a towel, set him down on the bath mat, and wash myself. And now that he was eating solid foods, I'd figured out which ones he liked best and forgot about the rest. Usually he was ferociously hungry, and I had to keep spooning it in as fast as I could. And Mrs. Peters really had cured him of his up-all-night ritual. He still woke up early, five or six, but even then he was sometimes willing to wait a half hour or so until he was fed.

Nights were the problem. Just knowing he was there seemed to rattle me. I remembered one of my father's friends saying "I'd sell my soul for a solid night's sleep." I couldn't even remember what that was like. *Maybe you just need to get laid.* Sure, when? And with who? A primal scene at three months? I know I could count on Mason to wreck that one in a hurry.

That night, emerging from my bedroom, I saw Vivian reading in the living room. Lindsay was almost always studying or doing her extracurricular activities. Fern studied in her

164

room. Vivian was the only one who, like me, used the living room to study, even though it had no door and anyone passing by could see into the room. She was a night owl, sometimes staying up until three. Occasionally, waking up because of Mason, I'd see the light under my door coming in from the living room.

"Listen, I'll store your books in my room, if you want. It's just . . . it's really hard for me, trying to sleep with Mason in the same room."

I must have sounded desperate because she said quickly, "Oh, sure, that's okay, whatever." Her eyes looked glazed.

I felt suddenly furious. "So why did you make such a big deal about your books? He could've been sleeping there all along."

"What?" She looked half asleep.

"I've been having trouble sleeping for over a month, but I assumed the storeroom was out because you said you needed it for your books, and now you're saying you don't even *care*?"

Vivian yawned. "Yeah, right." She shook her head. "What's the problem, Tim? Do you want the room or not?"

"Of course I want the room!" I yelled. "But why didn't you come to me, why didn't you say it was okay? What if I hadn't said anything about it?"

She touched her hand to her eyes. "I can't focus on this. I have a lit paper due tomorrow. Just take the room, will you?"

I went back to bed, seething. There was something about her that still, although I saw she could be humorous and entertaining at times, infuriated me. She seemed so blithely, totally unaware of other people. *Look, Mason's no concern of hers. You're the one who has to speak up if you want things. They just go their own way, they're busy, they feel they're doing you a good deed by letting you stay here.* I lay there, frantic with some kind of undefined rage which seemed to dart from Vivian to Mason to myself. *In over your head. No, I'll set up the spare room tomorrow. That'll make all the difference, some difference, anyway.*

It did make some difference. I did begin sleeping better. But my nerves felt as they had before, when I was on much less sleep: too tightly coiled. I realized on various levels I resented the girls. Their lives seemed so much freer than mine. Vivian was always going off to the movies, Fern sang Gilbert and Sullivan in the shower, Lindsay sat in her quilted bathrobe writing long letters to her boyfriend. They didn't impinge on my life, but it was impossible to ignore the contrast between their set of responsibilities and mine.

I began cutting chem class. I figured that was one subject I knew inside out. I'd even tutored kids in high school in it. The textbook was straightforward, I could just bone up for exams. And what I did in the time chem class met was: nothing. I just went off and had coffee by myself, sat there mooning into space, daydreaming. I didn't allow myself to use the time for any useful purpose, to catch up on other work. *I'm entitled to this. I need it*, I defended myself to some unseen judge.

Then came the shocker: midterm exams. Most of them I handled well. In Chinese history I even got an A minus. But when I sat down to take the chem exam, I had what I can only describe as a ten times worse version of the anxiety attack I'd had in the lab. My hands turned ice cold. I even had trouble seeing the page. *Look, this is pure, simple anxiety. You'll deal with it later. Right now just put it to one side and get through the exam. Get a C, just get through it.* But I was mortified. My best subject! And it was so weird, because I knew the answers, but in some indescribably strange way they eluded me. They seemed to come forward and go backward almost physically, like an object being dangled right in front of you, then withdrawn. I struggled, tried skipping certain questions. *If I break down they'll make me see the college counselor. I'll have to tell them about Mason.*

When the exam was over, I raced out of the room. *Look, you don't know how you did. And it's just a midterm. Don't blow it out of proportion.* A week later we got the results. I got a C minus, not the worst grade anyone's ever gotten, but for someone like me, to whom chemistry should be second nature, it was scary. *What if it's a pattern? What if I truly am unable to make it? You'll give Mason to . . .* I hated even batting those thoughts around. Blaming Mason seemed such an easy out. *You'll take a lighter course load next semester. Maybe five courses is too much.*

Then I got a call from the dean's office. The dean of students was a guy named Chambers Evans. I'd had no interaction with him one way or the other. For some perverse reason, after that first thrill of dread passed over me, I thought, Great. It finally happened. They'll find out about Mason, I'll lose my scholarship. After all these weeks of furtiveness, anxiety, sleeping badly, the idea of total public exposure and mortification was perversely appealing. They could put me in stocks, the way they did to sinners in colonial America. Let this be an example to you.

Still, I got Janie to stay with Mason while I went in to meet with the dean. He was a young guy, tall and skinny, with a red bow tie, spiky brown hair, and tortoiseshell glasses. "Mr. Weber," he said, shaking my hand. "Glad to meet you."

I just smiled and sat down in the chair he was pointing at. I decided to say nothing until he did.

"I'm sorry we haven't had a chance to have a talk before this," he said. "I make it a point to see all the incoming freshmen, but you know how it is—meetings, all of that. How do you feel things are going for you?"

I knew he had my record right in front of him. I hate cat-

and-mouse games like this. "Not too well," I said. "That is, I just got a C on my chemistry midterm, and it's my best subject."

He glanced down at the papers on his desk. "Yes, so I see. Well, any explanation for that? You are taking a heavy, though not unduly heavy, course load. But if, as you say, it's a subject that normally comes easily to you . . ."

I didn't want to get into my anxiety attacks, I didn't want to go see a shrink. "I've been thinking," I said slowly, looking at an Oriental print on his wall, "maybe I should drop chem this semester, if it isn't too late. I am premed, but I could make it up over the summer."

"I think we could arrange that," Evans said. "You feel it's just overload, then? The lab as well as the course work?"

"Yeah, partly." I hesitated. It was as though Mason were looming in the air above us, like the Cheshire cat, grinning malevolently.

"Sometimes personal problems make adjustment difficult," he said. "Is there anything like that operating here? I'm sorry to be probing. It's just that it's rare for a student to have trouble with his best subject."

Bite the bullet. I looked right at him. "I have a baby," I said.

For a second, from the expression on his face, I think he really thought I was crazy, as though I'd said I was pregnant. "A baby?"

"A son, Mason's his name."

"I didn't realize . . . . Is your wife at Columbia as well?"

"I'm not married." After a second I added, "My girl-friend didn't want to get married. She wanted to give the baby up for adoption, and so . . ."

His expression had changed, and he was frowning and leafing through his papers as though that would somehow

168

help. "This is an unusual situation. I don't believe there's any record of that in your files, is there?"

"No."

"Why *is* that?"

"Well, I—I'm on a scholarship and I was afraid it might not be allowed."

Evans smiled. "I doubt the scholarship people would have thought to anticipate a situation like this. There can't be many, if *any* precedents. I think their only concern would be: Can you handle this and keep your G.P.A. up?"

The instinctive "I can handle it" had been excised from my vocabulary. "I'm not sure," I said. "I think I can. It's just been harder than I expected."

"I would imagine. Goodness . . . But wouldn't it have been easier if you had told us? Just in terms of finding housing, day care, and so on?"

"I don't want to be considered some kind of campus freak," I blurted out. "It's my problem or situation or whatever. It's no one's business but mine."

Evans cleared his throat. "I realize that, I just meant . . . Why do you feel people would regard you as a freak?"

"Maybe freak is too strong, just . . . peculiar."

"Does the opinion of your peers matter that much to you?"

"Not usually, but . . ."

He looked at me carefully. "I think I understand your concern, Timothy . . . Tim. But please understand, if you wish this to be private, it will be. I'm glad to know it. And I would say, under the circumstances, dropping chemistry *might* help. You know some students take a fifth premed year at the end just to ease the pressure. You could consider that. Your son will be in school by then."

It was the first time, or so it seemed, that someone had said "your son" so easily, as though it were just what it was, a fact of life. Something in me eased.

"My son is four now," he went on, "and I'm not saying it's easy, but compared to the first year . . ."

I smiled. "He's basically a good kid."

"I'm sure he is."

I walked out of Evans's office feeling like I'd won the lottery. *Don't get too excited. You're just dropping one course. Who says you won't start getting anxious in English or Chinese history?* Maybe I would, but I wanted to savor the feeling, however brief, of freedom. And then I had a wonderful idea. I wouldn't go home for Thanksgiving. I realized I'd been dreading it, a week with my father hovering and questioning and getting on my nerves. I'd just stay in the city, get baby-sitters occasionally, relax.

When my father, in one of his thrice-weekly calls, asked when I'd be arriving, I hesitated. "I—I just don't know. We only get a week. It's a long drive."

"Fly. I'll send you a ticket. Charlie and Maureen are looking forward to it."

"I just—I need the time to relax, to rest." I knew Lindsay and Fern were going home, and assumed Vivian would stay with one of her parents, both of whom lived in Manhattan. The prospect of the whole apartment to myself was wonderful. "Christmas vacation is just a few weeks later," I said. "Dad, I want to, but—"

"Bullshit. If you wanted to, you would."

I hesitated. "Okay, I think I really need a week alone, time to myself—"

"That's what you've been having all along."

"No, not true. The apartment is busy and noisy. I'm working myself to the bone, I've lost eight pounds—"

"Aren't you eating? What's *wrong* with you?"

"I'm eating when I have time. It's been a lot of pressure.

I'm handling it, but I think I'm entitled to one measly week of just hanging loose."

"Do that *here*. I'll baby-sit for you. You won't have to look at the kid."

"That's not the point."

There was a long, angry silence. I didn't feel like breaking it, but finally, since my father's silences can be louder than most people's conversations, I said, "Look, I want to see you, it's not that, but—"

"I have a great idea," my father said heartily. "I'll fly *there*. You say the apartment'll be empty. You can put me up, or, if you'd rather, I'll stay at a hotel. I'll buy a turkey, I'll roast it, I'll do the whole thing. . . ."

"Dad!" I said. "I've roasted more turkeys than you have."

"Tell me one thing. Were you planning to have a real honest-to-goodness Thanksgiving, with all the trimmings, like we have at Charlie and Maureen's, pie, stuffing, cranberry sauce?"

"No."

"So what do you say? Take it or leave it. I won't get underfoot. You have some girl you want to see—no problem. Free built-in baby-sitting. Stay out all night. Dance the night away."

I laughed hollowly. "I'm not dating, or whatever."

"Whatever!" my father said cheerfully. "Call it what you will. What do you say? Yes? No?"

I looked up at the wall. Even I recognized a one-answer question. I tried valiantly to rise to the occasion. "That sounds terrific," I said. "When will you arrive?"

The change in my father's voice was almost pathetic. "Now listen, I'll leave the day after Thanksgiving. I just want a day. I won't horn in on your plans, your social life. I just want to see Mason, see my grandchild. I'll be invisible."

"Famous last words," drifted in billowy clouds in front of me. "Let me know when you'll arrive," I said.

"I'll call the airline the minute I set down the phone."

The minute I set down the phone, Mason, who'd been awake but quiet, let out a yell. By now he'd perfected a variety of yells. There was a yell of: I'm hungry and you better feed me pronto. There was a yell that just meant: I'm exercising my lungs and I want you to know they're getting louder every day. There was a yell of pain, either stomach upset, or something mysterious. And there was the yell he'd just given, which said: Pay attention to me, play with me.

I lifted him up. He'd been changed before my father's call. "Well, it looks very much as though we have no choice, Mase," I said. I knew I was alone in the apartment. "Grandpa is descending and we're going to eat turkey till it comes out of our ears. And you're going to get so much attention you'll probably want to be in solitary confinement until the New Year. But look, he's blood kin, he's a lonely old man. I shouldn't say old. He's a lonely, middle-aged man. His wife—your grandmother, actually—died. He's alone. You've got to make allowances, okay? Will you do that?"

The thing about talking to Mason was, he gave me the kind of undivided attention that you never get from another human being. Of course, the reason was that he wasn't really a human being in the fullest sense of the word. He hadn't the foggiest notion what I was saying, but when he looked at me with his round, blue eyes, there was a sense of human contact. "So we handle it, it's just a day. We'll have the whole apartment to ourselves, take some good walks. I know I've been kind of weird lately. I think I'm weird. I'm a weirder person than I know, or

172

than you know, luckily. But I'm doing my best, and I think you appreciate that, don't you?"

Talk about one-answer questions. Mason just gave me his crooked toothless grin. What did he know? Thank God.

CHAPTER 15

Thanksgiving vacation started officially on Wednesday, but on Tuesday afternoon Lindsay, her suitcase in hand, started out the door. Fern had already left. "Have a super time," Vivian called, coming to the door. "Hope things go all right with Kevin."

"Not to worry." She smiled at both of us. "Have a good Thanksgiving, both of you," she said.

We mumbled incoherent agreement. The minute Lindsay left, Vivian said, "Um, when are you and Mason setting off?"

I felt uncomfortable. "We're not, actually. I just thought I couldn't afford the time. Well, no, it's more I'd really like some time to myself; that is, with him, of course."

She stared at me, horrified. "You're staying here all during vacation?"

"Yeah, what's the problem?"

She sucked in her breath. "*I* was going to stay here . . . I was really looking forward to it. Total peace and quiet."

"But your parents live in the city. Can't you stay with them?" I couldn't believe my ill fortune.

"Oh, Mom is off to Pennsylvania, of all ungodly places, to meet her latest beau's family, and Dad has Moira and her two kids from her first marriage. She's such a pain, and they're just unbearably whiny, wretched *beasts*. I don't know. I really liked Alice, you know, the one who died of the over-dose, but I just plain don't have it in me to go through this again. I mean, stepmother, okay. But *step*-stepmother? Where does it end? He could go on like this till he's eighty!"

I tried to control my temper. "Look, Vivian, this really means a lot to me. I've been under so much pressure. Couldn't you, maybe, go to your father's just for a day or so?"

"No!" she exploded. "And I don't get why you can't pop on a plane and go home. You'd have your father there to help out with the baby and—"

"He's coming here instead."

She looked even more disbelieving. "Coming *here*? Not to this apartment? Not *staying* here?"

"Well, he *could* stay at a hotel, but I thought—I assumed I'd have the place to myself. He's a quiet guy, we won't get in your way. This is as much an imposition on me as it is on you."

"How can you *say* that?" Her cheeks were flushed. She had funny, dark eyebrows that shot up at the sides. "I'm just me, one single person. You're three people. How is that equal? And I don't scream at all hours of the day and night—"

"Mason doesn't scream, he only occasionally—" I started to protest.

"Look, Tim, I am at my fucking wit's end. I try to study at night and I just go in to make myself a cup of tea and I feel like I have to tiptoe around the apartment. I can't play music. I'm so scared he'll wake up and start howling."

"He doesn't—I mean I appreciate your thinking of all that but . . ." I felt grim. "I'm just asking for two days. Is that really impossible?"

"Yes!"

"Even knowing you won't have the place to yourself, that it'll be me, Mason, my father."

She eyed me levelly. "Even knowing that."

"You're so goddamn stubborn." I couldn't restrain myself.

At that Vivian exploded. "Look, Tim, you want a nice Thanksgiving? Go to my father and Moira's. She adores babies. They'd love to have you. They'll have a turkey as big as the Ritz. Should I call them? Should I?" She advanced menacingly toward me.

"No." I half turned away.

She started biting her nails. "What are you three doing for Thanksgiving? Ignoring it, celebrating it?"

"We'll do something. I'll let him handle it. Frankly, I'd much rather ignore the whole thing."

She looked sympathetic. "I *hate* holidays! All of them. They really suck. If you want to see every member of a given family act their absolute worst, give a holiday dinner."

"Well, I don't think it's *that* bad," I said, remembering dinners at Charlie and Maureen's.

"It *is* that bad," she said grimly. "It's worse. God, I wish they'd invent a pill that you could take before the holiday began and wake up when it was over."

I gathered we had reached a kind of stalemate agreement. "So we'll coexist, right? My father'll probably want to go out. I don't think it'll be too bad."

She shrugged.

Damn. If it could've been Lindsay who was staying, I think I would've taken it differently. Partly, of course, because she would've managed to be gracious and malleable about the whole thing. Then suddenly I remembered Vivian's saying her mother was going to visit her current boyfriend's family in Pennsylvania. I decided to give it one more try. I knocked on Vivian's door.

"Come in," she grunted.

I opened the door. She was lying under the covers, as though she had just begun a nap. "Okay, this is just a final try," I began from the doorway, feeling awkward. Had I woken her up? "You say your mother's going to visit her boyfriend's family. So doesn't that mean her apartment will be empty?"

Vivian stared at me with narrowed eyes. "Tim, don't you *ever* give up? No, the apartment will *not* be empty. It will have his cat, to which, to whom, I'm allergic. It will have all their crap; their plants, their stuff. They are both *incredible* slobs. I don't feel like living in a pigpen for two days! I want to be here, in my own place. Is that too much to ask?" Her voice was trembling.

I backed out of the room. "No, that's fine," I said.

She seemed a lot more on edge than I'd noticed, not that we'd had a lot of interaction, only it had seemed to me that I was living among three fairly carefree girls who seemed to have full, interesting lives. The way Vivian was lying there under the covers reminded me of how, after school, the year my mother died, I would come home and just get into bed for an hour, not to sleep, just to lie there under the thick, heavy blanket. I don't know if I associated the blanket with her, and I don't know what I was doing by lying there, but I always had the feeling I was doing something I shouldn't. Somewhere deep down, maybe I had the feeling that if I stayed there long enough, I could will her back. I would get up after about an hour, feeling groggy and strange. But it was a ritual I went through for at least a year.

When my father arrived on Wednesday night, I was shocked at his appearance. Of course, he's fifty-eight, no surprise, and off and on throughout my childhood I'd been struck, when comparing him to the fathers of friends, at how much older he looked. It wasn't just looks, then, it was his manner, his dry, caustic, detached manner, his seeming inability to interact on a casual level with other people. I knew it was just that I hadn't seen him for several months and had simply forgotten what he looked like. "So, here I am!" he said, hugging me awkwardly.

"Welcome," I said, trying to sound cheerful. "This is it."

He glanced around the living room. "Not bad. Quite a place. You were lucky." Then he started roaming down the hall, opening doors. I whispered after him, "Dad!"

He looked startled. I beckoned to him. "Look, we, uh, we're not going to be here alone, like I thought. There's one of my roommates here, Vivian. She couldn't go home for Thanksgiving." I decided not to mention any of the details of her private life mainly because it would strike my father as too peculiar. "So she'll be here. She may be here now."

"Should I stay at a hotel? Is there room here? Be honest."

"No, there's plenty of room. Fern and Lindsay will be gone the whole time. It's just her door is that last one on the end, and she might be in there. I don't know. I've been out with Mason."

My father's face brightened. "Where is he?"

"I set him down. . . . You can come in and see him, though." I took my father into the spare room. Mason was lying in his crib, just staring around, as he often does.

"Hey! Look at that!" my father exclaimed. "What a

178

change! He looks terrific. A lot better than you. *You* look like you've had the plague. . . . Can I hold him?''

"Sure." I lifted Mason up. He's pretty good with strangers at this point. Obviously he wouldn't remember my father from four months ago.

My father held him gingerly. "Hello," he said. "How're you doing? Remember grandpa? Remember me? I was the guy who picked you up at the hospital."

I watched them uneasily, relieved Mason hadn't let out a howl, which he's been known to do, more so with men than women. "Listen, I'm going to start dinner," I said. "I thought we'd just have a steak . . . unless you feel like going out."

"Sounds wonderful. You go on and I'll carry him around a little."

I went into the kitchen and started heating the oven for the potatoes, thawing the bread, trimming the fat off the steak. Dimly I heard my father's comments as he carried Mason around, talking quietly to him. I didn't hear the exact words, more a murmuring intonation. There was something strange about transplanting my father to New York City. It was as though you'd lifted up a cardboard or wooden play figure and placed it in an imaginary alien landscape. My father belonged to Haysburg; he seemed to fit in there.

Since the apartment was so empty, I set up the table in the living room and put out candles and wine. I convinced my father that Mason was better off in his crib. When he stayed up way beyond his bedtime, he could get fretful, and his night schedule could be ruined. "You're the boss," my father said, watching me light the candles. "Pretty nice. Gracious living."

Just as we were sitting down to eat, Vivian came wandering out of her room. It had been so silent and dark in that part of the apartment that I hadn't even been sure she was

179

there. She looked groggy, as though she'd just woken up from a heavy nap. She was dressed in her usual jeans and man's shirt, barefoot, her hair loose. "Oh, hi," she said tonelessly, raising one hand in greeting.

"Dad, this is Vivian Imhoff, one of my roommates."

"Delighted to meet you." My father looked slightly startled. "Have you eaten?"

"What?" her voice had a slow, spacey quality.

"Would you care to join us for dinner?" he repeated. "Tim here has fixed enough for an army."

Vivian yawned. "I just woke up. I've been sleeping all day. Catching up, I guess. . . . Well, maybe a glass of wine and a potato or something." She meandered over to the table and pulled up a chair.

I went into the kitchen and got another plate and set of silverware. She took them absently when I returned and handed them to her. I began carving the steak.

"I'm his father," my father said. "Abner Weber."

"Right," Vivian said. "He said."

"You were unable to return home for Thanksgiving?" my father asked.

"Kind of. It's a little complicated." She glanced at me, as though wondering how much I'd told my father about her family. "My stepmother died a year ago on Thanksgiving, so I don't have such great memories of it, and, well . . . a bunch of other things."

My father looked sympathetic. "Yes, well, holidays are difficult for us, too. My wife died some years ago, and somehow things are especially fraught on these supposedly joyous occasions."

Vivian was gazing at him fixedly. I couldn't read her expression. "Did she kill herself?" she asked.

"No!" my father said, horrified. "Why would she do that?

She was happy, young, she had a family. No, she had a cerebral hemorrhage.''

Vivian was poking at her potato. "It's just my stepmother, Alice, did, and so . . . But you're right, yeah, about 'supposedly joyous.' I wonder: Are they ever? Isn't that just a crock at heart?''

"Are *what* ever?" my father asked, bewildered.

"Holidays, family happiness, all that stuff that's rammed down our throats from birth onward,'' she rushed on. "I think ninety-nine percent of families are completely wretched on holidays or *not* on holidays. It's just holidays force them to be together so it makes it even worse.''

My father was cutting his steak in his usual precise way. "No, I certainly can't subscribe to such a cynical view, by no means . . . Perhaps your own family was. But not all, no, not all. I have the happiest memories of my own marriage. They were the most wonderful years of my life.''

Vivian was dissecting the potato as though it were a frog in a biology class. "So how come you didn't remarry?''

My father flushed. "Pardon me?''

"I mean, if you were happy, why not be happy again?''

"You think it's that simple?'' my father said dryly.

Vivian laughed hollowly. "No, I think it's impossible, myself. But I would think if I had ever experienced it, I might believe in it.''

My father sipped his wine. "I don't believe happiness is handed round that profligately,'' he said. "I was lucky, that was all. I would be incredibly presumptuous to expect such good fortune twice.''

Vivian shrugged. She twirled her hair around her finger. "My father just keeps on going.'' she said. "He's onto his third.''

"He's probably a great deal younger than I am,'' my father said. "And probably has a way with women.''

She snorted. "Yeah, he has. He shreds them. But then, some women want to be shredded, so it's a perfect solution."

There was a pause. My father looked at me. "Anything wrong, Tim? You're rather silent."

I suppose in my mind I was reinventing this whole Thanksgiving, transporting my father to Charlie and Maureen's, Vivian to her mother's empty apartment, in short, pretending I was alone. "No, I'm fine," I said.

"He's pretending we're not here," Vivian said, looking at me with that provocative directness. "Because that's what he wishes. Right, Timothy?"

I hesitated. "No," I lied. "Wrong."

She smiled, as though this were transparent. Then, to my father, she said, "I couldn't face going home, Mr. Weber. I hope that's all right with you. I know you wanted to be alone with Tim."

"On the contrary," my father said. "I feel I'm imposing myself on the two of you by staying here at all. I'm very thankful you're willing to put me up."

Put that way, it seemed curiously to link Vivian and me as a couple. "There's just a lot of pressure with work and all," Vivian said vaguely.

"Well, all work and no play," my father said, "is not a healthy combination, as they say. I never worked out the equation perfectly myself."

"At college?" Vivian pursued. "Or in general? In life?"

"Both, I'm afraid. And Tim here has been scarred by the same brush, I fear. The male side of our family lacks a certain playfulness, one would have to admit."

Vivian was looking at him in that same intent manner. "Not in *my* family. All the men in my family *do* is play. It's the women who keep the ship on course, to the extent it *is* on course at all."

"Oh, women always do that," my father said. "Yes, always. That's why I wondered, frankly, when Tim decided to keep the baby, how wise a decision it was. But he seems to be coping remarkably. Don't you think?''

Vivian looked at me with an expression somewhere between irony and compassion. "Yeah . . . We don't know each other that well. I mean, we all live here, but . . . I guess we all basically lead separate lives.''

"Of course," my father said.

Another silence.

Vivian jumped up. "How about coffee? Should I make some?''

"Decaffinated for me," my father said.

I decided to sit and let Vivian clear if she felt like it. Evidently she did. As the door to the kitchen swung shut my father said in a low voice, "A pity about her family.''

"Yeah. She's a little unstable. I'm sorry about her asking all those questions. She's just like that.''

"No, it all seemed done in good faith, genuine concern," my father said. He hesitated. "I'm not, uh, interrupting anything with the two of you, by any chance? Because I'd be glad, as I said, to go to a hotel—''

For a split second I had no idea what he meant. Then the light dawned. He thought we were lovers? He thought he was interrupting an erotic interlude? I almost burst out laughing. "No, no," I said. "Far from it. Very far.''

It was strange, though. I don't know if this sounds believable, but despite my total lack of a sex life since Cheryl, and despite living with Fern, Lindsay, and Vivian, I hadn't had any special sexual feelings about them, at least any of which I was aware. I felt I had to add the last because, according to my psychology professor, it's the feelings you're *not* aware of that are the most potent. And maybe what happened after my father's remark was an indication that something had been going on in my unconscious. Lying in bed after we had all retired to our separate rooms, I suddenly became acutely aware of Vivian's presence in the apartment. Not just that she was there, but that there was a girl in the apartment, that, as my father had suggested, there *were* sexual possibilities. And as though out of the blue, what I felt like doing, had it been possible, was going in and making love to her, providing she could remain unconscious throughout. I didn't feel I was attracted to Vivian in the way I'd been to Cheryl. First, her attitude to me seemed decidedly ambiguous at best, as well as her attitude toward men in general. And then she wasn't pretty in that soft, delicate way Cheryl had been. I couldn't even imagine her gazing at anyone the way Cheryl, at times, had gazed at me, with that longingly melting expression.

But there was something else, not a neutral thing, but her provocative directness, her intensity which, while not sexual in that she acted the same way with Lindsay and Fern, had sexual overtones. I felt furious with my father, which probably was a little like the king ordering the death of the messenger who brought bad news. I felt if he had not made that remark, I would never have had these thoughts, but since he had unwittingly unleashed them, I lay there, incredibly turned on in the worst kind of way because I didn't really see any point to it. *Maybe I should move to a hotel. Look, this will pass. It's normal. What's strange is that it didn't happen before this.* I tried to wonder why it hadn't. I think it may have been for the same reason they say kids growing up on kibbutzes rarely feel sexually attracted to each other. There was an informality to our interactions which didn't seem at all romantic. And then there was the fact of the three of them. And maybe I felt, although no one had ever said this, that having feelings like these was taboo, that they were only accepting me here as a sexless presence, not a man or boy or guy whom they would have to worry about making a pass at them or having to impress in some way. I felt I was the kid brother to all of them, especially in that they were all a year older than I was and they all had brothers. I had never honestly felt any of them coming on to me in any of the many ways girls can, whether they intend anything to result from it or not. If I'd had sexual fantasies at all since arriving in New York, they had mainly attached themselves to girls I saw in my classes, anonymous, lovely girls whom I just gazed at from afar. Mason was my constant companion. He seemed to effortlessly absorb all the emotional energy at my disposal. Maybe that showed, somehow.

CHAPTER 16

The next day, Thanksgiving, everyone slept late, even Mason. When I woke up, it was ten. I was horrified. Mason never slept that late. Eight at the latest. I charged out of my room and into the spare room, terrified, when I heard my father call from the kitchen, "We're in here."

I went in and there was my father, holding Mason against his shoulder. "Is he okay?" I asked anxiously. "He never sleeps this late."

"Oh, we've been up for hours, haven't we, Mase?" he said. "I woke up early and I was fixing myself some coffee when I heard him, so I went in and changed him and gave him a bottle. I assumed the box of bottles in the kitchen were the ones you used. We've just been talking and exchanging our views on the modern world."

I sat down. "I felt so panicked," I admitted. "He's never slept that late."

"I figured you could use the sleep," my father said. "You look exhausted. In fact, I was thinking of taking him out for a stroll. Do you feel like coming? Or shall the two of us go alone?"

"No, I'll come. Let me just shower."

It seemed almost promiscuous of Mason to look and act so relaxed with my father. I was amazed, also, at how relaxed my father seemed. He actually seemed to be enjoying himself, which is something I, at least, haven't witnessed that often.

After breakfast we went out and I showed my father the campus, Mrs. Peters' apartment house, some of the bookstores I frequent. When I go out with Mason now, I carry him in a backpack. He seems to like that. He still loves crowds. The noise and the number of strange faces we pass as we go down Broadway doesn't bother him at all. I could see my father felt aghast at the homeless people sleeping on the sidewalk, the addicts staggering around Broadway. I'd felt that way, too, when I first arrived. Now they were part of the urban landscape.

"I could never live here," my father said. "There's something so heartless about the city. All these people, and no one seems to care." He gestured toward an elderly woman, staggering along, talking to herself.

"I think people do care," I said, "only it's done by big organizations rather than by individuals."

"That's the point," my father said. "In Haysburg take Alice Monroe, for instance. She's mad as a hatter and probably should be institutionalized, but somehow she manages. People look in on her, make sure she gets meals. Here you could die and no one would notice."

Even though he was just expressing opinions I'd felt when

187

I first arrived, it all sounded more prejudiced and small-townish than I wanted to consider myself. "I always felt claustrophobic in Haysburg," I blurted out, "as though whatever you did, people were watching. Here at least you're anonymous. And that can be freeing."

"I suppose you're right," my father said. "There *is* some of that. For instance . . . well, I hadn't mentioned this"—he looked uncomfortable—"but I've been seeing Margaret Hansen a bit. Don't get alarmed, it's no big thing, just an occasional dinner, but at least ten people have made 'knowing' remarks to me. It drives Margaret crazy." He chuckled. "She says she's going to start wearing fright wigs when we go out so people will think I'm with a mysterious stranger."

For some reason the one sentence that caught at me was "Don't be alarmed." I wasn't alarmed, just startled. "Is this—because I'm here?"

"Well, it has something to do with that," my father said. He still looked embarrassed, as though he were confessing something extreme. "But, even I, antiquated and stiff as I am, feel the need of feminine companionship. Now, I know that probably strikes you as grotesque, at my age."

"No, not at all," I said.

But he went on as though I hadn't spoken. "This is not, Tim, please understand this, I am not now, nor will I ever seek to replace your mother in any sense of the word. Do you understand that? You have my solemn promise."

"Dad, listen, I don't care. You can do whatever you want."

But he just continued with his monologue. Maybe he'd been rehearsing it in his mind for weeks. "I am lonely, Margaret is lonely. She's an intelligent, cultivated person. There is no need to read more into it than that. It is simply what it seems, no more, no less."

I glanced at him, trying to figure out how to say what I

felt. "I think it's great," I said finally. "Whatever it is. You're *not* old."

My father was silent. His face was red with cold, and yet he looked younger and more alive than he had the night before. "I *feel* old," he said, "but then I always have. I felt old at twenty. I felt old when I met your mother. Probably it's a defense of some sort. . . . Don't do the same thing, Tim."

I frowned. "What do you mean?"

"I feel afraid at times, that maybe I've infected you somehow with my . . . my tendency to withdraw. It's a trap. It doesn't work. I—I tried to make it seem like a choice, more than it was." His face had such a tormented expression that I felt touched.

"It's hard for me, too," was all I could manage.

Somehow the conversation exhausted both of us. We so rarely talked about anything, even indirectly. It was a relief to go into stores, buy a turkey, discuss what kind of stuffing we should make. My father offered to make a pumpkin pie, one of the few things he can make, and to assist me with everything else. "Will your friend be joining us?" he asked as we inspected turkeys.

"Vivian? I don't think so."

"Well, it can't hurt to have a little turkey left over. How about this one? You can have turkey sandwiches after I leave."

In the afternoon we stayed in, listened to music, talked in a random way. I let my father feed Mason since he seemed to get a bang out of it and Mason didn't mind. In between feedings we'd put him in his infant seat and let him stay in the living room, or in the kitchen once we started cooking. "Too bad he doesn't have teeth yet," my father said. "Well, next year. Yours were late in coming, as I recall. Your mother kept a record. I should look it up."

Preparing the dinner, instead of being a chore, turned out to be a perfect way for us to interact without having to get into any complicated talks about life. I felt I had absorbed my father's remark about Margaret without having digested it, as it were. I didn't feel anything negative, only a mild relief that there was something in his life other than concern about me and Mason.

We ate by candlelight again, after putting Mason down for the night. Outside, it had turned black and cold. I drew the curtains across the windows. For the first time I wondered where Vivian was. It seemed presumptuous to knock on her door. If she was in there, she'd come out eventually.

Just as we were finishing dinner a tall, heavyset man with a black beard came staggering out of Vivian's room. He was dressed in a shirt and slacks. "Hi there, I'm Sandor," he said in an Eastern European-sounding accent, shaking my father's hand. Then he shook mine. "You're Tim?"

"Right." I looked at him, puzzled. How long had he been in there? Or was it *they*?

"Viv'll be out in a minute," Sandor said. His eyes lit up at the sight of the food spread out on the table. "Wow, a real feast!"

"Won't you join us?" my father asked politely. "We have a great deal left over."

"That would be great," he said in a loud voice. "I'm starved. And Viv's talents, as you no doubt know," he said, glancing mischievously at me, "don't exactly lie in a culinary direction." With that, he pulled up a chair and just began diving into everything on the table. Instead of getting a plate, he just pulled the platter with the turkey in front of him and began wrenching off chucks of meat, scooping up mouthfuls of stuffing. My father stared at him, appalled.

A few moments later Vivian appeared. She had evidently just come out of the shower. Her hair was wet, and she was wearing a dress. "Sandor, what are you doing?" She sat down.

"What does it look like? I didn't have lunch, I didn't even have much breakfast. I was ready to pass out." He took the cranberry sauce and dumped a cupful onto the turkey platter.

"Yeah, but Tim and his father didn't invite us for dinner. They have to eat." She looked in a worried way at the two of us.

"We've finished," my father said stiffly.

Vivian went into the kitchen and returned with two plates and silverware. "Sandor, for God's sake, you're eating right off the platter! Don't be an animal."

Sandor grinned at my father and me as though Vivian were being incredibly delicate in her tastes. "If a man is hungry, he eats," he said.

She lifted the platter off the table. "Eat on a plate! This is disgusting. Did you even ask them if they had enough?"

I could see bits of turkey and sweet potato clinging to his beard. I felt repelled. This was the man she chose after claiming to be so fussy about the male sex? Jesus. Vivian sat down and took a tiny helping of everything. She smiled at me. "This is delicious, Tim. Thanks so much."

"We would have done it anyway," I said. I glanced at Sandor and then said, "I wasn't sure you were here."

Vivian set down her fork. She looked flustered. "Oh, we . . . yeah, we . . . Right."

We've been fucking, in short. At this point Sandor had managed to get down to the carcass of the turkey, what you would use for soup. It didn't look like there'd be any issue about turkey sandwiches. "I teach philosophy at Yeshiva," he said.

This appeared to be addressed to my father, who said, "I teach mathematics at Taylor."

Sandor frowned. "Where's that? Never heard of it."

"It's a small college in Massachusetts," my father said.

"Must be pretty small. I've heard of most of them. . . . I don't know. I got a few offers from places out in the boonies when I came over in '75—I'm from Budapest—but I just figured I couldn't hack it. The women all looked like they were carved out of trees, no movies, no bookstores."

"There are other compensations," my father said. "It's an unusually beautiful landscape."

Sandor was inspecting the bare carcass, which by now could have been polished and set up as a subject for a Georgia O'Keeffe painting. "Right, trees, lakes, I know . . . I'm just not into nature. It's not crucial with me. I see a tree and I think, 'Great, a tree.' But I don't have a tremendous yen to see another one."

Wryly Vivian removed the turkey carcass from his hand. "San, they were probably intending to live off this for a week. Now look at it!"

Sandor looked innocently amazed. "Were you? Listen, let me pay you. You went to all this work, all this time." He reached into his pocket and hurled a few ten dollar bills on the table.

Fastidiously my father shoved them back at him. "It's our treat," he said. "And now, if you still have room," he added sardonically, "we could have some pumpkin pie."

"Count me out," Sandor said. "I'm stuffed."

Vivian looked up at my father with a pleading expression. "I'd love some, Mr. Weber," she said. She stood up to help my father clear, leaving Sandor and me alone at the table.

He winked at me. "Well, sorry if . . . Viv said you wanted to be alone, your father came all this way. We didn't mean to impose. It's just my ex-wife is in town with her boyfriend and they didn't have anyplace to stay, so I figured—"

"It's okay," I said.

He seemed suddenly uncomfortable. "Viv's a lovely girl. I guess she's been having a hard time."

I shrugged. "We're not that close."

"Oh?" He looked surprised. Then he leaned back in his chair and burped. "That was some turkey," he said. "The best."

After coffee and pie, Vivian and Sandor left to go to the movies. My father glanced over at me. It was eleven. "Good lord," he said. "Who was *he*?"

"I gather her boyfriend," I said. "I've never seen him before."

My father's thin face wrinkled with disgust. "But he was so . . . and she's so refined, elegant seeming. I don't understand that, I never have. Some women seem to have that kind of taste in men. What is it? Some primitive thing?"

"Dad, seriously, I'm the last person on earth to ask. He seemed like a complete jerk to me."

"He smelled!" my father said. "I swear that man hadn't bathed in the last week. Incredible." We went into the kitchen and washed up, putting most of the dishes in the dishwasher. When we were done, my father said, "I'm bushed. I think I'd better turn in. My plane's at eleven tomorrow morning."

I could have urged him to stay another day, but I just said, "Sleep well. And don't feel you have to take care of Mason in the morning. I'll do that."

Suddenly my father's face lit up. "My dear boy, it's an honor, it's a delight."

After my father went to sleep, I stayed up reading. I felt roiled up inside from the unexpected end to the evening. Not that it was unacceptable for Vivian to have a boyfriend stay over with her, but she had made it sound like she was dismayed at my staying here because she needed time to be alone. I'd taken her at her word. Was needing time to be alone just a euphemism for making out with that boorish oaf, that jackass? *It's none of your damn business. Who cares what turns her on?*

I went to bed at one; Vivian and Sandor still weren't home. I slept fitfully, having snatches of dreams which seemed to collide together rather than to fit into each other. Then sometime later, I wasn't even sure how late, I heard yelling outside my room.

It was Vivian. She was screaming, out of control. "I said get the fuck out of here, do you hear me? You can dress outside. Just get out! I never want to see you again."

Sandor was pleading with her, saying something incomprehensible. Then his voice also was raised and there were epithets like "Bitch," "You crazy . . ." and finally Vivian let out a scream that could have been heard halfway down the block. There was a loud slam of the front door and then absolute silence. I lay in bed, so angry I was rigid. She knew Mason was right there, asleep. How could she be *that* insensitive? I waited, steeling myself for his "I'm awake and I want attention" yell. Looking at the digital clock, I saw it was four in the morning. No yell. How could he not have heard that? Was he alive? I got out of bed and tiptoed into the spare room, opening the door as quietly as possible.

There he was, sleeping contentedly, his fist pressed up against his mouth. I closed the door silently again. Then I noticed that there was a light on in the kitchen. I walked in. Vivian had her back to me. She was evidently fixing herself a cup of tea. The kettle was on and she was inspecting the box of teabags. I felt suddenly guilty at not having wondered if she was all right, not having rushed to protect her. What if she'd been in physical danger?

"Maybe I'll have some," I said quietly.

At that she let out a cry and whirled around, her eyes terrified. "My God, Tim, what are you doing creeping in here like that? You scared me to death."

194

"Well, it was a little hard sleeping with all that racket. Thank God Mason didn't wake up."

She poured some boiling water into a mug. "Do you want some?"

"Sure. God, don't you ever think of anyone besides yourself?" I blurted out. "You *knew* he was there. It sounded like the outbreak of World War Three."

She glared at me. "I was provoked."

"Why do you get involved with a jerk like that? He seemed like something that had crawled out of a cave."

"Hey, Tim, am I giving you advice about your love life?"

"I don't—" I began, but she rushed on.

"Am I telling *you* what I think you should or shouldn't do? Have I *ever* said a word about the presumed ethics of knocking up some girl in your hometown and then making off with her baby—"

"Making off!" I laughed. "Christ, you know nothing about it. She was going to sell the baby. I had to take her to court."

"So maybe she needed the money. Maybe she was poor. Maybe a million things. I'm just saying I'm not lecturing *you* on what you have or haven't done in your life regarding the opposite sex, so could you at least do me the favor of not butting into my goddamn business?"

I went over and took the teakettle to pour myself some boiling water. "You could do better, that's all."

"Oh, I could? Gee, I'm truly honored you think so. You know so much about me, right? You really know all about my tastes and my past and my hang-ups. You want to start a computer-dating service?"

"I just meant—"

Vivian was shivering. She put her arms around herself. "He's a despicable fool, all right? I *know* that. I have rotten taste in men. But . . . he also happens to be a wonderful lover and, when he's in the mood, an unusually kind, sensitive, appealing human being.'' She laughed hollowly. "Unfortunately, that's only a few hours out of every month, but . . .''

''Does he eat like that most the time? I was planning on having turkey sandwiches for the rest of the week.'' I rummaged around in the refrigerator for some lemon for the tea.

''Look, are all the girls you've been involved with such pinnacles of human intelligence and wonderfulness in every way?'' Vivian said. "It's hard to figure out why some people turn you on. It's mysterious.''

I thought back to Cheryl. ''True.''

She was still shivering, cupping her hands around the mug as though to warm her fingers. ''My stepmother, my friends, everyone says, 'Oh, wow, do I have someone for you!' But they're these . . . dead people. These little doctor types. They're *dead*. They wouldn't know what to do with a woman if you carved one up on a platter and served her to them! Don't you see? That's what it's like. You're some object and if they're in 'need,' quote unquote, they make a lunge at you. Who *needs* that?''

''Yeah, I, well, I know what you mean,'' I said.

''No, you *don't*!'' Vivian yelled. ''You can't! Because it doesn't work the other way around. Women are not physically lunging at you. Are they?''

''No,'' I admitted, ''but—''

''There *are* no buts,'' she said. ''It's just different. I hate it when men say, 'But we have problems, too.' One guy— this really took the cake—said, 'But don't men die?' And I thought, 'Sure, but women aren't immortal,' and even if we were, I'm not sure it would make up for it.''

I looked at her. ''Why are you shivering? Are you sick?''

Suddenly her face got that uncertain, tormented look.

"No, I'm just . . . It's something that happens to me. I guess it's psychological. I—"

"When does it happen?" I asked, concerned.

She turned away. "Oh, Tim, look, I don't know. I have problems, all right? Men make me . . . nervous. It's the shredding thing. I've just seen it so often and I've seen my stepmother go under and my mother put up with so much crap from guys, and when I see myself doing the same thing, I get so sick. Because that's the worst—knowing you're playing into it. It's one thing for guys to do it, but to play into it, to start feeding *yourself* into the shredder." She broke off.

That was such a horrible image. "What do you mean by the shredder?"

"Just—allowing oneself to be annihilated somehow. I can't explain it. It's that you're doing this thing, this act—sex—and suddenly you start to disappear and you get the feeling that if you're not careful you will literally disappear. Do you know what I mean?"

"No," I had to admit. "Or, sort of." I hesitated. "I always thought that was the point of sex, to lose yourself in some way." I had never discussed sex with a girl; it made me uncomfortable.

"But what if you never find yourself again?" she said urgently. "What if you just come to the ledge and fall over and you don't even know it's there?"

"You mean as a metaphor?"

"No, it's real." Her eyes were staring into mine so fixedly I had a peculiar sensation that she was entering me in some way. "I'm trying to explain it as a metaphor, but it's real."

I wanted to say something comforting, that wouldn't sound lame or inadequate, but I wasn't sure what. "Maybe it's just that you didn't really love him," I said.

"Maybe I've never really loved anyone," Vivian agreed touchingly. "I'm not sure I want to, either." Then, abruptly, in a totally different, warmer voice, she said, "I like your father. He seems like such a fine, kind person. Is he? Is that real?"

"Well, yeah . . ."

"I've never known men like that."

I tried to be flip. "We come in all shapes and sizes."

Vivian looked around the room. "I'm sorry I screamed. You know, I did think of Mason when I was doing it. That's what's terrible. Maybe I wanted to wake him up. I get so jealous of you, your connection with him. Your life seems so—together in a way. You know what you want."

"I don't," I said. "Absolutely not."

"You seem to."

"That's different." I noticed her shivering had stopped. "Are you okay now? I might try and get some sleep before my father—"

Vivian sighed. "Yeah, I'm fine. I feel very calm, actually. I'm going to try and sleep, too. Say good-bye to your father for me, will you? And apologize for Sandor?"

I walked back to my room with all of Vivian's comments swirling in my head, sure I would never get to sleep. But almost the minute I lay down I sank into a dreamless, heavy sleep that wasn't broken until my father leaned over me, saying gently, "Tim, I think you better get up. It's nine."

CHAPTER 17

I didn't feel apologetic for the fact that my father had once again arisen when Mason had and fed him and played with him. It was so clear he enjoyed it and would, in a second, have stayed on for the rest of the weekend. As he was packing I said, "Vivian said to apologize about her boyfriend. He's kind of an animal, but I gather once they had some kind of relationship."

My father was folding his sweater. "I'm concerned about her, that's all. She seems very high-strung."

"Yeah, well . . ."

I knew if I told my father a fraction of what Vivian had said last night, he'd want her to be shipped off to the psycho ward. And I didn't feel like betraying her confidences. I went downstairs and helped him get a cab. Mason was in my backpack. My father leaned forward and hugged me. "This has been a wonderful visit," he said. "Thank you."

"See you in a month or so," I said.

He leaned and waved out the back window of the cab. I knew it was Mason he was waving at, as much as me.

I took a long walk with Mason in Riverside Park. It was a mild autumn day and a lot of people were out walking their dogs or just strolling. You couldn't get the feeling of privacy you could in Haysburg, but the Hudson River looked beautiful, flat, shimmering, a translucent blue-gray. I walked all the way down to 79th Street, and then up again. By the time we got back to the apartment, Mason was starving. He put away two jars of cereal and an entire eight-ounce bottle, as though he hadn't eaten in weeks. His rash had vanished more than a month ago, after I switched formulas. Then, when he was done, he smiled up at me with his goofy, crooked grin.

I felt pleased at having survived my father's visit. Even though he'd been fine, exemplary in fact, there was a way in which he got on my nerves. I never knew how much of that was my mother's felt but unspoken presence, how much was just his idiosyncrasies, how much I felt his flickering attempts at advice about my life were more disturbing than reassuring. He seemed more human to me since Mason had been born, as though in some slow way he was coming out of his shell, but even though I would have thought that would be a big improvement, it unnerved me. I wished I could love him or hate him, have some clear-cut final attitude. Would Mason feel all this for me, no matter how I handled it: wishing he could have communicated with me better, differently, then suddenly wishing I'd get off his back and let him alone?

Vivian's door was open, so it was clear she was out. I dozed on the sofa, woke up when Mason did, then fooled around with him a little while I fixed supper. I knew I ought

200

to be working on my history paper, now that my father was gone, but somehow I didn't feel up to it. I decided that I was entitled to count today as a nonworking day since he had only left this morning. Looking in the paper, I saw there was a double feature on the cable channel: *Dead of Night*, an old thriller, and *The Lady Vanishes*. I vaguely remembered *Dead of Night* from when I'd been a child, but I'd never seen *The Lady Vanishes*. They were both terrific, involving, not as scary as I expected. I realized this was exactly what my fantasy had been: being alone in the apartment, not having to worry about who would come in or when. The silence seemed beautiful and relaxing, not eerie and unwanted. At midnight I got up to get a beer and then lay down on the couch again with some pillows under my head, my sneakers off.

The door opened. "Hi," Vivian said, coming in wearing her gray down coat, a red scarf around her neck. "I just saw a great double bill—*Baby, It's You* and *Lianna*. Have you ever seen them?"

"No, I never heard of them. But I want to watch the end of this." *Dead of Night* was still going.

Vivian settled into a chair. "Oh, I love that one, where it's all a dream and he realizes at the end—"

"Don't tell me, okay?"

"Okay." She sat silently in the chair and both of us watched the movie to its conclusion.

I sat up and reached for the beer. "That was excellent," I said. "I think I saw it when I was young, but I didn't remember it that well."

Vivian was slouched in the chair, her sneakers off. "And it's so true-to-life," she said. "I have that exact experience— I'll start having this awful dream which I know I've had before, and even in the dream I'll think, 'God, why am I having this dream again?' Sometimes I even wake up in the middle of it to go to the bathroom and I think, 'When you go back to bed, have another dream.' And I can't! It's like it's playing on some inner reel inside me, and it has to go on to the end.'' She shuddered.

''I never have dreams like that,'' I said, finishing the beer. ''I used to have nightmares, around when my mother died, but . . .''

Vivian sat forward. ''What were they about?''

I'd never told anyone about those dreams, not even my father, who sometimes would hear me yelling and come into my room at night. I swallowed. ''I guess the worst one, the one I had most often was my mother would appear and it would seem like I had this choice, either to go with her and be dead, or to be alive and to stay with my father. Once I even saw her in the doorway. I knew that was a hallucination. But I woke up and there she was . . . and then she walked away.''

Vivian was looking at me intently. ''I used to have somewhat the same dream, it's funny,'' she said. ''After my stepmother died. Only in mine she would come and make me promise that my father would never remarry and that I'd take care of my stepsister. I'd try to tell her I couldn't, and she'd get so upset, she'd plead with me. . . . It was awful.''

''Why did she kill herself?'' I asked. With Vivian I felt I could ask that kind of question, which normally would have seemed to me intrusive.

She frowned. ''I could say my father, but it wasn't, really. She was upset when she met him. She'd had a tormented life, ups and downs, mental hospitals, drugs, therapy. I guess that was the problem. Nothing seemed to work for her. She had this feeling she was doomed, and it really scared me because sometimes I've thought that about myself, but then I always think, 'No, it's a matter of will power.' And at least she wasn't my mother, so it's not like there's any genetic thing.''

I was silent. There are silences and silences. But in this

one the fact that we were alone in the apartment appeared like a presence and settled down in the center of the room. We were staring at each other and I was torn between wanting to look away and feeling if I did, it would seem cowardly.

Then Vivian got up and sat down, crosslegged, at the foot of the couch, where my feet were. She smiled at me. "Are you seducible? I just always wondered. You seem so . . . monklike. Or is it monkish?"

"I think I probably am," I said, trying to smile back. "There haven't been a lot of attempts made thus far."

"You don't invite them."

"Probably not."

She was looking at me with a mischievous expression. "So how did your hometown girlfriend do it? What was her technique?"

I laughed. "Just coming up to me in the hall and asking when Thanksgiving vacation began, and if I knew what our math homework was. Plus being pretty."

"Timothy, you're really easy. That's *all* it took?"

I turned red. "Sorry. I hate wrecking your image of me as the mysterious monk. That's kind of appealing."

"Yeah," she said. "You're . . . a challenge, anyway. For someone brave enough to attempt it." She paused. "It's a pity I'm a coward."

"No, you're not. You're less of one than I am."

"Then why are we just sitting here?"

I shrugged. I wanted her to make the first move, after all her comments about brutish men coming on to her. She did. She got up and leaned over and kissed me on the lips. I didn't put up any resistance. "Could we do this in a cut-and-dried way?" she asked softly. "I mean, I don't think I can handle any emotional stuff right now."

"Any way is fine."

We started down the hall to her room and it wasn't until

we were in it that I remembered that she and Sandor had been there just a day or so ago. "Maybe my room would be better," I said.

"Why?" She was starting to take off her top.

I hesitated, not sure I should say the real reason. "So I can hear Mason, just in case."

Vivian was standing there, bare breasted. "Look, Tim, are we going to do this or not? This doesn't have to be an all-night orgy. I thought it might be . . . I mean, I figured, God, he hasn't been with anyone since that girl in his hometown."

I felt suddenly totally turned off. "So this is some kind of charity thing?"

"Of course not. I just want your undivided attention, however briefly."

"Will I have yours?"

"To the extent I'm capable of it." She came over and kissed me again. It was hard not to get excited with her half undressed. I closed my eyes and let my mind wander off wherever it felt like going. *Mason doesn't exist, Sandor doesn't exist.* Vivian's body was thinner than Cheryl's, but her breasts were larger. She always wore such loose clothes I'd never noticed. And once we were in bed, she acted extremely turned on; it wasn't difficult to forget everything except what we were doing. Just occasionally bits of remembered conversation would dart through my head: *shredder . . . falling over the ledge . . . monkish.* And then we both seemed to vanish, only for me it was a wonderful kind of blanking out. Her body seemed so welcoming and undivided, compared to her mind, and for the moment, that was all that mattered.

Afterward we lay in the darkness, side by side. She didn't snuggle up next to me, her head on my chest, the way Cheryl had. "Did you come?" she asked.

I wondered if she was joking. "Wasn't that pretty obvious?"

"No, it's always hard for me to tell. Could you tell if I did?"

That seemed an equivocation. "Well, but it *is* harder to tell with women."

"Do you think I did or not?" she demanded.

"Are we playing twenty questions?"

"Just tell me what you think."

I wasn't sure what was at stake in what I replied, so I answered truthfully. "You seemed turned on . . . unless that was play acting."

"It's always partly play acting," she admitted, "but it was pretty real, too. It's just I kept thinking of Sandor—"

I turned away. "Thanks," I said coldly.

She touched me caressingly. "I don't mean it that way, comparing or whatever, just wondering why it so often ends the way it did with him, with such violent hatred."

"Because it's a violent feeling?"

"But hatred? Was it like that with you and your high school girlfriend?"

For some reason the scene of Cheryl coming up to me in the schoolyard that day and saying she would have an abortion on the spot returned to me almost in its entirety, the sick way I'd felt, her distorted, angry face. "She did seem to hate me," I said slowly.

"Because she got pregnant?"

"No, I don't think she blamed me for that. We used protection, I did anyway, it just didn't work. . . . No, maybe she thought I'd ask her to marry me. I don't know if she'd have said yes, but she would've liked me to ask."

"She would've said yes," Vivian said.

"I'm not so sure."

"Tim, get real! She'd rather go through nine months of pregnancy in her senior year?"

"That's nine months. If she married me, it would've been her whole life!"

Vivian laughed. "God, you're adorable. What a romantic! You would've split up in a year, but then she would've gotten child support, a whole lot of other things—"

"That seems like a fairly cynical view of women for a feminist," I said. "Out for what they can get."

"Just like men," Vivian countered. "Only in their own way. . . . I'm on the Pill, by the way. For someone who once knocked someone up, you seem pretty blasé about birth control."

"It's been so long," I said. "And I figured you were on something. I mean, you don't seem that self-destructive."

There was a silence. "Don't I?" Vivian said wryly.

"Not in that way." I half sat up. "What do you want? Do you want me to go back to my own room?"

"No, I'd like you to spend the night, but, just not necessarily to fuck our ears off, just because . . ."

"Would you be willing to spend it in my room?"

"Because of Mason?"

"Yeah." I decided to be as honest as I could. "I don't think I can be undivided totally, ever. He's just there, he's part of my life. I don't know how much emotional energy I have left, really."

"Isn't that an excuse?" But she didn't sound accusing, just questioning.

"In part, maybe. But I just mean I want you to know what you're getting into."

She began kissing me. "Impossible. It doesn't work that way. No one knows."

"Well . . ." We were sailing off again, I was starting to forget whatever it was we'd been talking about.

"We'll go in your room afterward," Vivian whispered as she stroked my body. "Is that okay?"

"It's okay."

But this time, after I came, I fell asleep about one second afterward, as though I'd imbibed some incredibly intoxicating, lethal drink. I dreamed about Cheryl. We were in my father's house, in my room, only Mason was there, and Cheryl would sometimes seem like herself, and sometimes turn into Vivian. My father was downstairs, sometimes with Margaret, sometimes with my mother. Then suddenly Cheryl grabbed Mason up from his crib and said, "This is what I really feel," and hurled him out the window. I sat bolt upright in bed, my heart pounding, frozen with terror. Mason was crying from the back room. For how long? I dressed hastily and went in to him.

He was lying on his back, kicking his legs, his face screwed up, red, ready to let out another scream, but when he saw me he stopped, his mouth open. "I'm sorry," I said. "I—just—"

Fumblingly I changed him. He was coated with shit. I wiped him off, put him in a clean stretch suit, and went into the kitchen to get a bottle. I sat in the living room, feeding him. The second he started guzzling, he went off into his own version of an orgasm, total, blissful, spaced-outedness. What a short memory he had. Or maybe he had just started to scream when I woke up. In one way I was glad he had awakened me. Or had it been the dream that had, trying to escape from it? I'd read once that you never dream your own death, that you always wake up before that happens. I think I couldn't have dreamed Mason's death either.

Vivian was still sleeping. She still had her own world, intact, and I couldn't help envying that.

Once Mason had finished eating, I put him in his playpen and lay down on the couch, hoping to fall asleep again. I knew if I left him alone he'd yell, and that if I stayed, he'd start his babbling sounds. But despite that, I managed to doze off. It was like hearing snatches of someone speaking a foreign language, too incomprehensible to be worth listening to. And I knew I didn't want to fall deeply asleep. Like Vivian, I had a feeling that dream might be lying in wait for me, ready to start up just at the point where Cheryl (or was it Vivian?) threw the baby out the window.

She came into the room just as I was waking up, a long T-shirt on, her hair unbrushed, tousled. It was strange. I really felt, though it didn't make sense from either direction, a sense of divided loyalties, that I should apologize to both of them for not being there as totally as I felt I ought to be.

"Have you been up long?" she asked.

"An hour or so . . . I heard him screaming."

"I'm glad—I mean that you could hear him, even from my room."

"He may have been screaming a long time. I had a dream that woke me up."

"What about?"

"Nothing special." I didn't feel like telling her because somehow she seemed implicated in it.

Vivian was looking at Mason. "So, what now?" she asked.

"About what?"

"I mean, was this a one-night stand? What was it? I just want to know." She had that edge to her voice again.

"I guess it can be whatever we want," I said, conscious of avoiding what she was really asking.

She sat down next to the couch. "Tell me what you want."

I glanced at Mason. He was wiggling his feet in the air and looked at me as though he, too, wanted to hear my answer. "The sex was great," I said. "I suppose I would . . . like more of that."

208

She laughed. "Only?"

"I don't want to hurt you, I don't want to be part of that pattern you were talking about, shredding women, all that."

"You're not a shredder, Tim."

"But I think what you said last night is true. You can't predict. Things do get out of hand . . ."

She looked stricken. "You think I can't handle it, I'll get hysterical, start screaming in the middle of the night—"

"What do you think? You know yourself better than I do."

She looked out the window, her face troubled. "I do want something. Part of me likes that you're not all there, whether it's really because of Mason or not. But also I'm just scared of a kind of neediness in me which always seems to be lurking there, beneath the surface."

"How about Fern and Lindsay?" I asked, moving away from that topic, because it seemed too tangled. "Wouldn't it be awkward if they know? Or would you want to do it so they wouldn't know?"

Vivian shrugged. "That doesn't bother me . . . Either way." She looked at Mason again. "Babies scare me. Their helplessness . . . Doesn't that get on your nerves?"

I smiled. "Well, I'd like him to get up, feed himself, sure—"

"No, I mean don't you ever feel angry, like you want to just hurl him across the room or something?"

I thought of the dream. "No, I don't think so." Was the dream about me, about my feelings, or about my fear of women's potentially erratic, even insane behavior?

Vivian sighed. "I'd hate to be your therapist, not that you'd ever go, but—"

"Why?"

"You're so cagey. I feel like you keep holding up verbal shields and foiling me, like I'm trying to get you with this sharp sword, and you won't let that happen."

I laughed. "If it's a matter of losing blood—"

"That's not the worst thing."

We let the conversation trail off without consciously resolving anything. That day I worked every minute Mason would let me, both while he was sleeping and while he wasn't. And that night Vivian, who'd gone out, reseduced me, or I reseduced her, and the next day was the same. I felt I'd been clear about what I felt my emotional deficiencies were, and it was up to her to decide what chances she felt like taking.

CHAPTER 18

Sunday night Lindsay returned from Boston. Vivian and I had fixed up the apartment, even vacuumed, taken down the garbage, done the wash. It was as though Lindsay were the mother whom we were afraid would somehow intuit what had been going on in her absence. Or maybe that was just in my mind.

"So, how'd it go with Kevin?" Vivian asked. She'd washed her hair and looked, I thought, beautiful, but clearly at some point over the weekend I'd lost the ability to be objective about that.

"I think it's over," Lindsay said flatly.

"Gosh, I'm really sorry," Vivian said. She sounded sincere.

"It wasn't that he met someone else," Lindsay said. "It's just . . . I think he just sees he has a lot of other options and

. . . well, we *are* young. He's right. Maybe in ten years we'll get back together, but to do it now would be too soon.''

"I agree," Vivian said. She glanced at me. "Don't you, Tim?"

"Yeah, basically." I was nervous that Lindsay would sense something between us.

She smiled in her friendly, sisterly way. "How'd it work out here?"

"My father came in. He had a really good visit."

"I met him," Vivian said. "He's such a sweetie. Like Tim, forty years later. Only Sandor was here, and he acted like *such* a pig! I was really ashamed."

Lindsay looked appalled. "I don't get it. You let Sandor come over? After all you've said?"

"I know," Vivian said. "He's gone for good now. We had a final blowout."

Lindsay made a wry expression. "Haven't I heard that before?"

"This time it's final. . . . No, seriously. I suddenly saw him through Tim's eyes, through his father's eyes, and I thought, 'This guy is an animal.' "

Lindsay raised her eyebrows. "So I guess it's celibacy for a while, huh?"

I looked at the carpet.

Vivian said, "What will be, will be."

For some reason Lindsay said, "Yeah? With who?"

"I think she just means you never know who you're going to meet," I intervened awkwardly.

"You never know," Vivian agreed. She let our eyes meet for a second.

But that night each of us slept in our own beds; I was relieved. I frankly wasn't sure what I could handle either.

In the week after Lindsay and Fern returned, I worked my head off. I'd let things slide; I had two papers due, plus two exams. I switched in political science from pass-fail to getting a grade; that, combined with dropping chemistry, helped but I still felt I was treading water, capable of going under.

Then Mason got the flu, or maybe just a bad cold. His temperature shot up to 105, then down, then up. At night he seemed to have trouble breathing, so I moved him into my room, even though I knew that would make my concentration a mess the next day. Then I got sick—either I caught his bug or just picked up one of my own. At that point he was almost back to normal, except for a strange, strangulated cough that worried me. I rarely have illness with fever, so when I took my temperature and found it was 102, I was surprised. I didn't have that many symptoms, just an overwhelming lassitude. In class I tried to take notes, and found I would doze off right in the middle. I borrowed someone's notes and then didn't have the energy to copy them.

By the weekend all I was fit for was feeding Mason and sleeping. Vivian looked into my room. "Tim, why don't you call a sitter? You look like death."

"I'll be okay," I murmured.

"Look, let me call a sitter for you. It's stupid. Do you want to get really sick? She can just handle things till Monday."

"Who would you call?" Janie had said she had to concentrate on studying now.

"Barnard has a service. . . . Let me."

"Just for tomorrow." When she left, I realized I was annoyed that she hadn't said, "Let me take care of Mason for you." It wasn't that much work, just a matter of feeding and changing him. *She didn't sign on for that. She made that extremely clear.* When she returned, that thought had drifted off into outer space. Vivian put her hand on my forehead. "You seem warm."

"My temp's down to one hundred." Her hand felt cool, comforting.

"Want me to pick up something for dinner? I've got to go to the library, but I'll be back later."

"I'm not really that hungry."

"You ought to eat something, soup at least. . . . Sleep well."

Toward evening, I felt worse. I still had no symptoms, but my fever was up again. The sheets on the bed seemed hot, but when I rolled the covers down, I started shivering. Vivian peeked in sometime during the late afternoon. "I think I hear Mason," she said. "Is it his dinner time?"

"Yeah, I better . . ." I tried to sit up, but the room began whirling around. I sat there for a few seconds, waiting for my sense of balance to return. "God, I feel like shit," I admitted.

She touched my forehead. "You're burning up, Tim! Did you take your temp?"

"It's a hundred and three."

"Then you shouldn't be handling the baby. Should I try and get a sitter for tonight?"

I lay back down again. The room moved, then settled into its accustomed place. "You couldn't—do you think you'd be willing to feed him? I think I can handle the rest, just keep an eye on him until he gets sleepy."

"What do I do?" Vivian looked alarmed. "I've never handled babies. I don't know anything about them."

"It's really not complicated. You just change him—there are fresh diapers in the spare room, and if he's a real mess, wipe him off and put some baby oil on his bottom. There are clean stretch suits in there, too."

"I hate the smell of shit," Vivian said, standing there hesitantly.

By now I could hear Mason's screaming as a steady, de-

214

manding roar. "No one loves it. It's not that bad. Just breathe through your mouth."

"I'm going to do a lousy job with the feeding part."

"Bring him in here, then, I'll show you."

"I'm just not good at this," Vivian repeated.

I felt annoyed beyond endurance. "Look, he's screaming. Either do it, or I'll do it."

I started trying to sit up again when she said, "No, I'll do it. You rest."

I lay down once more, thinking how much I used to love being sick when I was a child. My mother had certain days when she returned early from the library and those days, when I was sick, and had no school and my father was at the college, were about our only times alone together. She would fix a tray of food for both of us and carry it up to my room. Then she would sit at my desk, eating, while I ate off the bedside table. It was always ordinary food like cream of tomato soup and grilled cheese sandwiches, but there was something so enjoyable about my mother talking to me about her life, as though I were a grownup—at least that was how I perceived it. Usually she would ask about school and my friends and work, but on those occasions she just seemed curious about how my life was going, as though I were an interesting person she really wanted to know all about.

When she sensed I was getting tired, she would take the tray downstairs. Sometimes, if the sheets were hot, or damp from my having lain there a long time, she would make me go in and shower while she changed the bed. That was the most wonderful feeling, returning from a brief, hot shower, limp, and collapsing into a perfectly clean, cool bed that seemed to have some faint scent which my mother wore. She would bring a glass of ice water or orange juice and put it near the bed, then give me this special bell she had inherited from her grandmother, and tell me to ring it if I needed her, since she had to go downstairs to start dinner.

There were so many elements that made this magical: my father's absence, the bell, which was beautiful as an object— it was pewter and simply designed—the pleasure of ringing the bell, which I reserved for special occasions. The feeling it gave me was that I was a monarch in a small kingdom. Simply by ringing a bell, a beautiful woman would appear whose only pleasure, whose greatest pleasure, was serving me, making me feel better.

Going back to school, needless to say, was always a disappointment. So was my father's return at the end of the day, in part because my mother was no longer my sole property, but also because he would appear in the doorway and say heartily, "Well, Timothy, how's it going? Ready to bound out of bed yet?"

Maybe my father thought my mother was pampering me when I was sick. But I think he also felt that the reason he almost never got sick was because he wouldn't allow it. He was a great believer in long walks, cold showers, hot oatmeal in the morning. When I was sick, I always felt *he* regarded it as a sign of weakness, something I could have warded off if I'd been tough enough.

After what seemed like an incredibly long time, Vivian reappeared with Mason, a bottle in her other hand. "Jesus," she said, wrinkling her nose. "How do you stand it? The smell, everything. I thought I was going to pass out."

"You get used to it."

"He's so small. I couldn't believe how much shit there was! It was all over his back, even! Why can't they toilet train them at birth? Don't they do that in Japan or something?"

"Maybe at a year, not at birth. Are you up to feeding him?" I tried not to sound sarcastic, but she was making

216

such a production out of something I did a dozen times a day.

"I'll try. Will you watch me and see if I'm doing it right?" In a gingerly way she sat down in the ratty armchair I had in one corner of my room. Mason began drinking right away. Whether he sensed or cared that Vivian was a stranger wasn't apparent. Maybe he was too hungry to care. I closed my eyes. Vivian's dark hair fell forward, screening her cheek. Mason lay snugly in her arms. It was like a photo imprinted in my consciousness. *This is the way it ought to be—a woman taking care, the man just watching, helping.* I knew these were thoughts that were going to boomerang, ones that, if I hadn't been sick, I wouldn't have even let myself think, but it was like being sick as a child. In some primitive way I indulged the extreme pleasure of being cared for, as though I were both myself and Mason. I was being cared for because Vivian was helping me out, but Mason was also me, allowed to press up against a warm breast. Surely he could tell the difference.

"When does he stop?" Vivian asked. "He's practically down to the bottom."

"Don't let him start sucking in air. You can leave a little at the bottom. Pull it gently out of his mouth once he's done."

As soon as Vivian did this, Mason let out a piercing howl. "God, what's wrong?"

"Hold him up against your shoulder and walk around with him. He likes that."

I watched, eyes half-closed, while Vivian walked up and down the room, but Mason, instead of quieting down, just upped his screams a few decibels. Vivian approached my bed. "I don't think he likes me," she said mournfully.

"No, he can just get like that. Give him to me, okay?"

She handed Mason to me. The second he felt my hands on his body he stopped crying, just closed his mouth and settled down in the warmth of the bed next to me and looked up with an innocent smile.

"I don't have the right touch, I guess," Vivian said. "I'm an amateur. He can tell the difference."

"No, maybe he's just disoriented because I haven't been paying him much attention lately. Is that it, Mase? Feeling neglected, huh?" I grabbed ahold of his foot, a game he likes beyond almost any other. I pretend that I won't let go, that I'm going to bite his foot, and for some reason he finds that hysterically funny.

Vivian was still standing there, uncertainly. "Should I heat up the soup?"

"Why don't we wait until he goes down for the night? It might be simpler."

"Anything you say, boss." She gave a wave and left the room.

I decided not to worry about Mason's picking up my flu. I was now pretty sure that we had a version of the same bug. Anyway, he seemed so content just lying there, babbling, waving his arms in the air, and all I had to do was make sure he was secure in my bed. I didn't let myself fall asleep again, but I let images drift through my mind: Vivian sitting in the chair, Cheryl sitting in my lap, kissing my neck, womanly smells and soft hair touching my skin. It was less erotic than connected to those memories I'd just been having of my mother, or rather the two flowed together in a way I was too fuzzy to untangle.

At seven, Vivian took Mason again. As she lifted him up he let out a very brief howl, then subsided. "Men are un-fathomable," she said wryly, and carried him to the spare room.

"I'm going to shower," I said. "I think maybe I'd feel better—I'd feel a lot cooler."

When I returned to the room, Vivian had brought in the

soup and some crackers and cheese on a big tray. "Are you up to coming to the table?"

"I think I better eat in bed. Would you stay with me?"

She smiled in a tender, teasing way. "Of course I'll stay with you." She put her hand on my forehead. "You're much cooler. Maybe the fever's broken."

The soup tasted wonderful, even the dry crackers, crunching them up. And the glass of ice water was like the finest kind of champagne. I tried to tell her about how it had been when I was sick as a child. Vivian listened carefully. At the end she said, "I never had that. My mother was ill herself. There were always nurses looking after her. Now she's okay. But that was never her forte, looking after sick people or babies. Maybe that's why they make me so nervous."

"You did a great job."

"Thanks." She acted as though she were going to say something further, but didn't.

After we had tea and cookies, Vivian came over, kicked off her sneakers, and got into bed with me. "I'm not up to—" I began, but she said, "I just want to lie here, okay?"

"You might get my bug."

"I'll chance it." She curled herself around me and didn't speak again. We just lay there, entwined. It was comfortable, with none of the tensions or highs and lows of making love, just the feeling of someone being there. It was wonderful.

When Fern looked in some time later, both Vivian and I had fallen asleep. "Hey, I just wondered if you—" She stopped short, seeing us in bed together. "Oh, listen, I'm sorry. I didn't—"

"No, he's just sick," Vivian said sleepily, without even opening her eyes. "I've been taking care of him."

"She was helping me feed Mason," I faltered. "She got tired out."

Fern looked bewildered, probably more by our feeling we

needed to make excuses, than by whatever was going on. "I just wanted to say there's a great movie on at nine, if you feel like watching, *Kramer vs. Kramer*."

"I've seen it," I said as Vivian said, "It's dreck."

"I heard it was excellent," Fern said. "Well, anyhow, just wanted to let you know." She closed the door carefully behind her.

"Caught in the act," Vivian said, smiling.

"Not exactly."

"As good as. Do you feel like fooling around a little? Or are you too tired?"

I hesitated. "I am pretty spaced. Plus, I feel awkward, knowing she's in there."

"Why? She doesn't care."

"I do."

"Tim, you're so prudish sometimes! So, what do you want to do? Watch *Kramer vs. Kramer*?"

"I told you, I already saw it. . . . Why did you say it was dreck?"

"It was so unfair to the mother. She just vanishes without a word, then whisks back. I mean, in real life it's exactly the other way around—men vanish, women cope. Why don't they ever make a movie out of *that*? The guy would be *inundated* if he felt like it with offers to remarry. He earned a good living. What was the big problem? But you were supposed to feel so sorry for him."

"He wasn't inundated. Who inundated him?"

"I'm saying in real *life* he would have been! Most women melt into helpless pools at the sight of a baby or a little darling kid like that. Look, Moira's with my father because she felt so sorry for him when my stepmother died and left him with this six-year-old kid. And she's had to fight off a lot of would-be contenders."

Clearly she saw herself as superior to these innately maternal types. I felt irritated. "You think she *shouldn't* feel sorry for him?"

"If it were reversed, if *she* were left, what man would give a damn? My father just sees her as a potential mommy who'll help him out with his kid, fuck him occasionally, cook the odd meal. If it wasn't her, it would be one of a hundred other women."

This seemed like a personal attack. Was it prompted by her having helped out so minimally with Mason? "Are you talking about us? Because if so, you're wrong. I'm not looking for that from you or anyone."

Vivian sat up. "There's something tempting about it. I understand it. You looked so appealing lying in bed with him, I care about you a lot. And then I felt this horrible feeling, what a mistake that would be."

I wanted to say this was all her fantasy, but unfortunately I didn't feel it was. "That's not what I want."

She didn't speak. "But you come with him. You're a package deal."

"Yeah, but—"

"It's not you, Tim. What I thought was, 'What if I start liking this, what if I start getting attached to Mason?' He's kind of cute. I mean, it would be a nightmare!"

"Getting attached to a baby?"

"Yeah, with all that implies."

I reached up to pull her down next to me in bed. "I'm not a package deal," I said softly. "I'm just me . . . just the way you're you. I wasn't that different before I was a father."

"I feel so close to you at times, and then I get petrified," she whispered. Then we began kissing and sliding out of our clothes and even though I wasn't sure I had the energy, I couldn't resist being made love to by her.

Fern never came in to see if we wanted to watch *Kramer vs. Kramer*. At midnight, Vivian returned to her own bed.

CHAPTER 19

By the final week of classes I was better. But I had two make-up exams to take when I got back from Christmas vacation, and a long paper which I hadn't even begun to do the research for. Luckily the Taylor library would be open, because a lot of the books I needed were already checked out from the Columbia library.

Vivian was staying at her mother's. Or at least staying there part of the time. We agreed to speak over vacation. If someone had put a gun to my head and asked if we were in love, I honestly wouldn't have known what to answer. It was something important, it wasn't casual, and I had no clear image of where it was going. I knew she felt pretty much the same.

Mason and I were let on the airplane first. He was in his backpack, and I'd stuffed a lot of disposable diapers and jars of food and bottles in my carry-on bag, enough to last if we were delayed for several days. The flight itself was only an hour.

He was pretty well behaved on the plane. He decided he wanted to eat just as the stewardess was coming around with a snack, so I told her to come back later and devoted myself to feeding him, which, given his appetite lately, takes about three minutes. Literally the second you take the spoon out of his mouth, he's got it open again, like a perpetual motion machine.

"What a delightful little boy," the woman next to me said. She was middle-aged, friendly looking. "Is he yours?"

"Yeah, he's five months old."

"He looks much older. Look at all that hair! My daughter's baby is bald as a Ping-Pong ball, and he's almost a year. It makes such a difference. They look so much more human with hair."

"He was pretty small when he was born," I said, "but he's filled out a lot since then."

By now Mason had finished eating and let out a loud burp. "I can give him his bottle," the woman said, "if you want to have your snack."

"That would be great," I said gratefully. I felt ravenous. I handed Mason over to her; he accepted her with ease. Maybe he knew an experienced hand when he saw one.

"Is your wife traveling separately?" she asked.

I bit into the ham and cheese sandwich and hailed the stewardess to order a beer. "I'm not married," I said. "My girlfriend didn't feel she was ready for that."

The woman looked puzzled.

"Well," she said after a moment, "he's a lovely baby. I hope so much before too long you *will* meet, well, the girl you've been looking for, someone to help you—"

"I really think I'm doing fine on my own," I said defensively.

She patted my shoulder. "Believe me, it's easier with two. I'm speaking from experience. My first husband died and left me with two babies. I survived, but it was hellish. I didn't meet my second husband until they were both in high school, and those years were—I was frazzled. I worked, rushed home. Everything in my life was on hold."

"I think I can manage," I said.

At that, she suddenly smiled warmly. "I'm sure you can. But if someone appears, you won't refuse to even consider—"

I decided I didn't want to get entangled any further in the conversation. "My father's seeing someone," I said. "He's a widower. Was that the case with your second husband?"

"Yes." She looked away. "But, of course, everything has its problems. One has the idealized image of the dead wife to contend with unless, and no doubt this would have its own problems too, she was a true monster. My husband carried a photo of his first wife in his wallet for the first ten *years* of our marriage! Can you imagine?"

"Did he carry one of you, too?" I asked, bouncing Mason up and down on my lap. He was getting wet.

"Yes, the two of us." She laughed. "If people asked, he whisked out both photos and said, 'This is Helen, my first wife, and this is Janet, my second.' I learned to hold my tongue, and then one day I noticed her picture was gone. But ten years!"

"My father'll probably do it for thirty years," I said. "He adored my mother. But he's lonely, and—"

Again she laid a motherly hand on my shoulder. "Please don't give him a hard time the way my children did. They want you to be faithful forever. Unto death and beyond. They don't understand that it's a tribute to the person you were married to, to want to do it again.''

"I understand that," I said.

"I'm sure he feels guilty enough already."

I thought of my father and Margaret. He'd been so circumspect when he'd referred to her at Thanksgiving that I wasn't even sure what was happening. Marriage could be the furthest thing from his mind. They might not even be sleeping together. Maybe this was childish, but the image of my father as sexually active was too peculiar to me. Good friends was how I imagined it. Someone to go to the movies with and have dinner with from time to time. *No one will ever replace your mother in my life, ever.*

So it was a shock when I saw Margaret waiting at the terminal as I emerged from the plane with Mason sleeping in the backpack. I didn't see my father. "Hi, Tim!" she called out, waving. "Abner's at home. He's fixing dinner. He's so afraid you haven't had a decent meal since Thanksgiving, I think you're going to be force-fed for the next two weeks." We walked toward the baggage claim area. "How was the trip?" she asked. "Does Mason mind traveling?" I didn't think she'd ever seen him, but from the familiar way she spoke of him, I gathered he must be a frequent topic of conversation between herself and my father.

"No, he was fine." I was surprised that my voice sounded a little curt. Somehow I was taken aback at this, my father's making no remark in any of his recent letters about Margaret. Not that I assumed she had vanished into thin air, or that they'd stopped seeing each other, but there seemed to be something calmly proprietary about the way she referred to my father.

After we had picked up my bag and loaded everything into her car, she said, "I'll just drop you off. I thought you might want to spend the first few hours alone together."

Meaning that the rest of the time, we wouldn't? I had certainly had no fantasies about intimate tête-à-têtes with my father, but neither had I assumed that it would be the three of us sitting around the dinner table every night. "Thanks for picking me up," was all I said.

It was strange seeing our house again, even from the outside. Everything about Haysburg looked smaller, as though in just four months the houses had all shrunk. It looked like a toy village, almost a settlement. There was no one on the streets. Of course, the college kids mainly went home over Christmas, and a lot of the faculty visited relatives, but in Manhattan I was used to seeing a bustle of humanity at all times of day or night. The quiet was deafening.

I walked into our house, which was open. This, too, seemed peculiar, that there could even be a town like this in America, where people didn't bother locking their doors. And then, as I walked in, a thousand remembered smells assaulted me, too complex a mixture to sort out, smells of furniture, of food, of the walls. I felt as though even if blindfolded, I would have known in one second where I was. My father, hearing the door open, rushed out of the kitchen. He was wearing an apron! He hugged me and then reached for Mason. "Dad, he's asleep," I said. "Maybe I better just set him down somewhere."

"Right upstairs," my father said. "Come this way. Wait till you see what I've done!"

I followed him upstairs. He led me into the room that had been my mother's sewing room and study. It was a small room, and when she used it, it had always been cluttered with books and boxes of fabric. In the closet she kept stacks of construction paper and crayons, and I would sit on the floor, drawing elaborate scenes of battleships or dinosaurs, while her sewing machine hummed along. After her death, my father just closed the door. It seemed the equivalent of walling it up. And strangely, I had never opened it in all that time, as though obeying his superstition, or maybe just sharing some mutual desire to deny her death, or avoid dealing with it.

Now it had been transformed. All of my mother's things were gone, everything: the sewing machine, the books, the material. The room had been repainted pale blue, and now there was a crib in one corner, a rocking chair, a small painted toy box with several stuffed animals inside. For one startled moment I looked at him. Surely Margaret was beyond childbearing age? Her kids were in college, or even out of college, as I recalled. My father was beaming bashfully. "For Mason! How do you like it? Margaret and I painted it ourselves. The room was just sitting here, no use to anyone, and I thought . . . well, time to move on. How do you like it?"

I thought of the crowded room where Mason slept in my city apartment. "It's resplendent."

My father showed me how the side of the crib lowered. "Just put him in . . . Oh, and there are blankets and diapers and stretch suits in the closet."

"Dad, I *have* all that stuff."

"Yes, but I figured, why should you be constantly lugging things back and forth from one place to another? I enjoyed it."

After removing his snowsuit, I placed Mason gently on his stomach the way he likes to sleep. He kept on sleeping. There was a small light on in the room, which my father turned off. "How does the temperature strike you? I turned up the thermostat this morning. I think it should be at least 75°, don't you?"

Usually my father keeps our house temperature at about 50°. He considers anything warmer both a decadent waste of money and bad for your health. I remember winter mornings charging from bed into the bathroom, where at least the water was hot. "Well, thanks," I said, I hoped not grudgingly. When we got to the foot of the stairs I said, "My room you left as it was, I trust?"

"Sacred, of course," my father said. He walked toward the kitchen, turning to look at me inquisitively. "You're looking better, still too thin, but better."

"I was sick," I said. "A week or so ago."

"Sick?" He looked alarmed. "With what? You never mentioned it."

"I didn't want to get you excited. It was just a flu."

"Did you see a doctor?"

"Dad, it wasn't that big a thing. Mainly just exhaustion."

"Did you have a fever?"

"Yeah, for a few days."

"And what about Mason? How did you deal with that?"

"I got a sitter. And Vivian helped me. Remember her? The girl we had Thanksgiving dinner with?"

"Of course I remember her! Lovely girl . . . But that horrible man. She isn't still seeing him?"

"No, that's over."

My father glanced at me, I hoped not knowingly. "She deserved better," was all he said.

I sat in the kitchen watching my father cook. Even there, changes had been made. It had been painted a brighter yellow, there were new curtains, the garbage pail had been moved to some unseen place. "I'm cooking now," my father said. "I know that will anger you, all those years and I did nothing. I can't say I'm a master chef, but curiously I find it quite relaxing."

"I always did," I said.

"Did you?" My father peered into a large pot on the stove. "It seems shameful to me in retrospect. Imagine making a teenage boy do all the cooking! What was I thinking of?"

228

I smiled. "Forget it. At least now I know how . . . What's for dinner?"

"A lamb curry. I've gotten very inventive with spices. I even make my own chutney. Margaret gave me the recipe. Wait till you try it: apples, onions, a touch of turmeric . . ."

There was a pause. "So, Margaret isn't living here?"

My father flushed. "Living here? No. Who said she was?"

"No one. I just, well, wondered what your arrangement was."

My father looked so embarrassed I was almost sorry I'd asked, except I really wanted to know. "We, well, we do many things together, I think you could say we're a couple. We're regarded as a couple, not that what people gossip about matters, but yes we are. But she has her house which she's fond of, and neither of us wants to rush into anything. Why should we? Does it make you uncomfortable?"

I wasn't sure exactly what "it" referred to: that they were seeing each other at all, that they were regarded as a couple, that they might be sleeping together. "No, it's fine with me," I said.

My father's expression was conflicted. "Good," he said finally. "Margaret is very fond of you, Tim, but she has no desire to step into your mother's shoes. She has her own children, grown, of course, but still, what I'm saying is her maternal urge has been satisfied. She will not impose."

"Fine . . . Do you have a beer?" I really was thirsty, but also eager to escape from this conversation.

But my father still had his nervous expression. "You don't have any—"

I snapped off the beer can lid. "Any what?" Though I knew what he meant I still, in some weird way, enjoyed needling my father.

My father cleared his throat. He began fiddling with the

229

potholder. "I just wondered if any . . . Well, of course, it's none of my business."

"I guess I'd rather not talk about it," I said.

He retreated hastily. "Of course. No need to."

At seven Margaret reappeared, carrying a bowl of what she said was a coconut custard for dessert. She also brought a bouquet of flowers. The meal was excellent—my father really *had* turned into a good cook. In the middle of dinner Mason woke up. I went to change him and then brought him down for his dinner. My father and Margaret watched this procedure with fascination.

"It's really extraordinary," Margaret said. "He looks *exactly* like you, Abner! I can't get over it. Your eyes, your chin, even your expression."

My father looked delighted. "Really? I don't see it, myself."

"Oh, you have to!" she insisted. "Don't you see it, Tim?"

"In a vague way," I said.

My father was gazing at Mason with a slightly melancholy look. "I see something of Rebecca, just something. . . ." He trailed off.

During dessert my father brought a playpen up from the basement and put it near the table so Mason could lie there and watch us while we had coffee and the coconut custard.

"You know, I'm amazed at myself," my father said. "I never thought . . . I hate to say this, Tim, but when you were a baby, I didn't notice a thing. The whole experience passed me by. I couldn't have cared less. And now I feel like I could spend all day just looking at him."

"With one's own, one is too harassed," Margaret said. "It's only with grandchildren that one can relax enough."

My father sipped his coffee reflectively. "No, I wasn't harassed. I was oblivious. I never gave Tim a bottle, never

230

fed him, never changed him. I thought of all that as women's work. . . . What was wrong with me?"

Margaret gave him an affectionate, indulging glance. "You were a product of your time."

"I don't know if that's a sufficient excuse."

I smiled. "Anyway, I seem to have survived."

"Only because your mother did such an extraordinary job. . . . No, but what I'm saying is I missed out. I thought I was avoiding something onerous, tedious. I was blind."

I sighed. "A lot of it *is* onerous and tedious."

"Yes," Margaret said. "Don't go to the other extreme, sweetie. Tim's right. Getting up at night, trying to blow their noses when they're sick, the scary illnesses . . ."

My father accepted this. "Yes, there I go, idealizing as always."

What zinged out at me in this exchange was not my father's changed attitude toward babies, or being a grandfather, but Margaret's casual "sweetie." My mother always called my father either Abner, or "dear." Sweetie seemed more intimate somehow. Could you call anyone sweetie whom you weren't sleeping with? What does he call her? Can I take it if my father starts using expressions like sweetie? I'm not sure.

I had a sudden image of my father marrying Margaret, and me giving him away, the way fathers of the bride usually give them away. *Let them sweetie each other into eternity. What could be better? Let her inherit all his peculiarities and obsessions. It lets you off the hook. It's perfect.* I was surprised at the discomfort I felt. I decided it must have something to do with a final severing with my mother, a final, absolute recognition that she was gone and would never come back. It had been almost seven years, and yet that thought still had the ability to pierce me through and create such a sense of desolation that I sat there, almost immobilized.

"Did you like the room upstairs?" Margaret asked. I wondered if she sensed what I was feeling. I always have the feeling women can, somehow. "Pale blue seemed a bit cliché," she continued, "but I thought it was a warmer color than just white."

"It looks terrific," I said, maybe a shade too heartily.

"My daughter and her husband live so far away," Margaret went on, "in California, and I so rarely see my grandchildren. I think Abner is luckier than he knows."

"I *know* I'm lucky," my father said, giving her a fond glance.

Maybe it was just that I was so totally unused to seeing my father happy. Not that he'd undergone a total personality transformation, but the image of him that was fixed in my mind was the brooding, taciturn widower, sitting silent at his desk, staring off into space, not hearing me when I called him to dinner, or glancing up with an expression so blank and despairing it made my insides contract. Now—could it be?—he seemed a trifle smug, almost self-satisfied. Was it Margaret, or Mason, or some mysterious combination of the two?

I had always worried about forming an attachment to a girl, how my father would react, his being overcritical, finding her not up to his impeccable standards. Whereas now I felt I could bring home a two-headed girl with purple hair, and he would just say indulgently, "A lovely girl, Tim. I'm so glad you found someone."

Okay, admit it. You miss the way he used to be. Perverse and nonsensical as it is. And also, in a much milder way, I missed Margaret as she used to be. You could say this was a perfect extension of her former role in my life, a surrogate mother, suggesting books for me to read, seeming to enjoy my company. But before, she was comfortably sexless, a plump, graying, tired but basically genial woman whose only

232

function in life seemed to be to sit behind the desk in the library and check out books. It seemed to me that she also looked different. Was she tinting her hair, or maybe dressing more elegantly? Of course, here she was at someone's house for dinner, not at her job, but I noted her rose-colored dress, her gold pin. There was a definite feeling that some effort had been made, even, in the most mild way, a certain bantering flirtatiousness in the way she both looked and spoke to my father. *So? What's the big deal?*

After dinner, my father and I took Mason up to his room. He seemed at home or maybe just exhausted from the trip. Then we went downstairs and played some records on the stereo. My father sat, his eyes closed, in his favorite armchair. There was a fire in the fireplace. Margaret read a novel she had brought along. I took out one of my textbooks and half read at it. I was tired from traveling, or maybe from all the complicated reactions I was having to the new arrangement. I would read a sentence, go on to the next, and then realize I had no comprehension whatever of what I had just read. I gazed around the room instead, the familiar shabby, comfortable furniture. I was glad their nesting instincts hadn't yet attacked the living room. All the furniture was the kind that Goodwill might even hesitate to bother carting away, but I liked it, I was used to it.

Margaret glanced up at me and smiled warmly. "You look exhausted, Tim. Why don't you turn in? It's ten thirty already. Traveling is so tiring."

"I might," I said. "I've been sick, and I think I'm still not quite back to normal."

"Sick, and he didn't even tell me," my father said, opening his eyes.

"He didn't want to worry you," Margaret said. "You know how you are, Ab." She glance back at me. "I had a cold or flu or something last month, and you should have

233

seen him! Homemade chicken soup! I think you were a Jewish mother in another life.''

Okay, this is it, all I can take for one evening. First sweetie, now Ab. Then the image of my father making homemade chicken soup! *If I hear any more, I may become ill in another way!* I started up the stairs.

"Oh, Tim," my father called. "Don't feel you have to get up to feed Mason in the morning. I'd be glad—"

"Whatever," I said, yawning.

My room, also, had been allowed to remain the same. It looked a lot neater than it had while I was in high school, but probably that was because most of my stuff was in New York, and some had been stored in cartons in the attic. I had saved back issues of Spiderman comics in hopes that someday they would vastly increase in value. I got into bed slowly, half mechanically because I was so tired, but also looking at the room the way I had looked at my father. Had it changed, or had I changed? It seemed familiar, but also, in some indefinable way, alien.

I'd thought I would fall instantly asleep, as I used to before Mason was born, but somehow the mattress seemed lumpy. The room too warm. I got up to open the window, then tried to settle down again. Sometime around midnight I heard Margaret's voice saying, "I'll check the thermostat." After that there were just indistinct murmurings, but one salient fact imbedded itself in my consciousness: Margaret was spending the night, as no doubt she had before.

When the house became silent again, it seemed ominous. *This is dopey*, I argued with myself. *As Vivian would say: get real! What do you expect? They're in their fifties, people do it until they're ninety sometimes. Why should you care?* I felt like it was too sudden, as though my father should have had more respect for my feelings. *What does that mean? He tried to tell you over Thanksgiving. You're not twelve years old anymore. They're giving each other some comfort, some pleasure.* I started thinking of the evening I'd been sick, and how Vivian had gotten into bed with me and we'd just lain there snuggled together in a way that didn't seem sexual, the way animals must burrow next to each other in caves, not just for physical warmth, but for some sense of connection, being together. Suddenly I wanted to will Vivian into my room, beam her down, the way they used to do on *Star Trek*. Vivian in Haysburg? I could imagine her dry, sardonic comments as we drove through the main street and she started meeting some of the denizens of the town. *So, what do you do at night here? Where are the movies? . . . Well, about half an hour away there's a place that shows six movies at once. . . . No, I mean, where are the foreign movies? Where are the revival houses?*

I touched my body pretending my hands were Vivian's but, needless to say, it wasn't quite the same.

CHAPTER 20

At breakfast only my father was there, sipping his coffee. He had awakened early to get Mason up. Actually, I'd heard Mason wake up and then had heard my father pattering in there and had thought, What the hell, sleep late if you feel like it. It felt wonderfully decadent to get up at eleven, really well rested. Over breakfast I yawned. "It's funny," I said. "I slept twelve hours and I still feel sleepy."

"You were ill. Rest as much as you can while you're here. You need it."

"I have a lot of work."

"Don't push that, Tim. You must think of your physical well-being first of all."

Even though it's clear my mother's hemorrhage was a medical "accident," one of those unexplained things that happens occasionally, and doesn't make sense even after it's over, my father is convinced that it was because she'd had pneumonia several months earlier and had gone back to work almost immediately. "I couldn't reason with her," he would say. "She insisted. But I should have. She was run down."

My father had fixed fried eggs the way I like them, bacon, hot muffins. Half innocently I asked, "Where's Margaret?"

Instantly my father looked abashed. "Oh, she—she works today and . . . she'll meet us later at Charlie and Maureen's for dinner—do you mind that? They're so eager to see you."

"It's fine," I said. "How are they?"

My father lowered his voice. "Well, it's been a difficult fall for them. I didn't want to mention this, but it seems that Joely, their daughter, you know—the one you took to the prom—well, she's having some sort of problem with her sexual identity."

I tried to look surprised. "You mean she's gay?"

My father sighed. "Well, she says that, but of course she's so young, how can she tell? She hasn't given men a chance! If she'd had some bad experience, one could understand it, but—"

"Dad, some people are born that way."

"Nonsense!" my father cried. "What does that mean? Men are born men and women are born women. The other way doesn't make sense. No, it's just a way of rebelling, of causing them distress. She deliberately left a letter around for them to see, a love letter from another woman. You can imagine how they feel. Charlie especially! He's devastated."

"I *can* imagine," I said dryly.

My father was staring out the window. "You were a cause of concern to me about many things," he said, "but at least not that. At least I was spared that."

I was onto my second muffin, slathering it with strawberry jam. I looked at Mason playing in his playpen. "I don't care what Mason is," I said. "It couldn't matter less to me."

My father looked horrified. "That's an absurd thing to say!

Of course you would care. Tim, don't try to provoke me just for the sake of it. You want him to have a happy, normal life. Every parent does."

"Maybe I define that differently than you do. Maybe 'normal' doesn't mean as much to me. Or maybe I think there are more ways to be normal than you do." I was getting angrier than seemed worth it.

My father's lips tightened. "Well, this is a profitless discussion," he said. "I just wanted you to know, but also, please, *not* to refer to it in any way. I believe Joely will be there, hopefully not with her female friend. But if she is, just treat it as an ordinary event."

I laughed. "That's what I think it is, so I don't think I'll have a whole lot of trouble. . . . How was Mason this morning? I appreciated the chance to sleep late. Thanks." I wanted to get him on another topic. My father can be like a bulldog with a bone once he gets onto a subject that concerns him, and about as unyielding and stubborn.

"He is wonderful!" my father exclaimed. "What a child! I've never seen him cry."

"Dad, you have so. You've seen him cry lots of times."

"Only for perhaps one second, if he's hungry. But the moment he sees me, you ought to see his face! What a smile! He just lies there, lets me change him. Where did he get that kind of sunny disposition, that sense of trust for people? Not from you or me, that's certain. Even Margaret noticed it. He's not her grandchild, but she said she'd never seen a more winning, delightful baby in her entire life."

I gave up. "Yeah, well, I think he's pretty good."

My father stood up to clear. "Tim, I know this is none of my business, but I think it would be good if you were to give your little friend from high school a call."

For one second my mind went blank. Little friend? "Cheryl?"

"I see her from time to time. She has a job in Joe's Phar-

238

macy, and, well, she has such a wistful air, such a sweet little face. I think it would mean so much to her if you called.''

"What for?" I felt instantly wary.

"I'm sure she'd like to see Mason, how he's progressing. How can one deny that to her?"

"It might just be painful."

"That's for her to decide. . . . But for you to show her there were no hard feelings."

I sighed. Only there are, on both sides. "I'll think about it," I said. I really thought my father was wrong, that the last thing in the world Cheryl would want would be a rehashing of a painful memory which maybe, by now, she'd buried or at least come to terms with. And frankly, I didn't feel that eager to see her: there were a lot of ugly scenes I felt I'd just as soon let sink beneath the surface. But my father's comment inadvertently opened up a Pandora's box of memories, some erotic, some neutral: Cheryl in her bikini at the beach after she'd given birth, Cheryl and Henrietta having dessert with me and my father that evening after the movies.

Since my father's classes were over until January, and he seemed so eager to baby-sit, I decided to take him up on it. I went for a long walk, one of the kind I used to take in high school, into the woods. It had snowed, and then the snow had thawed so the ground was covered with a hard thin sheet of ice. I saw some kids ice-skating down at the lake. Parents always worried that the ice wasn't thick enough, but as soon as December came, kids were down there. It was a windless cold, and I had my hooded parka and gloves. Despite that, the air bit into my skin, and I realized my lips were getting chapped and dry. I passed by Joe's Pharmacy. My father hadn't said when Cheryl worked there. Probably he had some Vaseline at home. I stood, jumping from foot to foot to keep warm. Then I pushed open the door.

I saw Cheryl as soon as I entered the store. She was behind the counter helping a customer. Even then I hesitated, began looking through the magazines that were placed near the entrance. *Jerk. Get moving. You don't have to invite her over. Do whatever you feel like.* I approached the counter slowly, feeling like my feet were weighed down with lead. Cheryl was behind the cash register. She didn't see me until I was right in front of the counter. When she looked up and saw my face, her mouth dropped open. "Tim?" she said in a questioning voice, as though I might be someone else.

"Hi," I said. "It's really cold out there."

"Yeah. It was warmer last week, but now it's awful again."

I remembered how she hated the cold, how she got goose pimples in bed unless I covered her with a blanket, how we always made love under a sheet. "I wanted some, uh, Vaseline . . . No, Chap Stick. Do you have any?"

"Sure." She disappeared in one direction and came back with it. "How's college?" she asked, seemingly lightly.

"Well, it's . . . pretty hard. A lot of studying. And the city is—I'm not that used to it. I'm getting used to it, but—" It was as though I were back in high school, insanely inarticulate about the smallest things.

She was ringing the purchase up. "Yeah, well, high school was bad enough. Do you want anything else?"

I remembered the dinner at Charlie and Maureen's and went over and selected a two-pound box of chocolates. "We're going over to Charlie and Maureen's tonight, my father and Margaret Hansen and myself."

Cheryl was holding the box of chocolates. She was still incredibly pretty, especially looking down that way, her long dark lashes, her faintly pink cheeks. "Your father's going with her, isn't he?"

"Kind of."

"My mother thought they were married."

"No, just . . . for company." I cleared my throat. "I was wondering, well, I don't know if this would interest you, but would you want to come over and see Mason? He's at my father's, and if you wanted—" Where else would he be?

I had no idea what was going through Cheryl's head in the long silent moment in which she gazed at me. "Could I bring someone?"

"Sure," I said, assuming she meant Henrietta or her mother.

She looked me right in the eyes. "I'd like to bring my fiancé," she said, underlining the word "fiancé" with proud, defiant emphasis.

"Sure," I said. I hesitated a moment. "Who is he?"

"Harry Tyson," she said.

I reached for the package. "That's great news," I said. "I hadn't heard, but then my father doesn't pick up on things that much."

Cheryl blushed. "We just decided last month. The wedding won't be until the spring, so we can have time to get ready."

"Right." Maybe I was too stunned and perplexed to be making much sense, but still I wondered: why did she need six months to "get ready"?

Cheryl was still staring at me, seeming to want to fire a final salvo. "Do you have a girlfriend?" she asked.

I shrugged. "Well, kind of, yeah . . . Not in that . . . I mean, we're not . . . ."

She smiled, clearly enjoying my discomfiture. "What time would be good for us to visit?"

"Tomorrow morning, around eleven?" Tomorrow was Saturday.

"I'll ask Harry, but I think that would be fine," she said. Again I detected a certain pride in the way she emphasized, "I'll ask Harry."

"Great. See you then." I gathered up my purchases and left.

241

Harry Tyson? Harry was the son of Joe, of Joe's Pharmacy. I'd say he must have been thirty, early thirties, a short, thin man with glasses and an oddly bald head. Just as I could only picture Margaret behind the library desk, stamping out books, I had Harry Tyson fixed in my mind behind the pharmacy counter, jotting down prescriptions or repeating doctors' phone numbers in his firm, monotonous voice. I don't know why, but I'd always assumed he was a permanent bachelor type, not gay, not even necessarily celibate, but there was something dry about him that made it hard to imagine his falling for Cheryl or, needless to say, her falling for him. But looked at coldly, it was a step up for her economically. The store did well, his family was respected in town. And love is blind, right? Did it make less sense than me and Cheryl, or me and Vivian for that matter? Still, on the way home, I kept twirling it around in my mind, scenes of the two of them in the back room, Cheryl giving him one of her innocently sultry glances, him clearing his throat and working up the courage to say, "Miss Banks, I wondered if by any chance . . ." But that was as far as I got, or maybe as I wanted to get. It was impossible to imagine Harry Tyson in bed with Cheryl, or with anyone else, for that matter.

Still, it was a disturbing thought.

When I got home, Mason was asleep. My father was working in his study. I peered in. "Have a good walk?" he asked.

"Yeah, it's pretty cold out. I took your advice, by the way."

He looked amused. "About what?"

"I invited Cheryl over to see Mason tomorrow morning." I hesitated. "She's bringing her fiancé."

My father looked startled. "Fiancé? Who is he?"

242

"Harry Tyson."

"No! Harry Tyson? Why, he's thirty-five if he's a day."

"Dad, I'm not planning the marriage. She seemed pretty pleased about it."

My father was shaking his head. "Don't tell me *he* knocked her up, too! Didn't that girl learn *anything*?"

"There's no evidence that she's pregnant, not that I asked. She said the wedding wasn't until spring, so I would doubt—"

My father was still shaking his head in disbelief. "So she nailed Harry Tyson, did she? Well, really, not such a bad choice, now that I think of it. A stable, hard-working man. Probably always wanted a family. They'll have six kids before the decade is out."

I shrugged. "Maybe."

My father smiled. "You see what you drive women to, Timothy."

"Not exactly."

"The rebound! The rebound! But, as I say, why not? Who cares about the motives? Let them be happy! We don't bear any grudges."

That was big of him. Why should *we* bear grudges? "I hope they're happy," I said.

"She wasn't right for you," my father said, "wasn't your equal in any way. It would never have worked, but I will always, in some corner of my heart, cherish Cheryl Banks for giving us Mason."

"She didn't exactly *give* him to us," I said. Had he forgotten the court case?

Suddenly my father looked at his watch. "We're due at Charlie and Maureen's in an hour. You're going to change, aren't you?"

"If you think I should. Are we picking up Margaret?"

"No, she'll come by for us. She doesn't mind night driving and I hate it, as you know."

I changed into my good slacks, a fresh shirt, and a jacket. A tie seemed superfluous.

CHAPTER 21

Nothing seemed changed at Charlie and Maureen's. He still looked ruddy-faced and genial, she warm and maternal. Peg wasn't pregnant, but Sylvia was, and her three tiny children were running around making a racket. From the way Charlie greeted my father and Margaret, I could tell he was glad they were a couple. "Look at you!" he said, kissing Margaret on the lips. "What a beautiful color." Margaret was in a bright purple dress. "You look splendid, my dear. What are you doing with an old codger like this fellow?"

Margaret smiled. "Thanks. I hesitated, the color seemed so bright, but then I figured, what the heck."

"You should wear it all the time. It makes your eyes look like violets. . . . Make her wear purple every day, Abner."

My father smiled. "You think women obey everything we say so readily?"

Charlie winked at Margaret. "Sure they do, if you treat them right. Is he treating you right, my dear?"

"Perfectly," Margaret said with a trace of irony.

Everyone rushed over to look at Mason as I put him on the couch and got him out of his snowsuit. "Oh, what a darling," Maureen said. "Look at him! Look at him, Charlie!"

"I'm looking, I'm looking. The spitting image of you, Timothy, my boy."

"I think he looks just like Abner," Margaret said.

Maureen bent down to pick Mason up. "And just a trace of Rebecca, in the eyes."

Evidently Cheryl's genes had vanished without a trace, although I saw them clearly in Mason's long dark eyelashes and rounded pink cheeks. My father reached for Mason. "The friendliest baby you'll ever see," he said. "Where did he get that disposition?"

"Search me," Charlie said. He looked at me. "Now, I ask you, Tim, did you ever expect this geezer here to turn into such a marshmallow as a grandpa?"

"I can't resist him," my father said. At that moment Mason reached out and playfully grabbed my father's nose. "Hey, watch that! He's got quite a grip. This is my nose, not a removable object."

"No," Mason said, patting it.

My father's face lit up. "Did you hear that? He said it! He said 'nose.'"

Charlie laughed. "He did? I didn't hear him. Say it again, Mason."

Maureen said chidingly, "That's how they begin, darling. Here you've had three children and three grandchildren, and you can't remember a thing."

Charlie tapped his head. "Soft up here. Okay, Abner, I'll take your word for it. The child's a genius."

246

Suddenly I noticed Joely wasn't there. I remembered the conversation I'd had with my father. "Is Joely around?" I asked.

Charlie looked just slightly uncomfortable. "She and Courtney are off ice-skating. They said they'd be back by the time it got dark."

Maureen sighed. "I get so worried about the children going down there before Christmas. The ice isn't thick enough. But they promised to stay close to shore."

"Oh, I wouldn't worry," Margaret said. "It's well lit. And I think someone is down there, keeping guard."

My father held Mason, which was fine with me. Clearly he enjoyed it, Mason was happy, and it was nice not to have to carry him everywhere or worry about him. I followed Maureen into the kitchen.

"Having any time to cook?" she asked, peeking at the turkey.

"Not much. He keeps me pretty busy. Plus studying. It's a tough school."

"Oh, I can imagine." She began stirring some gravy on the stove. "Are you enjoying it, though?"

"Yes. It took me a while to get used to the city, but now I like it."

She frowned. "Is it safe? One hears such terrible stories!"

"I think it is during the day. And I found a good daycare place for Mason, so I don't worry about him during the week. It's weekends that can be tricky."

She was looking at me with her lovely, sympathetic blue eyes. "Abner says you're living with three girls. That must be a help."

I smiled. "Not really. I mean, we each have our own room. Baby care isn't included in the rent."

"Oh, but how can they resist? If I had him around, I'd be tempted to spend all day just playing with him."

"They're in school, too. Their schedules are as tough as mine."

Maureen sighed. "Yes, modern girls. They're not the same. They have so many other things on their minds."

She hesitated and then looked up at me. "I heard Cheryl is getting married . . . to Harry Tyson. Had you heard about it?"

I nodded. "I ran into her today at the pharmacy. She told me."

"How do you feel about it?" Maureen's voice was lowered, tentative.

"Well, it seems a little fast. And he doesn't seem her type. But then, I guess I wasn't either."

Maureen opened the oven door again. "It's a good, wise choice. He'll take good care of her; he's an honest, respectable man. Romance only goes so far."

"I guess he just seems old to me." I wondered why I was pursuing this.

"Old? No, hardly. Harry must be . . . thirty-three, thirty-four."

"Cheryl's just eighteen."

"Oh, that doesn't matter. My mother was twenty years younger than my father, and you never saw a happier marriage. He's lucky. Cheryl's lovely. I'm always struck by that when I drop in at the pharmacy. Skin like velvet. And if you look at her parents, you can't help but wonder where that came from. . . . Do you mind?"

I shook my head.

"I don't think she would have been right for you, Tim," Maureen said. "But some day you'll find the right girl. Don't worry."

"I'm not . . . Can I help you?"

"Yes, I was just waiting for Joely, but I think I hear them now. Here, why don't you take in the rolls and butter?"

248

Dinner was even more hectic and noisy than ever, with toasts and jokes, and gravy spilled on the good lace tablecloth. I put Mason in his highchair, which we'd brought in the car, and placed him at the end of the table, between my father and myself. He appeared to be in high good humor.

Courtney and Joely sat side by side at my end of the table. Clearly they were being presented not as a couple, but as friends. And it would have been hard to tell the difference. I wondered if Joely would make any physical gestures, but she didn't. Maybe she didn't want to add to Charlie's discomfiture. It was enough just to have Courtney accepted as part of the family.

"It's so funny to think of you as a daddy," Joely said to me. "You still look about twelve years old."

"Thanks," I said wryly.

"I don't know how you do it," she went on. "I've been working my ass off and just pulling in C's."

"Yeah. I've been having a hard time, too," I said.

"In what way?" my father said, pricking up his ears. "Your grades are all right, aren't they?"

I knew if I said anything, he would go off just like a rocket. "It's just a lot harder than high school. Here, you could sleep your way through classes and do fine. There, some of the lecture classes have a thousand kids. No one knows who you are. You aren't given any special attention."

"Well, that's the real world," Charlie said heartily. His white hair had fallen onto his forehead. "I want to make a toast. First, to Margaret and Abner, then to Timothy and Mason, to Sylvia and Mack's new baby to be, and, of course, to myself."

Everyone clinked glasses and drank. My father had brought three bottles of German white wine, as he always did. I thought of last year with him getting combative and irritable, me stalking off on a walk, Joely running after me, Mason only existing in Cheryl's womb. I suppose that last transformation seemed the most miraculous, that now he really existed, that out of a bunch of teenage fumblings had come this actual person who perhaps already, in some unconscious way, was forming memories and impressions of everything. I glanced at him, realizing he probably needed to be changed. I got up and pushed the highchair tray outward, unbuckling the belt that held him in place.

"I have to change him," I said. "I'll be back in a second."

"Let me help you," my father said, leaping up.

"That's okay, Dad. I can do it."

But he followed me into the living room, where I'd deposited Mason's carry cot and some diapers. He just stood there, watching intently as I changed Mason. "That rash of his seems to have completely cleared up," he said.

"Yeah, I think that cream really worked. Can you keep an eye on him while I take this away?" I took the soiled diaper and the cotton balls soaked in baby oil into the kitchen, dumped them into the garbage, and returned. My father was gazing down at Mason, wiggling his tie at him while Mason tried to yank at it.

"Look out," I said. "He can pull pretty hard."

"Oh, I can take it," my father said. "I'm a tough old bird, just like that turkey."

We returned to the table. Margaret seemed to fit right in at Charlie and Maureen's. I didn't even think of it until dessert time, when she brought out a mincemeat pie she'd baked. Watching her and Maureen come into the dining room simultaneously looked like a familiar scene. Margaret is much smaller than Maureen, and less pretty, but there was something of Maureen's homey friendliness in the way she said, "Abner has to have the first piece. He made the mincemeat for me."

"No!" Charlie roared. "I won't touch it then."

Clearly he was just joking, but Margaret said indignantly, "Abner's a fine cook. He was just out of practice."

"I'll say," Charlie said. "Remember that beef stew you cooked for my birthday, Abner? I was sick as a dog for a week afterward."

"Now, Charlie," Maureen said. "This smells absolutely delicious to me. Give me a big piece, Margaret. I love mince pie, and I just never quite got the hang of it."

"It takes patience," my father said. "You have to chop everything very fine: apples, orange peel—"

Charlie took a bite. "Don't reveal your culinary secrets, old man. You may tempt me into trying to best you."

"I'd like to see *that*," Maureen said dryly.

It was ten thirty when we set off for home. Mason had fallen asleep in his carry cot. He didn't wake up when I put his snowsuit on, just let himself be stuffed into it like a floppy doll. I carried him out to the car while my father carried the cot. Margaret got in front to drive, and my father sat next to her. I sat in the backseat next to Mason, my hand resting on Mason's foot, steadying the cot.

"What a lovely family," Margaret said wistfully.

"Yes, well, they've had their troubles, like all of us," my father said. "But whenever Charlie goes trumpeting off, Maureen manages to bring him down to earth again. Without her, lord knows what kind of life he would have had."

Sometimes I think of my father like a symphony: there are certain refrains and counterpoints that come up again and again, depending on the occasion. One of them is that men without women are helpless wrecks, destined to drift through life without human connections, but, once redeemed by a "good woman," they can put their shoulders to the wheel and get on with it.

"I'm sure if he hadn't met Maureen, he'd have met someone very like her," Margaret said in her sensible way. She was wearing sheepskin gloves as she drove. "Men don't remain single long around here."

"Like her?" my father said. "Never! How could that be? Maureen is special, just as you are, my dear. I never understand what people mean when they make a remark like that, as though people were just stamped out of cookie cutters. There's no such thing."

Margaret gave him a quick, fond glance. "You have a romantic streak."

I'd thought my father would deny this. "Every man does," he said. "It just takes the right woman to bring it out."

I had expected Margaret to get out with us, but she just stopped her car in front of the house, let us out, and called, "See you tomorrow."

"She has to be at the library in the morning," my father explained, or half explained, as we proceeded slowly up the driveway. "A lot of paperwork. They're piling administrative duties on her and, I fear, taking advantage of her good nature. Just the way they did with Rebecca. I've told her: Make them at least pay you more."

We were inside the house, which my father had left at a comfortably warm temperature. I realized his comment didn't really explain why Margaret wasn't staying over. But I gathered sometimes she did, sometimes she didn't. And perhaps when I wasn't around, he stayed at her house. I had never seen it, though I knew the part of town it was in.

I carried Mason upstairs and put him in his crib. In the dim light I took off his snowsuit. He slept through the whole thing, as he always does. Maybe my father was right. There was something amazingly trusting about the way he let you do whatever you wanted with him, the way he snuggled into the arms of strangers, as though he expected nothing but goodness and friendliness from the world. I didn't want to become sickeningly fatuous like my father, but alone in the bedroom I allowed myself a few moments of quiet pride as I contemplated him.

As I was leaving the room the phone rang. My father answered it, then called upstairs. "Tim! It's for you."

I went into my father's bedroom and picked up the phone. "Hi," Vivian said. "It's me."

"Oh, hi." I waited one second and then there was a click as my father put down the receiver. "How are you?" I felt absurdly excited, just hearing her voice.

"Okay. I'm still at the apartment, but I'm going to my mother's tomorrow. It's silent as a tomb here."

I thought of the night before. "I miss you," I said impulsively. "Last night I pretended I was Mr. Spock and beamed you down into my bedroom."

"To what purpose?"

"Guess."

She sighed. "I know. It's the same with me. I don't want to betray my feminist principles by saying anything horribly slushy, but I'd give anything if you were here right now."

I looked at my father's clock. "It won't be too long," I said. "My father has a woman friend who sleeps over. I guess I was getting jealous or envious. At any rate, I'm having some kind of complicated reaction."

"Oh, all your reactions are complicated!" she said with a laugh.

"He's in his fifties. Shouldn't *I* be the one who's sneaking someone into bed with me?"

"Your time will come."

I sat there looking out at the cold, dark night. "Why don't you drive down and visit me?"

"Would you really want me to?"

"Sure."

"But I'll strike everyone as unbelievably weird."

"They'll strike *you* as unbelievably weird. No, it'd be great. I could show you the town, all my favorite walks." Since there was a silence I said, "But I guess it's a pretty long drive."

Vivian hesitated. "I'd like to, in a way. Maybe after Christmas? The twenty-seventh or eighth?"

"We could go back to school together." I was feeling elated at the prospect.

"Well, let's speak again." Her voice lowered. "Love you," she said in that quick, you-don't-have-to-take-this-too-seriously way she had.

"Same here."

I hung up wondering if I'd been foolishly impulsive, which is exceedingly rare with me, or had possibly done something sensible.

CHAPTER 22

When I got into bed that night I slept like a log and awoke refreshed and calm. It was only as I was showering before breakfast that I remembered Harry and Cheryl's visit at eleven, and a slight, uneasy sense of foreboding glazed over my good humor. I went downstairs after getting dressed and found my father reading in front of the fire with Mason, obviously fed and contented, in his playpen.

I went over to him. "Hey, remember me? The guy who's been taking care of you all these months?"

He gave me that lopsided, delighted grin which said: How could I forget? Then he put his hands over my ears, a game he likes, while I put my hands over his ears. "All quiet on the western front?" I asked my father.

"Excellent." He stood up. "I'm going to the college for

255

an hour or two. Is that okay? See you around one, I imagine.''

I couldn't tell if he remembered Cheryl and Harry were coming or not. I suspected not, and decided not to remind him. Somehow it seemed easier to deal with them without my father's input.

But once he had left, the house seemed curiously, ominously quiet. There are times when you look around at a very familiar room and all the objects take on a slightly surreal quality. Maybe this just comes from staring at them too hard. I looked at Mason playing in his pen. He was freshly changed, and dressed in a clean, light blue terrycloth playsuit my father had bought for him. I tried to see him through Cheryl's eyes, and it seemed to me he would have to look attractive. Or would she just see a round, obnoxious baby whom she was relieved she would have nothing to do with?

I sat nervously, reading my Chinese history textbook, half concentrating, taking some notes until the doorbell chimed. It rarely does because my father doesn't lock his door. Usually people either knock or just push the door open tentatively and call out, ''Anybody home?''

I went to open the door. Harry Tyson was in a broad tweed coat, hatless, his ears bright red with cold, his bald head amazingly shiny. If I had no hair, I'd wear a hat in this kind of weather. I wondered if it was some kind of macho gesture. Cheryl was in a fur-trimmed coat with a hood. Her face looked bright-eyed and pretty, and her dark curls peeked out. ''I'm glad you could come,'' I said formally, closing the door behind them.

Cheryl shivered. ''Umm, it's so nice and warm in here,'' she said.

''There's a fire,'' I said, indicating the next room. ''Here, let me take your coats.''

While I was hanging their coats up, they moved into the

living room. I followed them. "Well, this is Mason," I said. He seemed to have fallen asleep on his stomach, his fist stuffed up near his mouth.

"A fine-looking youngster," Harry Tyson said stiffly. He was wearing a tie and a suit made of some grayish material, as though he were going to a reception. Cheryl also looked oddly formal in a grayish dress with a white collar. It was as though, by wearing the same dull color he wore, she was trying to blend in with him. In one gesture they sat down side by side on the couch.

I took my place in the armchair. "I'll wake him up later," I said. "He just takes catnaps sometimes, if he's up early."

"How early does he get up?" Harry Tyson asked. His voice had exactly the same intonation it had in the pharmacy, as though it was really important to get all the facts straight.

"It depends. Usually he's pretty good, he can make it through until seven or eight. But when I'm here, my father gets up to feed him in the morning. He's an early riser and he—my father—seems to enjoy it."

Cheryl looked at me with a smile. "He never seemed the grandfather type," she said. She crossed her legs. She was wearing nylons and boots, but between where the boots ended and her dress began was an area of skin.

It struck me in the most subdued way that there was, inevitably, though I hadn't anticipated it, a sense of sexual rivalry in the room. Two men who have slept with the same woman. I assumed they must be sleeping together. I don't think I felt jealous, just aware of the oddity of it. And there was the sense that Harry Tyson was from another generation, not my father's, obviously, but clearly not a kid. It was accentuated by the way he spoke, the way he sat there, his prematurely bald head. He seemed to ooze a sense of firm, unshakable propriety. I felt, too, that there was something proprietary in the way he let his hand rest on Cheryl's shoulder as though he couldn't resist a feeling of pride in having acquired, for whatever number of complicated reasons, this lovely creature. I wondered if I was imagining the fact that whenever Cheryl's eyes caught mine, there was something in them beyond mere friendliness, some glint of emotion that I couldn't exactly interpret.

"I understand your wedding is in the spring?" I said, turning to Harry because Cheryl's expression made me uneasy.

"Yes, well, we need time to plan it and to plan our honeymoon in relation to the store." He smiled, I thought, smugly. "I don't like doing things in a rushed way. This is once in a lifetime, after all."

For the first time I noticed Cheryl's ring, a gold band with a small cluster of diamonds. "That sounds like a smart idea," I said.

There was a pause.

"So, do you like having a baby?" Cheryl asked. Her cheeks flushed, as though she'd asked me something very intimate.

I smiled, trying to appear more at ease than I was. "I do. It has its problems, of course, but he's a great kid. He's extremely good-natured, and, well, I guess I've been lucky."

Harry Tyson sat forward, his hands crossed over his knee. "You don't find it a problem, taking care of him and pursuing your studies?"

I cleared my throat. "Well, it can get . . . . sure, sometimes it's hard. But he's well cared for during the day, and on weekends I get sitters when I need to. I'd say it's working out."

"Would you?"

What kind of question was that? I'd just said I thought it was. I just looked at him, puzzled.

"I don't know if Cheryl has said anything to you," Harry Tyson said.

"About what?" For some reason my heart started thumping wildly.

"About the situation. . . . about Mason."

I shook my head. I glanced at Cheryl, but she was studiously examining the carpet.

"From what Cheryl tells me, you wanted her to have an abortion," Harry Tyson said.

I decided to go very slowly. There were land mines in this conversation; I wasn't sure yet what they were. "Only if that was what she wanted," I said. "I knew she didn't want to be burdened with a child."

Harry Tyson's eyes were fixed on mine. "How did you know that?"

"She said so." I felt we were in one of those arm wrestling matches where you try and ease the other guy off balance, twisting his arm so slowly and quietly he doesn't even know until it's too late.

He smiled unpleasantly. "Wasn't it simply that you weren't willing to assume the responsibilities involved in being a husband?"

"Partly that, yes."

Harry Tyson looked down at Mason, then across at Cheryl, then back at me. "What I'm getting at, Mr. Weber—Timothy— is that we feel, *I* feel, an injustice was done to Cheryl."

"The judge didn't feel that way," I said coldly, catching on by now where he was going.

He smiled triumphantly. "Perhaps he'd feel differently now, if he had to choose which was a more suitable home, a married couple with a real mother, or a footloose bachelor living with three college girls in a city apartment."

God, what a bastard. "Are you saying you're going to take me to court?" At the thought of that, at the thought of losing

Mason, a feeling of blind, sick terror flew through me, as though he'd taken out a loaded gun and pointed it at my heart.

For the first time in the exchange Cheryl leaned forward, licking her lips. "No, we decided not to do that," she said softly, demurely. "We thought of it, but we decided not to."

"We could have done it," Harry Tyson said, "and I have no doubt we would have won the case." He squeezed Cheryl's shoulder. "But then we thought: Turn the other cheek. You caused Cheryl pain and anguish. Why should we, just for simple justice, cause you similar pain?"

"That's magnanimous of you."

But my sarcasm seemed to be unnoticed. "Cheryl and I intend to have a large family," Harry Tyson said, glancing fondly at her. "I come from a large family, as she does. We both love children. We've already bought a four-bedroom house on Elm Street so there'll be plenty of room. Our children will want for nothing." Again he looked at Cheryl. "Cheryl is made to be a mother. Not many girls like that left, you know. She'll be wonderful."

Cheryl beamed at him. "You'll be wonderful, too, Harry."

At that note of sickening accord, Mason woke up. Seeing the two of them, he opened his eyes and let out a howl. That was interesting to me, because in general Mason is so friendly to strangers. But maybe he sensed something in the conversation. He howled steadily until I bent down and picked him up. "Hey, it's okay," I said softly. "Take it easy. Have a bad dream?"

He was soaking wet, but the second I picked him up he settled down. "I'd let you hold him, but he's pretty wet," I said. "I really should change him."

Harry Tyson rose. Cheryl stood up next to him. "Oh, I think we've taken enough of your time," he said. He reached out and pumped my hand vigorously. "Good luck to you," he said.

"Same to both of you," I said.

Cheryl hesitated. Then she leaned over and quickly gave Mason a kiss on the cheek. "Merry Christmas," she said. Her eyes looked blurry.

When they had gone, I carried Mason upstairs to change him. Jesus, what a sinister guy. How could Cheryl marry someone like that? *He'll take command, the whole macho trip, maybe that's what she wanted.*

To my surprise, my hands were shaking. He had scared me. More than that, he had terrified me. Now that they were gone, I wasn't positive he was even right that they could get custody, though I knew there was a chance that he was. But what was clear was the satisfaction he'd gotten out of his quiet demolition job on my ego. It reminded me of the way we used to feel, as kids, watching a building in town being razed to the ground.

"Anybody home?" my father called from downstairs.

I brought Mason down, and my father, who'd taken off his coat, reached for him. "So how did it go?" he asked. "With Cheryl and her intended?"

"I wasn't sure you remembered."

He smiled. "The art of discretion," he said. "I didn't think you'd want me around."

I hesitated, then told him about the encounter.

"That swine!" my father exclaimed. "Who is he, coming here, to *my* house, issuing idle threats like that? I wish I had been here. He would have been out on his ear before he could get that sentence out of his mouth. Well, that's the last time I ever go to Joe's Pharmacy, you can depend on that. I'll drive all the way to Cardoba."

"Dad, it worked out okay. He was just trying to scare me."

"He's a sadist, a petty tyrant. If I were friends with Banks, I'd call him up and give him a piece of my mind. Imagine

allowing a lovely young girl like that to marry such a . . .
He's bald! He's balder than I am!''

All my father was doing was expressing the sense of out-
rage and fear that I had managed to hold in check. ''They're
planning a big family,'' I said.

''Oh, I'll bet they are. Only they can have babies from
now till doomsday, but one thing is clear as crystal: not one
of them will have one iota of Mason's charm, intelligence,
and physical attractiveness. Not one!''

I shrugged. Probably they would, if they looked like
Cheryl, but I knew how he felt. What had surprised me was
the sick feeling of shock that had passed through me when
Harry Tyson began threatening to take Mason away, a feeling
almost akin to sexual desire, a sinking sense of total and
disturbing vulnerability. I realized I was holding Mason, even
though I didn't need to, almost too tightly.

My father, perhaps with the same emotion, reached for
him. ''There are people like that in the world,'' he said.
''People who enjoy instilling fear in others, just for the pure
joy of it. It's one of the many things that makes me wonder
about the human race. Luckily Mason knows nothing of that
yet.''

I relinquished Mason to my father. ''Should I put on some
soup?''

''Thanks, Tim. Cream of tomato would be good on a day
like this, I think.'' He followed me into the kitchen and sat
in a chair playing with Mason while I added milk to the
canned soup and started making some grilled cheese sandwiches.

''Tim?'' My father was not looking at me but at the bird
feeder right outside the window. ''There's something I
wanted to ask you.''

His voice was curiously stiff, and the fact that he wasn't

looking at me added to the feeling of something being amiss. "Yes?"

"I don't want you to take this the wrong way," he said carefully. "I think you're doing a splendid job with Mason, perfectly splendid. His condition shows that. He couldn't be this way if you weren't. . . . It's just, well, it has occurred to me, I've talked this over with Margaret, it did occur to both of us, though it was my idea, that possibly it would be easier on you, this would be just while you're pursuing your studies, you understand, or for whatever length of time would be convenient . . . that Mason could stay here with us."

I was stirring the soup, waiting for it to simmer. "Leave him here, you mean? Permanently?"

My father cleared his throat. "Not permanently. Just while college is in session. You'd be home on vacations, and of course we'd come to see you as often as you'd like, more often, probably. As you see, I have lots of room and now that Margaret is around to help . . . not that that's the main thing. Really, it's something that would give me great pleasure. . . . And I thought it might make life easier on you."

For some reason I had never contemplated this, even though the newly fixed up nursery might have been a clue. It was tempting. Mason would be well cared for, loved. Clearly my father wanted a chance to have the relationship he'd never had with me. Yet at any moment I could reappear and claim him. Probably even with an arrangement like the one my father was suggesting, Mason would see me as often as some babies saw their fathers. It wasn't as though he would forget me, or be taken away forever. I thought of my slipping grades, of the possibility of having long stretches of time with Vivian without having to gauge when I had to rush in for the next feeding. I could be, in short, a normal student, to the extent my character would permit that.

"Youth is for having fun," my father went on. "You've

always been so responsible, especially since Rebecca died, cooking, taking care of me. Why not just indulge now? Not that I expect you to party all night or burn the candle at both ends, but—''

''No, I know what you're saying,'' I said. ''It's a really generous offer. I appreciate it.'' I lowered the flame under the soup. I looked at my father and Mason, who were sitting there together so comfortably. ''I think you'd do a great job, it's not that, and in a lot of ways you're right, it would make things easier, only . . .''

My father smiled painfully. ''Only?''

I sighed. ''I guess I want to keep on trying. Maybe it'll just mean I won't give anything my all, Mason or my studies or . . . whatever girl I might meet. But I . . . It's strange to say, but at this point I can't imagine life without him. Or maybe I just don't want to.''

''I understand,'' my father said. He bounced Mason on his knee. ''It's probably greed. Here I have something good and I want something better, or more, anyway. Margaret thought you'd say no.''

There was a curious lack of tension in the conversation, as though almost for the first time, my father and I were talking to each other as fellow human beings. I reached up to get the soup bowls. ''Dad, listen,'' I said. ''There's this friend of mine, Vivian, you met her. She might drive down to spend part of Christmas here. Would you mind?''

My father smiled. ''Mind? How could I mind?'' He looked at Mason. ''What does he take me for?''

Mason reached out and put his hands over my father's ears.

ABOUT THE AUTHOR

Norma Klein was born in New York City and graduated cum laude and a member of Phi Beta Kappa from Barnard College, with a degree in Russian. She later received her master's degree in Slavic languages from Columbia University.

Ms. Klein began publishing short stories while attending Barnard College and since then has written novels for readers of all ages. The author gets her ideas from everyday life and advises would-be writers to do the same—to write about their experiences or things they really care about.

Several of Norma Klein's books are available from Fawcett, including MY LIFE AS A BODY, OLDER MEN, FAMILY SECRETS, and GIVE AND TAKE.

Ms. Klein lives in Manhattan with her husband and their two daughters.